THE BED WAS IMMENSE, LUXURIOUS . . .

When Ben joined her, she said, "I feel wicked wallowing in all this luxury. Positively wanton."

"That's good." He kissed her. "Tell me what to do."

If he wasn't teasing, then he was a strange one. "Don't you know?"

"How would I know? Every woman is different. Take my hand and show me."

"Oh, Ben—"

She took his hand and guided it over her body. The sensitivity of his touch was surprising, considering the size and strength of his hands. It produced some stimulation, rapture; she wanted, needed more. She whispered to him. He pretended not to understand her, but she knew he did.

SHADOWS OF PASSION

PATRICIA GALLAGHER

AVON
PUBLISHERS OF BARD, CAMELOT, DISCUS, EQUINOX AND FLARE BOOKS

AVON BOOKS
A division of
The Hearst Corporation
959 Eighth Avenue
New York, New York 10019

First Avon Printing, July, 1971
Third Printing

AVON TRADEMARK REG. U.S. PAT. OFF. AND
FOREIGN COUNTRIES, REGISTERED TRADEMARK—
MARCA REGISTRADA, HECHO EN CHICAGO, U.S.A.

Printed in the U.S.A.

SHADOWS OF PASSION

part **1**

chapter
1

ANGER PLUNGED THROUGH BEN HALE, swift and sharp as a knife, followed by deep-gutting disgust. Suddenly he felt a vital need for fresh air. In spite of Paris perfume, the place stank. The people stank. The whole goddamn world was a stinky sump, and he had to escape it, at least temporarily.

He took a few turns about the room and then walked out on the terrace. To the average tenement dweller, he thought, this forty story resident hotel must appear to be an annex of heaven, high enough that on a smogless day you could see the sky in all directions and breathe the air without insulting your lungs. Ben couldn't guess at the annual rental, nor how many other "Eddie Edens" Silver Haddington, currently in her singer syndrome, had intermittently housed there, though her critics claimed them legion.

The Haddington penthouse, from which the mistress had discreetly absented herself while the men discussed business, occupied the entire top floor of the Regal Towers, and the terrace was on solid construction, not one of the cantilevered balconies hung like eagles' nests on the sheer stone walls, as those of other tenants were.

Ben Hale stood on this broad balustraded platform in

the clouds, in a synthetic paradise of plastic plants, gazing down at Central Park. It was green and busy in the afternoon sun: pedestrians, equestrians, automobiles, taxis, hansom cabs, tourist buses, rowboats on the water. They all looked like miniatures. Curiously, the pools, ponds, reservoir had a greenish-yellow cast, like slime, in spring and summer, and a brownish-gray one, like mud, in autumn and winter. Still it was considered one of the more spectacular sights in this city of spectacles.

The view did not improve Ben's mood or perspective, however. He went back inside, where the head of the agency, Harvey Dobbs, was talking with the prospective client, and freeloading Miss Haddington's private stock as if he were a guest there on her personal invitation. Well, what the hell! So his job stank, too. It was a living, and he had to earn a living. There was no wealthy benefactress propositioning him as Silver Haddington was Eddie Eden, if indeed she was. Ben didn't quite believe it, but he was skeptical by nature and suspicious by profession.

Harvey Dobbs, plainly annoyed by his meanderings, demanded brusquely, "What's bugging you, Ben? You're prowling around like a hungry tiger."

"Yeah," Eden agreed. "What're you so tense about, man? You'll be escorting my wife, not the President."

Ben sat down and lit a cigarette, but nervous energy kept him toying with the lighter, igniting the flame and immediately extinguishing it. "Why do you want protection for Mrs. Eden? Have there been any threats on your life or hers?"

"Sure, plenty. I get crackpot calls and warnings all the time. Every public figure does. The world is full of nuts and weirdos."

"You can say that again," Ben said.

Dobbs interrupted, "Look, Ben. You know our motto: any assignment, any place, any time. Mr. Eden's asking for an escort for his wife from Louisiana to New York. What's so wrong or unusual about that?"

"Nothing, ostensibly," Ben said, appraising the client through smoke-narrowed eyes. "Level with me, Eddie. What's behind this? I've read your publicity, I'm familiar with your background and circumstances. You're not famous, and you're broke. So nobody's going to try to snatch your frau for ransom, and if you had some phony publicity stunt in mind you wouldn't want a private dick around to queer it. The truth is, you don't want Mrs. Eden to come at all. You've been in New York three months without her, you're involved with the Haddington Enterprises, and hope to make it permanent. But you've got a little legal impediment down South, right? You'd like a divorce, but maybe it's not mutual, correct? Well, that's your problem, man. What do you expect me to do about it?"

"I'll answer that," Dobbs said, helping himself to a fistful of expensive cigars. "I expect you to do the job you're paid for, Ben, and you're not paid to heckle, analyze, or challenge clients."

"Then send another boy," Ben said. "I don't want this assignment."

"Mr. Eden wants you, Ben. It's a legitimate service, Dobbs offers it, and I assign the agents, nobody else."

"But it's routine stuff, Harv! A simple escort job. Anybody could handle it, why me? I'm in the middle of that insurance investigation."

"I'll take it over."

"Harvey, Mrs. Eden could get up here in a few hours on a jet! This travel-by-auto bit is a delaying action, and you know it. I'll just be a chauffeur to give Eden more time with Miss Haddington."

"That's his business," Dobbs said. "He has a valid request, and I'm satisfied with his reasons."

"Sure, but it still smells to me," Ben muttered.

"You want an affidavit?" asked Eddie Eden. "I'll admit I didn't exactly invite Marcie up here, Ben. But she's my wife and she's got a vacation, and she insists on spending it with me. She's never been to New York and she thinks she can travel cheaper in her chariot than any other way; she's got a frugal streak in her. But she's helpless as a child, doesn't know a damn thing about a car, couldn't even change a tire, and God knows what could happen to her in fifteen hundred miles alone on the road. I could forbid her to come, of course, but that'd only make her more eager and determined."

"And suspicious?" Ben suggested. "Tell her about your new love, and she may change her mind."

Eddie shook his head. "Not a chance. She's got a thing about marriage, believes that biblical forever muck, and so hung up on me I couldn't pry her off with a crowbar. If I told her about Miss Haddington, she'd come on a rocket, weep and wail, and then understand and forgive like she's done a dozen times or more. She's the noble type, the long-suffering spouse bearing the cross of an incurable chaser. She's a drag and sometimes I wish she'd just relax and let go, but that's got nothing to do with this business."

"You're lying in your gums, Eddie. You think throwing her together with some guy for a few days might loosen her grip on you, maybe? If so, you've got the wrong agency, man. We're detectives, not professional lovers. And if you're looking for an exterminator, call Orkin."

"Oh, that's funny," Eddie said. "Is there any extra charge for the jokes, Harv?"

Ben turned to Dobbs. "If you accept this cuckoo's case, count me out. I'm not a stud. My sexual services are not for hire."

"You flatter yourself," Eddie drawled. "I doubt if you or anybody else, including Sean Connery, could get to Marcie that way, Benny boy. And if I were trying to hire *that* gun, believe me I'd find a more likely prospect. A lady-killer, you ain't."

Dobbs grinned at that. "He's got you there, Ben."

Ben sat smoking and glowering at his boss, a big bald bellied man spilling like over-risen dough out of a tub-chair. He'd worked for Harvey Dobbs for five years now, he'd drawn some bizarre assignments and encountered all kinds of proposals and propositions, particularly in the domestic cases, but generally the client was honest with the agent if no one else, and Ben could spot a sham readily. He considered Eddie Eden a fake and thought Dobbs did too, and only Eden's present connection with Silver-Haddington, a profitable client in the past, could have induced Dobbs to accept this petty case. The agency specialized in more complicated civil and criminal investigations, most of which fell in Ben's bailiwick. Some were highly interesting and challenging, and all would benefit him in his future ambition.

Long ago he had discovered that detective work, even on an amateurish scale, was good training for a creative writer. It developed an inquiring mind, honed the faculties and instincts. It taught him to probe for motivation and minor detail, to create plot and promulgate it through curiosity and suspicion, to sustain suspense, and not be satisfied until a satisfactory conclusion was reached. In this respect Harvey Dobbs, a master in the field, was a valuable tutor, and Ben had learned much from the association, as he had from his previous tenure on the police force. And though he thought Dobbs' personal ethics were somewhat synthetic and fragmented, he liked to think his own were reasonably real and intact; that he still possessed some self-respect, principles, and integrity, if few ideals. When you dealt with humanity in this capacity, you soon lost your youthful ideals. If there were times when he didn't enjoy his work, when he actually hated it, that was all part of the game. Lots of men had the same problem. He'd known Treasury boys who didn't relish nailing income tax evaders, and FBI agents who disliked some of the undercover tactics to which they must resort, and soldiers who despised war yet fought it. There were many undesirable jobs in the world, created primarily by undesirable people, and somebody had to do them. Ben Hale was one of the

13

somebodies. Still, he wanted the right to refuse a job in which he had no professional interest, or felt was patently dishonest, and ordinarily Dobbs obliged him. His adamancy this time was arbitrary, Ben thought, a test of wills and tempers, a show of authority more to impress the client than discipline the agent. Nevertheless, it irked him and he defied Dobbs.

"I've met some bastards in my time, Eden, but you've got to be Number One. The supreme sonofabitch of the ages."

"Stop with the insults," Dobbs warned, sipping Chivas Regal on the rocks.

But Eddie Eden was either impervious to insult, or conditioned to it. He smiled smoothly. Ben Hale wasn't the first person to question his paternity, and he rather enjoyed bandying wits with him. "And you've got to be the champion cynic and skeptic, Hale. But if you got the impression that Marcie's some kind of angel with clipped wings, a tragic heroine wasting away in the swamps while her villainous mate swings in Manhattan, perish it. She doesn't need any pity. I've been hitched to her seven years, and I'm the one that's shafted. A clinging vine can smother and choke you. Like that honeysuckle that grows wild around her aunt's place in that Dixie dump on the banks of the Bayou Teche. I used to sit on the front porch with her, fighting mosquitoes big as vampire bats and as bloodthirsty, and smelling that sweet vine, watching how it crawled over the trellis and banisters and posts and everything else, until you couldn't see nothing but honeysuckle and smell nothing but honeysuckle. On a still summer night the fragrance was enough to make you puke. I couldn't stand it. I'd have to cut out somewhere, anywhere, and when I came back, I'd want to tear that goddamn vine down and stomp the roots to death. And I'd think, 'That's what's going to happen to you, Eddie Baby, if you hang around here long enough! Marcie'll wrap her tentacles around you like that octopus vine, and you'll suffocate in the sweetness!'

14

"Jeez, how tired I got hearing her syrupy voice nagging the hell out of me! 'Eddie, when're you going to give up show business and get a steady job and settle down? Eddie, when're we going to have a house of our own? Eddie, when're we going to start a family? Eddie, Eddie, when, when?' Christ! It was like being caught in a whirlpool of molasses, trying to swim in sorghum, and drowning in the sticky sweetness. A miracle I didn't go ape and strangle her. Yeah, man, you can get too much of a good thing."

Ben didn't know about that. His own marriage had been a brief and bitter disaster ending in divorce and his custody of his son. Dale had been Eddie Eden's female counterpart, a bitch from the beginning, born one, and nothing he'd ever done had pleased her. Because she didn't like being married to a cop, he'd resigned from the police force and gone to work for Dobbs Detective Agency. But that didn't satisfy her, either, because it wasn't as glamorous and lucrative a profession as it was supposed to be, and he had this crazy compulsion to write in his spare time, selling enough of his output to keep him interested but not enough to please Dale. He'd accumulated several thick notebooks of "authentic background material" for reference—most of it sordid stuff, the unbelievable rottenness of humanity. This episode would be just one more entry.

"I wouldn't know," he said. "I never had that problem."

"Well, it can be more of a curse than a blessing," Eddie assured him. "Down in Teche Country, they have voodoo rites and potions to remove such curses. However, as some poet once said, one man's poison can be another man's meat. ..." He took a snapshot from his wallet and passed it to Ben. "Here, have a look, and believe me, that pic doesn't do her justice. She was just a kid when it was taken, seventeen, fresh out of high school. She's twenty-four now, a woman, matured and how. That shouldn't be too hard to escort, should it?"

Ben studied the snapshot as if it were a clue, a piece of evidence. A pretty, innocent-looking girl, smiling rather timidly and enigmatically, as if life both intimidated and mystified her at that age. Wearing a summery print dress and sandals, standing before a small frame house with a vine trellis and an empty rocking chair on the sagging front porch. Ben found himself feeling sorry for her, and wondering what kind of woman would want to hang on to this kind of man. He thought he'd met all the types, in every strata of society, all the ghouls and deviates, fools and fanatics, kooks and maniacs. But Eddie Eden was a special swamp breed, unique in his emotional construction, apparently without heart, soul, or conscience, dedicated utterly to self, a complete narcissist and hedonist.

He returned the picture without comment. Eddie glanced at it fleetingly, showing no visible recognition, as if he viewed a stranger, then put it out of sight and, presumably, out of mind.

"What do you expect to happen, Eddie? If she's as shy and faithful as you say, and eternally in love with you, three days on the road isn't going to change that."

"That's not your mission, man. But who knows? The world was made in six days, and a lot can happen in three. It can be a lifetime if you know how to live. Trouble is, Marcie doesn't. It's high time she learned, and I'd have no objection to you as a teacher. Could be an interesting project, Ben. Silver wasn't much of a challenge. She came to the Amber Alley one night like a pussy in heat hunting a tom and took an immediate fancy to this Cajun cat. All I had to do was serenade her the rest of the evening. Easy conquest. Takes something out of the chase. Know what I mean?"

"No," Ben said. "I'm not interested, Eddie."

"How do you know, man? You haven't met her yet, and she hasn't met you. Might be instant love." He laughed, enjoying Ben's discomfort and disgruntlement. "I'm joking, of course. I repeat, that's not your mission.

However, I don't want her to know you're a detective, Ben. It'd scare the poor kid to death to think she was in some kind of danger."

"Then you wouldn't have to worry about a divorce."

"Can't you shut this comic up?" Eddie addressed Dobbs. "I'm not hiring a clown."

"You wouldn't have to hire one," Ben said.

Dobbs scowled, puffing a cigar, which protruded from his slack mouth like a miniature cannon. "Stop this shit, and get down to business, boys."

"Right," Eddie nodded. "When I left Marcie the last time I told her I'd send for her when I got settled and could afford all the domestic things she wanted. Well, I reckon she got tired waiting, because yesterday I got a letter saying she was coming up on her vacation. But I think she means to stay longer than two weeks—that's why she's bringing the car, to have room for some household stuff. She's probably planning to rent one of those cross-country trailers and move up here *in toto*. If so, I expect you to talk her out of it, Ben. Naturally, you'll drive the chariot."

"Who am I supposed to be—Ben Hur?"

Eddie laughed. "Just a friend of mine, a writer between assignments who volunteered his help in order to soak up some southern atmosphere."

Ben frowned skeptically. "You expect her to swallow that? You make her sound stupid, Eddie. Is she stupid? I'd hate to play nursemaid to a moron for fifteen hundred miles."

"No, she's bright enough as broads go. No genius, mind you, but not retarded. She'll take the writer bait easy enough, though. You got the starving artist look, you know. Lean and hungry. Too bad you don't have artic pallor to match. Ought to wear your hair longer too, shaggy around the edges, and a seedy tweed jacket with worn elbow patches. I saw Truman Capote rigged like that once."

Dobbs snickered. "Don't let his appearance fool you,

17

Eddie. He could break your neck with a karate chop. He trained with the city bulls, you know."

"I'll remember that," Eddie said, "when I hire a bodyguard. You know Sinatra has one? And Presley? And the Beatles? Status symbol in show biz; sign of real success."

Dobbs was impatient with the persiflage. "It's settled, then? You're going, Ben?"

"Do I have a choice?"

"Sure, you can quit. But don't make any rash decisions, Ben. You got no angel like Miss Haddington to pay your earthly bills, and you got a kid and a widowed mother to support. Debts and obligations."

"You're cracking the whip," Ben bowed.

Eddie poured another round of drinks, the jolly host very generous with his mistress's goodies. "Don't pressure him, Harv. A fella knows when he's financially strapped, nobody has to remind him. And this isn't going to work any personal or professional hardship on Mr. Hale. He'll be well paid for his services."

"Don't quote any prices, Eddie. If I could afford to, I'd do it gratis, because I think you're going to be the loser in whatever shabby game you're playing—and that'd be payment enough."

"Careful," Dobbs cautioned again, like a diligent referee constantly separating the opponents.

Eddie gestured deprecatingly. "Oh, let him blow off his steam, Harv. Spew it out of his system, purify himself. And let him clobber me. Should make his work easier. Some men have to justify their actions. Mine justify themselves."

"That's pot philosophy," Ben observed. "Acid acumen."

"Man, he uses pretty words, don't he? Could shame some of those petty poets in the coffeehouses."

Ben began prowling the living room again, which was actually a salon, a *chambre par excellence* in the continental sense. He had been there before, a year ago, when Miss Haddington, then a French countess, was a client of the agency, but this cloud-castle still impressed him. Despite his other faults, his unorthodox pleasures and pursuits, which had filled a thick dossier when finally accumulated, the Count had been an accomplished decorator, and his wife's own considerable talents in this respect had matured under his expertise and guidance.

A huge portrait of the former Countess de Martinique dominated the room and set the theme and color scheme, but the count's effeminacy prevailed in the appointments, all of exquisite detail and texture, perfect symmetry and harmony. The paintings, sculptures, objets d'art were priceless, collected in world travels and at private auctions. The result was an elegance uncommon even in penthouses, where wealth did not necessarily signify taste or intelligence, and opulence often reflected ignorance and vulgarity.

Ben's shoes sank ankle-deep in the luxurious white carpet, the cleaning bills for which probably exceeded his annual income. Two people could easily sleep on the long jade velvet sofa and no doubt had on occasion, when too beat or too bombed to make it to the boudoir. No wonder Eddie Eden had fanciful designs on the lady. This kind of pad could spoil a man for walk-up flats and frame cottages.

"Just get this straight, Eddie. You're not contracting for a co-respondent, remember. I've helped get that kind of evidence, but I've never been a part of it. So if you think you've got a catalyst for a court action, forget it."

"Hail, hero!" Eddie lifted his glass in mock salute. "Where do you find such moralists, Harv?"

"His father was a preacher," Dobbs said.

"Jesus Christ," Eddie muttered.

"No, just a preacher." Dobbs grinned and excused himself to visit one of the four bathrooms equipped with sunken marble tubs and gold-plated fixtures.

During his absence, Ben asked, "Who's picking up the tab for this operation, Eddie, as if I didn't know?"

"Jeez, you're curious and suspicious!"

"I make my living that way, Eddie, and for the present you're suspect. You haven't got a sou, not even a job. You were closed at the Amber Alley yesterday. I saw them changing the marquee this morning."

"Released by mutual agreement," Eddie corrected.

"That's the same as resigning by request," Ben said. "The old hook."

"Not quite, but so what? It was a lousy job. No future. No prestige. A third-rate club."

"You're a third-rate entertainer," Ben said, smiling brutally. "I've seen your act, Eddie." His hands described a big zero. "Nothing."

"I got a theory, Ben. Most knocking is done by people who don't know how to ring the bell. That's your problem. You're not exactly a bell-ringer yourself. You've got no right to criticize me."

"Oh, you've got the temperament all right, Eddie. But not the talent. And while you might fake the talent, there's something more important you lack. That certain charm, that old magic. Charisma, and without it there's no real or lasting success in show business. You'll never make the big scene, unless your angel buys a piece of the action, and I doubt if she's silly enough to invest in a dud. You're just a new and amusing toy to that multimillion dollar baby, and when the novelty wears off she'll discard you on the junkheap of her other playthings. But the Eddie Edens of the world never underestimate themselves, do they, nor profit from precedents? Dig this lode for all it's worth, man, because your strike is going to peter out, pun intended."

Of all his words, only one registered with any force on Eddie Eden. He stood before a large Venetian mirror framed in gold-leaf, examining his capped teeth and his black curly hair and as much of his fine profile as was possible at that angle, the narcissist hooked on his own image and paying homage at his personal shrine.

"No charisma, huh? I'm gilded with it, Ben. What do you think put me on this magic carousel? It's going to keep me here, too. Don't worry about me, pal. Marcie's your charge. She's at work now, slaving away in that sugar mill as much as any nigger ever did when it was a plantation, but she'll be home this evening, and I'll introduce you on the horn. Meanwhile, up in the tower, we have time to kill, so why don't we amble out for grub and return for booze and cards?" His grin was infuriating. "You play poker, don't you, Ben? Stud?"

chapter
2

MARCIE WAS IN THE BATHTUB when the telephone rang. She heard her aunt stir out of her rocker on the porch and hurry to answer it, banging the screendoor in her haste. Probably one of Aunt Beth's cronies, she thought, and they'd chat for hours in the way of lonely ladies. It was too much to hope it might be Eddie. She hasn't heard from him in weeks, no letter, not even a postcard. Maybe he wasn't in New York any more. Maybe he was in Chicago or Los Angeles, or on the road, chasing that dream which so far had successfully eluded him, seemingly as vaporous as the will-o'-the-wisps of his native marshlands, yet continuing to lure him with the same fascination.

The evening was hot and still, the kind of night that came early in the season to southern Louisiana and lingered late. The bathroom window was open, and Marcie smelled the blooming honeysuckle and thought wistfully of her husband. Eddie hated the summer heat, the stillness, and especially the swamps, although he was a native son of Teche Country, born in the same parish, the same town, as Marcie. He'd pretended to be from New Orleans until a publicity agent had convinced him that he might register better on the marquees if he created an image for himself, an identity, A Personality. There were hundreds of singers and guitar players, and most of them faded swiftly from anonymity to obscurity to oblivion. To remain in the race a potential contender had to explode on the scene like a rocket, grab the public's fancy and hold it, create a loyal cult. Eddie Eden had some Acadian blood and the dark brooding picaresqueness that appealed to romantic older women, and though this wasn't the stuff of which current fads were fashioned, the agent decided to play that angle. He culled a long list of possible titles, trying to conjure a sensational one, dredging up such gems as "the Cajun Cat", "the Teche Troubadour", and "Eddie Eden, a Little Bit of Paradise", all of which Eddie scorned as swamp muck that would serve only to drown him, suck him under like quicksand, and he fired the PR genius, although he did eventually use his Acadian background in his publicity.

Between engagements Eddie Eden had worked in the local sugar mills. He'd worked in the cane fields. He'd driven a truck. He'd developed his physique and his swarthy complexion at outdoor manual labor and despised and resented every hour of it. He considered the town of Rainbow, and especially its name, a mockery and made the same contemptuous observation every time circumstances forced him to return: "There's only one kind of pot could be at the end of this dump, and it ain't filled with gold." His origins haunted him, permanent escape became an obsession, and his attempts seemed futile to everyone but Eddie Eden. The fact that he was thirty and still batting zero in the major entertainment leagues appeared no handicap to Eddie. It wasn't talent holding him back, just luck. Bad breaks. He'd never had that golden opportunity, that choice chance. What were the stars before they became STARS? Bums, some of them. Bums, most of them. One hit record, one appearance on a high-rated TV show, and they were famous. Celebrities. NAMES. Kings enjoying the pleasures and privileges of crowned heads, and there was always room at the top of the throne for one more. Why not Eddie Eden? All he needed was luck, the fond smile of fate rather than the old fickle finger he'd been getting so much of lately.

Marcie sympathized with him through his rejections and depressions and agonizings over "Kismet's conspiracy against Eddie Eden." She traveled with him when he wanted her along, and stayed in Rainbow and worked as a secretary in the sugar mills and sent him money when he didn't want her with him. Sometimes she thought he survived on hope and ego alone and would perish utterly without them, for of course they were prerequisites in the career Eddie pursued. An entertainer had to believe in himself, had to have faith and confidence in his ability and the courage of his ambitions, if he was to persuade and convince an audience of his worth. To Eddie, ego was the aura of his masculine mystique, rationalizing and excusing his frequently boorish behavior, and Marcie had learned to accept it as an integral part of his personality, indeed the essence of it. And perhaps he *would* make it big some day, on sheer arrogance alone. . . .

"It's for you," Aunt Beth said at the bathroom door. "Hurry up, Marcie. Long distance from New York."

"Eddie?"

"You know anybody else in New York?"

Marcie couldn't find her robe. She tied a bathtowel around her hips and ran, dripping bubblebath, to the telephone in the hall. Beth brought another towel and draped it over her bare shoulders.

"Hello, Eddie? Oh, Eddie, I'm so glad you called! I've been so worried. Haven't heard from you in so long I thought you'd moved on somewhere else. Have you been getting my letters? Are you all right, darling? Are you there? Eddie, Eddie?"

"I'm here, baby, in person. Got all your mail, just been too busy to write." In the penthouse in Manhattan,

24

Eddie covered the mouthpiece of the phone and grinned at Ben Hale, who was holding an extension, and his eyes gloated, "See what I mean?"

"Now be quiet, honey, and listen. I got good news for you, but this is long distance and you got to let me do the talking, see?"

"Sure, Eddie."

"First, there's someone I want you to meet, sugar. He's here beside me, a new friend and a pal. A writer named Ben Hale. Meet Ben, Marcie. Ben, meet Marcie."

There was a garbled exchange of self-conscious responses. Ben liked her voice. Soft and low, even when it bubbled with joy and excitement, and with only a trace of southern accent, unaffected, apparently as natural as her breathing. Ben waited for her reaction to the plan Eddie outlined, hoped for her objections, protests, refusal. But as Eddie had complacently assured him, there was none. She was all wifely subservience and compliance. She didn't even question the feasibility or discretion of the arrangement; if that was her husband's wish, it was her desire. And it was so kind and thoughtful of Eddie to let her bring the car; she was afraid he would insist that she fly and then she couldn't bring the things she wanted, including the rest of his clothes and his other guitar. But she wasn't afraid to travel alone, she could manage, and he need not put his friend to the trouble of escorting her. Mr. Hale had business in New Orleans? Well, in that case, it would be all right, she guessed. Rather convenient, in fact, since she might possibly need some help on the road. Yes, she understood the plan. Mr. Hale would fly down and they would drive back to New York together. ...

As simple as that. A round of garbled goodbyes, and Eddie hung up. Ben held the instrument a few seconds before replacing it. Eddie was smug and triumphant, as if he'd pulled off a terrific coup, his face seeming swarthier and even more piratical than before, his dark eyes as murky as the swamps that had spawned him. He topped six feet in height, and Ben knew his brutish build was part of his appeal to Silver Haddington, who had a thing about muscles. Eddie Eden didn't look like a singer—but then he didn't sing like one, either.

"Did I tell you, pal, or did I tell you?"

Ben had the taste of dirt in his mouth and would have spat if there were any place but the floor. "You told me," he said and went out on the terrace for fresh air again.

Lights glowing mistily, the city appeared to have a celestial nimbus about it when viewed from the pinnacles at night. You had to see it from the pits to know its darkness and ugliness. When he'd first come there, a latter-day Green Mountain boy, he'd been fascinated and inspired, enchanted as a youth with his first love affair, moved to poetry, and then he'd learned that he'd fallen in love with a whore. Within a few months New York had seduced him, stripped him of his boyish illusions and countrified ideals, tempted, tormented, tortured and tried him, dissected him, and left him for dead. Dale, another beguiling bitch with the instincts of a whore, had finished him.

He surveyed his nemesis grimly, wondering why it still impressed and even awed him. Ten years of exposure to its ills and infections should have immunized him. He'd been intitiated into its mysteries, brutally hazed in its cults; he'd suffered its ironies and defeats, its satire and sadism. He'd witnessed subtle changes in its appearance but not its character or spirit. The innate attitudes and atmospheres prevailed. The lovers were loving, the muggers mugging, the conspirators conspiring, the rats racing, the whores whoring. He balled his fists in his pockets and went back inside, to buoyant white carpets and authentic paintings, to art and culture as another harlot, Eddie Eden's new patroness, practiced it.

"When do I leave?"

"Soon as possible," Eddie replied.

Dobbs, burdened with weak kidneys, had just returned from the john. Hearing the news, he happily helped himself to brandy and cigars. And soon Eddie was settling the monetary details with Dobbs, delivering the retainer, and Ben knew it didn't bother Eden in the slightest that the money was not his own.

He and Dobbs rode the automatic elevator down to the marble-and-gilt lobby. A doorman, rigged out like a costume-ball general in a blue twill uniform with gold-fringed epaulets, bowed them out. In the street, Dobbs hailed a cab and offered Ben a lift to his apartment. Driving away, Ben said, "Isn't that ridiculous? That poor devil in all that brass and braid, as if he were a footman to royalty. Why couldn't they give him a simple uniform?"

Dobbs was preoccupied. "You mean the doorman? That's so nobody could possibly mistake him for a resident. You got any angles on this other thing, Ben?"

"Angles? It's not a case, Harv. I don't intend to keep a dossier. Eden's the one with the angles. Boy, he's an odd duck, psychologically in the class of a pimp married to a prostitute and getting a queer kick out of peddling his wife. That's what he was trying to do with that picture and build-up of Mrs. E. you know. Sell her to me! But that's not going to happen, and he's just paying a hell of a high escort fee, or Silver Haddington is."

"She can afford it," Dobbs said. "And as long as I get my fair share, I couldn't care less about the final outcome. Naturally, I couldn't tell Eden that. I had to get tough with you up there. You understand, don't you?"

Ben smiled wryly. "You're all heart, Harv."

"Yeah. Well, don't forget, you're not the only guy with scars from a dame, Ben. I was mauled and mangled by one too, and I'm even more bereft than you, because I don't have a mother to enshrine. *She* was the female that gutted me."

"We all have traumas and complexes, Harv."

"Mine began in the womb," Dobbs said. "I entered

this world a bruised baby, and I been bruising babes ever since. Biting boobs and banging bellies. I don't feel I owe womankind any allegiance, and neither should you after Dale's claws. If you get a whack at Eden's broad, take it. You've laid your share since Dale. Compromising one more shouldn't tax your integrity too much. Bang her once for me."

Ben lived a few blocks east of the Park, and the cab was soon there. Dobbs wished him luck. Ben waved him on, and stood a moment looking at his residence. Sometimes he thought there were only three kinds of places to live in New York; penthouses, remodeled brownstones, and tenements. The last two were familiar to him through experience, the first by profession; and while his present address was anything but prestigious, it was a big improvement over his initial cave in the catacombs.

He climbed the steps, which had worn places in the stones and nicks in the banisters, and entered the dimly-lit vestibule. Another flight of stairs brought him to his door, and he admitted himself with his key. His mother was watching television, her only diversion other than taking Timmy to the Park. The child was already in bed, in the cubicle sandwiched between the bedrooms, once a butler's pantry, now serving as nursery.

"Hi, Mom."

"Hello, dear. Did you have supper?"

"Yes. At Lindy's."

"Isn't that expensive?" Mrs. Hale asked, always mindful of the budget.

"I didn't pay for it. A client did."

Ben went to see Timmy, trying as he had since the divorce not to see Dale in him. But she had left her genetic imprint, her personal monogram, in the shape of his head and his small flat ears and the generous curve of his mouth; with his wide gray eyes open, he resembled his mother even more, but as Ben's eyes were also gray, of a deeper slate hue, he could recognize himself in his son, too. And he hoped as the boy grew older and lost his childish features and characteristics, he would develop more of his father's, until by maturity he would bear no maternal resemblance at all.

Mrs. Hale had not moved from her position before the TV set. Ben saw her silhouetted in the dim light, profile sagging, gray head slightly bent, shoulders sloped, like Whistler's mother. She appeared older than her sixty years, primarily because of her dated clothes and outmoded hair style. After five years in New York, Agatha Hale still retained her small-town appearance and attitudes and would probably never lose them. The wife and now widow of a New England minister, she was not especially pleased with the pattern of her son's life, but wise enough to know she was limited in her power to change it. Actually, Ben had not wanted her to come to New York after his divorce, had believed he could manage for Timmy and himself with hired help, but she had insisted that her place was with her son and her grandson. And since his father had died only a few months previously, collapsing in his pulpit during a Sunday sermon, and she was expected to vacate the parsonage as soon as possible to the Reverend Hale's successor, it was really more a case of necessity than choice. And soon Ben was glad and grateful for her presence and competent management of his household and his son. She brought order and economy and the required discipline, rescuing dignity and serenity from what often threatened to become clamor, chaos, and bankruptcy.

"I'm going out of town tomorrow, Mom."

"Business?"

Ben fished a cigarette from his half-full pack. Mrs. Hale frowned as his lighter flared. She worried that he smoked too much and was always clipping articles on lung cancer and emphysema from newspapers and magazines, which Ben read to please her and then ignored.

"Yes. New Orleans. I'll be gone for several days, possibly longer."

"Is it a dangerous mission, son? Are you investigating a murder or other crime?"

"Mom, we agreed long ago that you wouldn't pry into agency business," Ben reminded gently. "The cases are confidential, you know that."

Mrs. Hale sighed, rose to switch off the television program in which she had suddenly lost interest, sat down again and twisted her hands in her lap, thin, nervous, almost gnarled hands showing prominent blue veins and dark age spots. "Oh, I wish you'd quit that job, Ben! Stay home and write stories like you always wanted. Nothing bad can happen to you at a typewriter."

"Not according to the critics," Ben mused.

"You could write a fine book," Mrs. Hale encouraged. "A biography of your father—the country minister, like the country doctor and lawyer. It could have humor and pathos and nostalgia, all the qualities that make such works memorable. Why, it could be a classic!"

"Sure, Mom. Book of the Month, and all the rest. Meanwhile, there's a little matter of food and shelter. Dad didn't leave much insurance and no securities or annuities—that could be the chapter on pathos—and you're not eligible for Social Security. I've got to have a steady job, a steady income."

"But you have two years of college, Ben! You should have a big job with big money."

That was another of her illusions Ben had frequently to dispel. "Almost everybody has two years of college, Mom, and some of them are pumping gasoline and sweeping streets and driving trucks. The people with the status positions and pay have four, six, eight years of college." But he knew his explanations did not change her mind on the matter, nor ease her concern about the trip, and he had to mollify her. "This isn't a dangerous assignment, Mom. Nothing to worry about." He paused a little grimly. "I'm just going to be a lady's traveling companion."

"Her bodyguard? Is she in some kind of trouble?"

"No, Mom. Just forget it, will you? I hope I have some clean white shirts?"

"Of course, dear."

Of course, Ben thought. He always had clean shirts and darned socks. Mothers were like that.

"Well, I'm beat, Mom. I'm going to sack-out early. Good night."

"Good night, son."

The window of his room looked out at another remodeled brownstone. Ben recalled the view from Silver Haddington's tower, and Eddie Eden's roach-ridden flat in the Village, and could understand and almost condone his desperation. In a sense, he and Eden had something in common. He'd knocked around and been knocked around too, hunting success. Eddie Eden was a stillborn singer, and Ben Hale was that unsung hero, the freelance writer. He'd tried to convince Dale that knocking around was a part of the education, experience, preparation for a writer. He'd cited notable examples—Hemingway, James Jones, Norman Mailer, among others—but Dale had only laughed and uttered her favorite expression of contempt: "Crap." He was as frustrated in his hopes and ambitions as Eddie Eden was in his, and he ought to feel some fraternal camaraderie and compassion for him. Maybe they were both talentless, predestined failures in their preferred professions, and if he had the opportunity Eden had now he might be just as much of an opportunist. He didn't think so, but how did a man know his reactions in any situation until he was tested? Gigolo, protégé, stud—how did they classify kept men these days? What was the chic "mod" designation for that ancient game?

His typewriter sat on a small olive-green metal table in a corner, a battered portable with a sheet of yellow paper on the platen half-filled with black print. "Stay home and write." Poor Mom. How simple she made things sound. Probably because life was simple to her, a matter of living simply and simply living. She was never tormented by goals and ambitions, had never struggled or competed in the endless rat race for recognition. She wouldn't understand Eddie Eden's desperation, nor his own, which was sometimes like a vicious tapeworm gnawing in his guts, a relentless vise squeezing his skull. Maybe it didn't even occur to her that if he quit this job tonight, refused to go on this assignment tomorrow, he'd have difficulty paying next month's rent and buying food and clothing for them. His father's income, pitifully inadequate by today's standards, had been stipulated by the church deacons and tithed from the parishioners; it had provided the necessities of life, and both the Reverend and his wife had been convinced that if they needed more, the Lord would provide it. Their son, however, had no such blind or rockbound faith. Experiences and needs of a different nature had taught him that he must do battle with reality if he would conquer or even cope with it.

It was stuffy in the small room. Soon the nights would be unbearable in the city, and the annual exodus of those fortunate enough to flee would begin. Ben switched on the electric fan. One of these days he was going to live in airconditioned comfort. One of these days he was going to have a beach or mountain retreat in which to escape and write. The fan fluttered the yellow sheet in the typewriter, so that it sounded like the old-fashioned razz-berries. He stared at it ruefully. This was the eighth summer he'd promised himself success.

He removed his coat and tie, opened his shirt and lay down on the narrow bed—virginal as far as any sex life there was concerned—and smoked. Marriage, whatever its other drawbacks, had its compensations. Even a set-up like Eden's had its advantages. Variety might be the spice of life, but it could also be the boredom and despair. There was plenty of variety in the Madison Avenue office building that housed the Dobbs Detective Agency, a regular smorgasbord for the sexual appetite, and he'd sampled his share; but seconds were rare, and he'd found nothing so far tasty enough to want to make a steady diet of it. Oh, Dale had left her imprint, all right, and not only on Timmy!

chapter
3

BEN GOT OFF THE DELTA JET at New Orleans,
wearing a dark dacron suit and dark glasses, and feeling
like a member of the Mafia. There was no flight to
Rainbow, not even a shuttle or air taxi, a good indication
of its size. He made connections with a Greyhound, and
after four hours and twenty minutes through some of the
most beautiful country he'd ever seen, left the bus and
caught a cab to the address Eddie had written down for
him on a piece of Miss Haddington's monogramed sta-
tionery which, like everything else in the penthouse, was
permeated with her specially blended Paris aphrodisiac.

The town, developed from a plantation over a century
ago, lay on the banks of the tortuous Teche, in a region
of rivers and lakes and glades, forests and fields of
sugarcane and rice, old mansions and shacks and shan-
tyboats, of jungle density and almost mystic beauty and
enchantment. The inky waters of the bayou were like
black mirrors reflecting the tangled, semitropical growth
on its banks. There were floating gardens of ferns and
elephant's ears, waterlilies and hyacinths. Moss seemed
to drape the entire landscape, trailing long gray veils that
shimmered iridescently in the sunlight and turned a misty
mauve at dusk.

The house, a small frame bungalow begging paint and repairs, stood on a quiet street shaded by monarch magnolias and ancient live oaks bearded in Spanish moss. Hydrageas, camellias, jasmine bloomed in the yard, amid other flowers and plants that Ben did not recognize. But the trellis of honeysuckle, against which the young girl was wistfully posed in the snapshot, was immediately familiar, and Ben knew what Eddie had meant about the cloying fragrance. In the hot humid afternoon, it was almost palpable, overpowering.

There was no doorbell and no answer to his knock. He heard activity in the rear and went around and found Marcie Eden packing the car. She was barefoot, wearing blue jeans and a plaid shirt with the tails out. Her dark hair was mussed, her face innocent of makeup. She looked sixteen, and suddenly Ben felt old and dirty and depraved.

"Hello," he said.

"Hello." She eyed his bag, mistaking him for a canvassing salesman. Peddlers were persistent in Rainbow; failing a reception at the front, they usually tried the back.

"I'm Ben Hale."

"Oh," she cried, immediately flustered. "Oh, good grief! I didn't expect you so soon. I—I didn't even know you had arrived. Why didn't you call me from the airport?"

"Sorry. I should have. Just didn't think of it."

"When did you get in?"

Ben was cautious; one loose lie, one careless slip could betray him and his job. "About midnight."

"And the business in New Orleans?"

"All settled this morning." He smiled his apologies. "I shouldn't have surprised you this way. Shall I leave and come back?"

Her smile forgave him. She had nice teeth, small, white, even, and her well-defined mouth needed no lipstick. Despite the flush of the heat, sun, and embarrassment on her face, it was a lovely, appealing face, with a delicate tip-tilted nose and deep blue, almost violet, eyes accented with crisp black lashes. And the boyish clothes did not quite camouflage a very female and equally attractive figure.

"No, it's just that I'd have made some effort with my appearance if I'd had time. First impressions, you know— and I must make an awful one."

"On the contrary, delightful. Refreshing."

"It is hot, isn't it? We have long summers down here. Come inside and I'll get you something cool to drink. I think there's a beer on ice. Aunt Beth went to the store to shop for supper. It's not far. She walked. But she'll probably be hours, because she visits on the way. No one's in much of a hurry here. It's the climate. Eddie says it's enough to cause mold and mildew and damp-rot in people as well as things, and I reckon you couldn't find a more leisurely or languid town in the South."

Her chatter was nervousness, Ben knew, and wished he could put her at ease. He followed her up the wooden steps into the kitchen. You didn't see kitchens like that much any more. Big and square. Open cabinets with fancy woodwork and lacy shelf-paper. Ruffled calico curtains at the windows. Old-fashioned range that probably turned out some of the best old-fashioned meals in the parish. The last such kitchen Ben had seen had belonged to the parsonage in the Vermont hills and his uncle's farmhouse in the valley.

"Sit down," Marcie invited, "if you don't mind the informality of the kitchen."

"I prefer it," Ben said. There was no dining room in the remodeled brownstone in New York; all their meals were eaten in the kitchen, not because his mother preferred it, but the extra space was needed as a bedroom.

Marcie found a beer in the refrigerator, opened it and brought it to him with a glass from the cupboard. Then she sat opposite him at the table, cupping her chin pensively in her hand, and asked seriously, "How is Eddie?"

"Fine."

"No, I mean, really."

"Fine, really. Why?"

"Well, he sounded fine on the phone. Good spirits and all, like he was pleased and happy about something. But it's hard to tell about Eddie. And I hadn't heard from him in so long, I was imagining all sorts of things. But he's really all right, Mr. Hale?"

"Ben," he said.

"Ben," she agreed. "Eddie's doing well?"

Ben poured the beer, trying not to put too big a head on it. "You could say that, Marcie. Yes."

Marcie contemplated her fingernails; the pale polish was chipped, she'd have to manicure them tonight and frequently in New York. Eddie liked well-groomed hands; they symbolized leisure to him. "I'm glad, because I plan to stay with him awhile. I didn't quit my job, though, just took a leave of absence. Precautions, in case I have to come back. I don't believe in burning bridges."

Ben wondered if experience had taught her this wisdom; if rebuilding those she'd unwittingly destroyed because of Eddie had instilled caution. "Wise girl," he said.

She raised her eyes and studied him. "Since I talked to you on the phone I've been trying to imagine what you'd be like, if you were anything like your voice."

"Am I?"

"Yes. I liked your voice immediately."

"Thanks. I liked yours immediately, too."

"But voices can be deceiving, can't they? The nice ones don't necessarily mean the person is nice."

"I guess not."

"I'm sure you are, though. Nice, I mean."

Ben gazed into his beer; the froth was melting. He wished she'd leave that subject. He thanked her again.

"How long have you known Eddie?" she asked.

"Not long," he hedged.

"How long?" she insisted.

"Ever since he's been in New York, more or less."

"That's three months."

"About."

"No, exactly. I've counted every day, marked them off on the calendar. I began to think he'd forgotten me, that he'd never send for me as he promised, and I'd just have to go on my own. Which I intended to do, even if he hadn't finally called me the other night. Do I sound stubborn?"

"Practical," Ben said. "Are you ready to leave?"

"Almost. But I think we'd better wait until morning, don't you?"

The reasons behind that suggestion were obvious enough. If they left this afternoon, night would soon overtake them on the highway. Evidently she wanted to get better acquainted before starting a lengthy journey with him. She wasn't as naive as Eddie thought, and he didn't know his wife as well as he imagined. Maybe he didn't know her at all, because in seven years of marriage he'd never taken the time, the interest, or the love. It appeared that Eddie Eden was not only a prime bastard but a prime fool as well.

"That would probably be best," Ben agreed. "Is there anything I can do to help, Marcie? Anything you want me to pack or carry out?"

"A couple of boxes of Eddie's things," she said, "and his guitar. But I'm not sure there's room enough in the car, Ben. We may have to rent a trailer."

Ben finished his beer. "Eddie said you might want to do that, and I shouldn't let you. He doesn't want you to bring too much, Marcie, only the essentials. Your aunt can send the rest later, if you find you're going to stay put awhile."

"I see." Her face clouded. "Then he isn't doing so well, after all?"

"Marcie, it isn't that, exactly. It's just that—well, he's afraid you'll cart along a lot of unnecessary stuff, like women are prone to do, and you'd have to find a larger apartment right off. His in Greenwich Village is rather small."

Yes, she had that fault. No matter how temporary her homes with Eddie, she'd always tried to add something personal and permanent: a picture or knick-knack with some special significance for her, something to which she was attached and could feel some attachment. Somehow, it made things easier. But Eddie was never happy with her attempts at homemaking. Just more junk to bother with on the next move, he'd complain. Apparently his future in New York wasn't too secure, either, and he was anticipating another, perhaps imminent, move.

"I understand," she said, suppressing disappointment. "It's settled, then. No excess baggage."

Ben was relieved. At least he'd softened that blow; the return trip would be less burdensome for her, if nothing else, and he still hoped she'd change her mind and decide not to go at all.

She was pensive, eyes downcast, one slender finger tracing a geometric pattern on the tablecloth. "Anyway, it'll be nice to have the car in New York. We won't have to ride the taxis or subway."

How could he tell her that that little green Chevrolet she'd worked to pay off wasn't Eddie's idea of an automobile, now he was coveting Miss Haddington's silver Jaguar?

"Yes," he said.

Aunt Beth returned with two bags of groceries and the latest neighborhood gossip, which she curtailed when she saw company. She was a slight, wiry woman in her late fifties, with sun-streaked hair and faded eyes behind gold-rimmed glasses. Her husband, Danton Ames, had been dead five years, and she was subsisting on a widow's pension from the Rainbow Sugar Mills, where he'd worked as a foreman, and some room-rent from her niece.

Marcie introduced Ben Hale. Mrs. Ames wasn't much

surprised at the traveling arrangements her niece's husband had made for her. Nothing Eddie Eden did surprised her much. She'd known him since he was in rompers, and some of his childhood and adolescent antics were not pleasant to contemplate. His family were plain people, swampers of mixed ancestry, mostly Acadian, poor but humbly proud, and Eddie had inherited the pride and poverty without the humility. Ironically enough, it was the Edens, a closely-knit clan, who had objected most to the marriage on the basis of religion. A renegade who'd last attended Mass at his grandmother's funeral when he was eighteen, they'd hoped for a staunch Catholic wife to return Eddie to the fold, not a Protestant who, they felt, would only lead him farther astray. Furthermore, Marcie Landers, orphaned early in life, had neither a substantial inheritance nor a proud heritage of traditions to recommend her, and no one expected anything of the union but an early failure.

Beth Ames had viewed the whole affair with misgivings, equally skeptical that it would last, and amazed by each month it endured beyond the honeymoon. But she hadn't reckoned, nor had the Edens, with the girl's tenacity and perseverance. The neglect and loneliness she suffered while Eddie was away pursuing his crazy career, tagging along with him if it suited his fancy or convenience, remaining behind if it didn't, but always ready and eager to run to him like a faithful dog when he snapped his fingers, as he had via long distance telephone last night. And so this was the mastiff he had sent to fetch her?

"Pleased to meet you, Mr. Hale."

"Same here, ma'am."

Mrs. Ames liked the way he said "ma'am" like a Southerner, but she wasn't interested enough to explore his background. Eddie met a lot of people in the towns he played, and some of them visited him in Rainbow. But she didn't bother to try to know them, for most were plainly not worth knowing, and those who might be never stayed long enough to cultivate acquaintance. Ben Hale, she thought, might be an exception in worthiness, but she'd have to wait and see. He appeared to be a gentleman, but that could be surface polish like the shine on his shoes. She suggested that he and Marcie go out on the veranda while she fixed supper. She didn't like strangers in her kitchen while she cooked, or in her house at any time, but she didn't say this. She only said it would be cooler outside, and Marcie agreed.

The Teche was visible from the porch. Sometimes, when Marcie was restless or lonely, she walked down to the bayou and wandered in the vicinity until the mood passed. You could lose yourself literally and figuratively in the swamp, and Eddie had often accused her of escaping life and reality there. He could never understand her affinity with this country, her congenital attachment to it, the intricate way it was woven into the fiber of her being, for he felt no such native sentiment, only resentment, revulsion, and rebellion at the thought of spending his life there.

Marcie sat in a rush-bottomed chair, Ben in its mate beside her. "The mosquitoes get pretty bad after dark," she said. "They breed like mad in the marshes."

"Don't they control them?"

"Sporadically, but not methodically unless an epidemic threatens. This used to be yellow fever and malaria country, you know. It's interesting, though. You must see more of it before you leave."

"I'd like to," Ben said, offering her a cigarette.

Marcie declined. "I don't smoke."

"That would please my mother very much," Ben said for some unknown reason. "Mind if I do?"

"Of course not."

"I'm glad to hear that, because I could never drive all the way to New York without smoking." He smiled. "It's one of my bad habits."

"One?"

"I have several," he admitted. "How long have you lived here, Marcie?"

"I was born here," she said. "My mother died before I was a year old, and my father was killed in an accident when I was ten. Aunt Beth raised me. She and Uncle Danton never had any children, and they were wonderful parents to me." She paused, as if she expected some comment, watched him light a cigarette, then continued, "Eddie's a local product too, though he doesn't like to admit it. He likes to consider himself cosmopolitan, and this parish is too provincial for him. He thought show business was the way out, and I guess that's the main reason he went into it.

"Anyway, he had some natural talent for the guitar and developed a kind of singing style, which a booking agency in New Orleans liked enough to get him some out-of-town spots for a year or so. He improved and moved up to Baton Rouge and Shreveport, then to Biloxi and Mobile and other cities, and finally to a club in the French Quarter of New Orleans. Then he hired a publicity agent and thought he was on his way to the stars. But he hit a detour and went on the circuit. Texas, Arizona, California. He wanted Las Vegas—God, how he wanted Vegas! But no dice. The big and spectacular places were just out of his reach." She broke again and gazed earnestly at Ben. "What kind of place is it in New York? He never told me much about it. Does it swing? Has it a reputation in the 'in' circles? Can it bounce him to bigger and better things?"

"It's called the Amber Alley," Ben said. "A combination coffeehouse-nightclub tourist attraction in Greenwich Village. Not big time, Marcie. Far from it. But I don't think Eddie is ready for top stuff, do you?"

"I guess not," Marcie agreed reluctantly, thinking that the Amber Alley sounded like another dead end for Eddie. "Of course I could never tell him that—his ego would be bruised. Oh, Ben! If he'd only give up show business altogether. He's had so many disappointments, so much disillusion and failure. And he's not young any more. Most people make it early in this business or not at all. The Fabians, Ankas, Presleys, Wayne Newtons—they were in their teens! And the big rage now is groups of weird-looking teenagers."

But talented, Ben thought, and with charisma. But no point telling her something she probably already knew, that Eddie Eden had little of either quality. He smoked in silence.

Marcie hoped she hadn't said too much, given him the wrong impression. "I'm sorry, Ben. I just met you and already I'm pouring out personal problems like I'm seeking a shoulder to cry on. I'm not, Ben. Don't think that." She waited. "Well, you have a fairly complete dossier on Marcie Eden. What about Ben Hale?"

Her choice of the word "dossier" was ironic, Ben thought, almost as if she were psychic. "I'm a very dull fellow," he said.

"I doubt that. I understood Eddie to say you were looking for a writing assignment in New Orleans?"

"Yes, I freelance," Ben said, glad that it was at least half-true.

"That's marvelous. I've never known a writer before. You make money at it?"

"Some. So far, however, income taxes haven't been a problem."

"What do you write?"

"Fiction. Articles. Whatever."

"Well, I hope you write a best seller."

"Thanks."

Shadows fell across the yard, and the swamp creatures began their evening serenade: tenor crickets, bass frogs, tremolo birds. The bayou looked deep and dark and ominous, and Marcie said, "You really should see more of Teche Country, Ben. You might get some ideas. Some classics have been written about it. It's the setting of Longellow's *Evangeline*, you know, and the characters were taken from life. I never did like the poem, though.

43

Hat in hand, the lieutenant was studying the face in the portrait, the enigmatic Mona Lisa quality which the obviously enchanted artist had exaggerated, the ethereal beauty and perfection he had no doubt been well paid to create but was only an illusion which, he suspected, the subject herself realized perhaps better than anyone else.

"Don't leave town," he advised.

"Am I under arrest?"

"No. Just be available for questioning."

"Only to the police," Silver said. "I shall be incommunicado to everyone else."

The other men were waiting for Lieutenant Morse in the foyer. He put on his hat. "Take him out the back way," he told the stretcher bearers. "There's a crowd out front. I'll send the wagon to the rear."

Exit Eddie Eden, Silver thought. No flowers, no applause, no encores. On a litter, under a sheet, through an alley. Dear God, what a way to go!

chapter
4

MARCIE CLEARED THE TABLE and washed the dishes, her chores when Aunt Beth did the cooking, and Ben insisted on helping her. Armed with insect repellent and aerosol bomb, standard outdoor equipment in Teche Country, Beth went out to sit in her rocker, her favorite summer evening pastime.

"What time shall we leave tomorrow?" Marcie asked.

"Early as possible, I suppose. Has the car been checked? Gas, oil, tires, battery? Is it ready for the road?"

"So the service station attendant assured me, and I have to take his word. I don't know anything about machinery. I have a very untechnical, unscientific mind."

"But still you'd have attempted the trip alone?" Ben said, admiring her courage if not her logic. "I heard you tell Eddie that on the extension. What would you have done in the event of car trouble?"

"Called a garage if a phone was handy. Otherwise, just sat and waited for a good Samaritan to come along and help me." She emptied the dishwater and began scouring the sink. "You dry dishes like a married man, Ben. Are you married?"

"I was," he said. "Three years. Divorced now. I have

a son, Timmy, five years old. We live with my mother, or rather she lives with us. I prefer the country, though."

"Why don't you live there, then? Writers can write anywhere, can't they? Isn't that one of the advantages of that profession?"

"Country places cost money," Ben explained. "I haven't made that much yet, might never make it."

"I hope I meet your family in New York," Marcie said.

"I want you to meet them," Ben told her. "Mother'd like you. Timmy, too."

"It's a date, then." She hung the dishcloth in the pantry. "You're going to bunk in the living room, Mr. Hale. There's a fairly comfortable sofabed, vintage model. Come give me a hand with it."

The house was built seventy years ago, in the parlor era. It too was a perfectly square room, high-ceilinged, with rambling red roses on the faded wallpaper and starched white lace curtains at the tall narrow windows. Crocheted antimacassars protected the velour upholstered chairs, and the sofabed was a brown leather relic splitting at the seams. A muted floral carpet covered the floor, which was centered with a round pedestaled mahogany table holding a milkglass vase of plastic flowers. The parsonage parlor all over again, and Ben felt as if he had come home.

"You have to pull that tab there," Marcie instructed. "Together now. Heave ho!"

The mattress popped up like a jack-in-the-box and stayed in the air, and Marcie said, "Sometimes you have to retrieve it. I reckon this is one of those times."

They brought it down safely and Marcie went to the hall linencloset and returned with clean white sheets, a pillow, and embroidered case. Ben watched her. She might not be technical or scientific, but she was definitely domestic. She'd be easy to travel with and probably fun, even if they camped along the way; and he rather wished now that he had defied Eddie and encouraged the trailer rental, plus the purchase of a couple of sleeping-bags.

"There," Marcie said, smoothing the last visible wrinkle from the linens. "The bathroom is down the hall, to the left."

"I'll find it," Ben assured her. The great big private eye dick will find the pot, ma'am.

"Good night, Ben."

"Good night, Marcie."

Ben was awake when the alarm sounded, but feigned sleep when she came into the living room and gently shook his shoulder. "Ben? It's time to get up."

He had a sudden gallant impulse to grasp her hand and tell her to go back to bed and forget the trip, forget everything Eddie had told her on the phone and everything he'd told her since his arrival.

"All right. Do we toss for the shower?"

"No. Me first. Then you, while I fix breakfast."

"Oh, don't bother. We can catch it on the road."

"Nonsense. Aunt Beth'd be insulted. No overnight guest leaves the Hilton Ames on an empty stomach. Besides, she's a habitual early riser, already up and making biscuits."

She padded off in her pajamas and bare feet. Ben wished she'd put on some shoes, so she'd seem less like a child. And when next he saw her, she was quite womanly in a yellow linen dress, her dark hair smoothly brushed, setting the table with the same blue willow dishes he remembered from supper.

Mrs. Ames was in checked gingham and apron, scrambling eggs, and the biscuits, which hadn't popped out of a can, smelled delicious baking in the oven.

"Good morning," she greeted him. "Looks like it's going to be a nice day. Hot, but clear."

"Yes," Ben agreed. "We should make good mileage."

"I hope you like grits?"

"Love 'em," said the Vermonter, who'd been raised on pancakes and maple syrup.

Beth indicated a chair, flatteringly at the head of the table. "Sit down, Mr. Hale. I don't know if you say grace or not. We do it silently, to each his own."

Ben's mother was big on grace, but usually Ben forgot, or was in too much of a hurry grabbing a meal on the run. He made a conscious silent effort this time, and then Aunt Beth passed him the bowl of steaming hominy grits.

"I picked up some maps at the service station yesterday and charted a couple of courses," Marcie said, as they were leaving. "There're several ways we can go to New York, Ben, and no great difference in mileage. I'd sort of like to go via Birmingham and Chattanooga, but you can study the routes and see which you prefer."

"Your preference suits me fine," Ben said.

"Well, just stay on Highway 90 to New Orleans. But of course you know that—it's the route you traveled on the bus out here. And if you'd like to see more of Teche Country, any of the sideroads will do it. That one coming up, for instance, leads into the heart of it."

It seemed important to her to show him this land, as if by doing so she could show him a part of herself, and Ben was interested in both aspects—intrigued, in fact. He turned where she indicated, and for two miles and more traveled what must have been the lonesomest, most isolated and enchanting road in the world.

"Here," Marcie said finally, signaling ground high and dry enough to park, a knoll on the banks of the Teche.

Live oaks hoary with moss arched in a canopy overhead. Cypress, exposing gnarled roots like giant knobby knees, stretched ferny green arms across the bayou. Purple hyacinths floated on the dark glassy surface. Everywhere vines crept, crawled, entwined. Morning mists still clung to the marshes, although the sun was rapidly burning it away, releasing in its vapors the unique miasma and chimeras of the swamps. Tree frogs trilled in the thickets, and marsh birds cried plaintively. Now and then a vagrant breeze fluttered the mossy draperies like gray ghosts, and the eerie cry of a loon was startling.

"Well?" prompted Marcie, as proud of the scenery as if she had personally created it. "Does it give you ideas? Inspire you to pen and paper?"

"Is that why you brought me here?"

"One reason."

"Well, I'm speechless."

"Then you're properly impressed. But do you feel anything special, Ben? I mean, the swamp has a definite effect on me. I think it's a place of tremendous peace and beauty and enchantment. Eddie thinks I'm crazy, because it's ugly and oppressive to him, just a big tangled bog, and he hates it. Some of his relatives still live in the interior, fishing and trapping muskrat, but he never visits them. Says it depresses him. He wouldn't even claim this land as his birthplace, if he didn't consider it expedient to his career."

"Eddie's not very sensitive," Ben said, which was unusual in an artist, even a mediocre one. "It is serene and beautiful and enchanting, Marcie, but it has other aspects as well. Dark, brooding, somber, sinister. Almost human moods—don't you feel those, too?"

She hadn't until he mentioned them. She recognized loneliness and isolation and sadness in the swamps, because they had been kindred spirits from childhood, and especially after the loss of her father; following his funeral she had sought solace and solitude there, venturing as far as she dared into the watery wilderness alone, turning back when the shadows became too deep and the growth impenetrable. But she had never experienced fear or dread in the Teche until this weird moment, when she heard the man beside her saying quietly, "Ideal spot for a murder."

Apprehension tensed her and suddenly she felt chilled, as if a cold wind had swept across the bayou. Why had he said such a thing? Was that how this lovely land affected him? And what was she doing here with him, a man she hardly knew, a rank stranger! He seemed normal and rational enough, but God knew Eddie was no judge of character or sanity. He'd taken up with some kooks and weirdos in his time, and this guy might be the prize of them all.

"You mean setting for a mystery?"

"Yes. Suspense yarn. I ought to take notes."

Marcie relaxed somewhat, although her heart continued its excited flutter. "You can always come back."

"But I may not feel this same impact and fascination. First impressions," he reminded her. "I should record them, mentally at least. Second experiences invariably lose some vitality and enthusiasm, it's inevitable. Let's get out and explore a bit, shall we?"

"Oh, no! We might get lost if we wandered off the path. You need a guide in Teche Country. Lots of curious folks have gone in too deep and never come out. Even the natives sometimes get confused and lost without a compass. There're a lot of superstitions about the Teche, and some people think it's haunted."

"That's understandable," Ben said. "I wish I had more time to know it."

"But we haven't," Marcie said abruptly, anxious now to leave the swamp. "We have to hit the trail to Manhattan." She reached into the dash compartment. "Want to look at the maps?"

"No, navigation will be your department," Ben said, starting the motor. "I'll be the pilot."

"I'm sorry I'm rushing you, Ben. It was my idea to come here, and then I hurry you away before you're ready. That's not very hospitable."

"I can always come back," he quoted her.

"Do you think you will?"

"Depends."

"On what?"

"Lots of things. An invitation, for one."

"Well, if that's all—"

"Not so fast, Marcie," Ben interrupted. "When you

know me better, you may not want me to come back."

Not knowing how to answer that, Marcie remained silent. And soon they were back on the highway, heading toward New Orleans, where they would pick up the route to Birmingham, Alabama. Ben had lit a cigarette and was smoking pensively, ignoring the pine forests paralleling the road and the water flowers that grew wild in the glades and ditches, masses of purple, sometimes a nuisance choking the bayous and impeding water traffic. Marcie was struggling with her short yellow dress, which had risen far above her knees, exposing her thighs, and then she was saying, "Ben, there's something we haven't discussed yet, and I think we should. It's important."

"Sleeping arrangements?"

Her glance seared him. "Why do you say that?"

Because after that tantalizing display of flesh and dimples it was on his mind, naturally, and he had assumed it was also on hers. "Isn't that what you meant?"

"Why, no. What other arrangement could that be but separate rooms? I meant money. I have some, but not much. I presume Eddie gave you enough for gas and other expenses?"

"Yes."

"Are you sure? He tried to sound flush on the phone, but Eddie hates to admit he's broke, ever. I don't want you financing any part of this trip, Ben."

"Eddie provided the funds, Marcie. But I don't see what choice you'd have if he hadn't."

"None except to borrow, Ben. But I'd pay you back. I wouldn't stick you with it. Neither would Eddie. He's proud that way."

Sure, Ben thought. Proud as Lucifer. Only a real proud devil would allow himself to be kept.

"I don't expect to get stuck with anything, Marcie. Let's forget that end of it, shall we? It's all taken care of. Watch the map—there's a junction coming up."

"I haven't lost us yet."

"We haven't gone very far, and except for that interesting detour in the jungle—" he paused, glanced curiously at her—"What happened back there, Marcie? Why did you freeze up on me? Did I scare you?"

"A little," she admitted. "With that remark about murder. Then I remembered you're a writer. Maybe you'll return for research and write a classic mystery or suspense story?"

"Maybe," Ben mused. "And dedicate it to you."

"Oh, I wasn't hinting for that, Ben."

"But you wouldn't object?"

"I'd be honored," Marcie said. "Where do you think we'll spend the night?"

"Wherever it overtakes us."

"The motels in small towns are cheaper."

"Marcie, will you stop worrying about that? We can afford good places."

"Just making a suggestion, Ben. Don't get mad."

"I'm not mad."

"Well, something's wrong. You're tense."

"It's the heat."

"I know. It's devastating down here. I wanted aircondtioning in the car but couldn't afford it."

"I'm not complaining, Marcie. I don't have all the comforts and conveniences in New York, either. I don't even own the car I drive. The agency does."

"Agency?"

Ben swallowed. "My literary agent lets me use his car when I need one," he said and felt the sweat pour under his arms and down his back. That was close! "It's damn decent of him, considering I don't earn enough in commissions to pay a fraction of the overhead in his office."

"No doubt he considers it a long-term investment, which he'll recoup with interest some day," Marcie said. "Want to take turns driving?"

"Not yet."

"Well, let me know when you get tired."

"I will. Pick out a café in the next town, and we'll stop for coffee. That's another of my habits."

"You can have a beer this evening or cocktail if you prefer," Marcie offered like a bribe for good behavior.

"Don't be so nice to me, Marcie. You may regret it."

Again he'd caused her apprehension. She stirred uneasily, tugging at her creeping skirt, her breath impaired. "What?"

"Forget it," Ben said, angry with himself.

A crazy thing to say! He was uttering a lot of wild and ambiguous nonsense. She'd think he was some kind of nut. He had to be more careful. Trouble was, this farce was getting sticky, and he despised his gum-shoe role in it. One lie led to another, one pretense to another, one hypocrisy to another, and they were pyramiding. There was no rationale, no logic to this trip. For Eden's purposes, his wife would have been better left in Rainbow. He could have forbidden her to come, or found some excuse to keep her away. Discounting the transparency that he hoped she would become interested in another man, apparently any man who might conceivably let him off the hook, what was Eden's real game? Ben recalled a sentence which the office stenographers used to test their typing skills: Monstrous motives motivate monsters. In his estimation, that fitted Eddie Eden pretty well. What annoyed Ben most was that he could not readily decipher and fathom the monster's motives, and it made him feel inadequate.

He stubbed out his cigarette in the tray and immediately craved another. God, he was tense! He had to relax and concentrate on the hidden aspects of this case. After they checked in somewhere this evening, he'd call Eddie and see how things were faring with Silver Haddington. Somehow Ben felt that she didn't even share, much less encourage, Eddie's marital interest. It was just difficult to believe that she wanted him to that extent. Perhaps they'd had a fight by now, and she'd jetted off to another lover somewhere, and Eddie'd be glad to welcome his faithful wife. Comforting himself with this possibility, Ben flipped on the radio. Frank Sinatra was singing

Strangers in the Night. Now there was a voice. By comparison, Eddie Eden was a bullfrog croaking in his native swamp; he should have stayed in the sugarcane fields, the rice paddies, the muskrat marshes. His tensions easing, Ben hummed and sang along with Frank.

"I like that song," he said, and Marcie thought his baritone wasn't bad, better in fact than Eddie's.

"Me, too," she said. "But my favorite at the moment is the theme from *Love Story.*"

They discussed that motion picture awhile, and the book which had inspired it. Then other books and films. A newscast came on, and they turned to Vietnam and the Middle East, foreign and domestic policies and politics, and Ben was surprised at her knowledge of these matters. As a Southerner, her views on civil rights differed somewhat from his, but she wasn't bigoted about it, or rabid, as some he'd known. She said there'd been no racial riots in Rainbow so far, perhaps because there were no ghettos and the other grievances were not sufficient provocation. But of course, as summer deepened, the aggravations and tensions might build with the heat and tempers erupt in violence. She lamented the lost summers of leisure and languor in the South, the new seasons of discontent and despair, rebellion and disaster, which people had come to expect and dread.

"Not only in the South," Ben said, recalling Los Angeles, Detroit, Newark, New York.

"It's significant, I guess, that geography isn't important any more," Marcie said. "An indictment of the whole country, in fact. But there has been progress, Ben. The liberals say not enough, the conservatives too much. The real progress will come when both races realize they have to compromise rather than conquer. Not white power or black power, but combined power is the way to overcome."

Ben had never heard a profound thought more succinctly expressed. She had vision and common sense and far more wisdom and intelligence than Eddie allowed her. One more thing, evidently, that he hadn't bothered to discover about his wife: that she possessed a brain. Probably never got past her body and had tired soon enough of that.

"You're right," he said. "And I think the older generation, conditioned by a century of procrastination, understands and appreciates that. But youth hasn't the time or the patience—this is their age for action."

"What would you do if we met a freedom marcher on the road?" Marcie asked.

"Offer him a lift."

She shook her head. "He wouldn't accept, Ben. That would defeat his purpose. What he'd want is a salute in passing, a nod of recognition, a cheer."

"That's not much to ask, is it?"

"Not much," Marcie agreed. "I guess the great puzzle to them is why it's so hard for some people to give."

chapter
5

MARCIE HAD ALWAYS ENVIED other women their sophistication and nonchalance; she had the misfortune of appearing guilty even when she was perfectly innocent. Her signature on the motel register that evening was almost illegible, so timid was the hand that wrote it. She wondered if some mute signal had passed between Ben and the desk clerk, a sort of gentlemen's agreement, resulting in the assignment of adjoining singles with connecting doors, presently locked but hardly a barrier unless the occupants desired it so. The bellboy seemed to stress this convenience as he carted in the luggage, going from one room to the other to deposit the individual pieces, checking the bathrooms for towels and tissue, and then holding out his hand for his reward. Marcie could hardly wait for him to leave.

"They suspect hanky-panky," she said. "I bet they always suspect hanky-panky in situations like this."

"Situations like what?"

"A couple coming in together, the way we did. The pretense of separate rooms."

"Pretense?"

"You know what I mean, Ben Hale! I'm not used to

this sort of thing. I've never gone to a hotel with a strange man before, never."

"Am I all that strange, Marcie?"

"Stop twisting the issue," Marcie said. "We met yesterday. We're not exactly old friends."

"You know the fellow next to you on the other side?"

"Of course not."

"Then he's a stranger too, isn't he?"

"That's different. A technicality and a coincidence."

"Life is full of differences, technicalities, and coincidences, Marcie."

"And you handle them all so easily, don't you?"

"Not all," Ben said. "There's a cocktail lounge and restaurant here. Why don't we gussie up a bit and sample the fare?"

Marcie agreed and met him an hour later in a pale blue silk sheath, heels, and a string of crystals that reflected new depths in her eyes. Her perfume was a delicate floral fragrance, sweet as a summer garden and as appealing. Ben had showered and shaved and wore his dark dacron suit and a fresh white shirt. Marcie thought he was a personable escort and was proud to be seen with him; the way he looked at her, she thought the pride was mutual.

The lounge had paneled walnut walls and simulated bronze fixtures, a synthetic elegance. The booths were small and intimate. Ben ordered a double bourbon on the rocks, Marcie a vodka martini. A girl with luminous eyeshadow and a long fall of misty-blonde hair sang and accompanied herself at the piano-bar, the deep décolletage of her black sequined gown obviating any vocal requirements. Somehow the atmosphere was not conducive to the kind of conversation they'd pursued on the road. Marcie supposed this was intentional on the part of the proprietors, making it easier for guests to forget their extraneous burdens, or ignore them. But it was also easier to magnify personal problems and attractions. The couples all seemed so wrapped up in each other, she felt as if they had inadvertently stumbled into a lovers' rendezvous. She dawdled with the olive in her martini, trying to decide whether or not to eat it, and soon Ben finished his drink and ordered another.

"You're not saying much," Marcie said.

"Talked out, I guess. We took the world to task today, didn't we? Too bad we didn't solve or change anything. It's still the same lousy rotten world."

"The world, Ben, or its inhabitants?"

"You're right," Ben said. "There's nothing wrong with the world that people couldn't make right if they tried. But that would involve a universal crusade, and the average person is too concerned about himself to give a damn about anyone else. He gets involved only when he's forced by some calamity that threatens him personally." His second drink arrived, and he raised it to Marcie in a wry salute to superior wisdom. "Marcie, what's your philosophy of life?"

"I don't know that I have one, Ben."

"Everybody does," he said. "They may not call it a philosophy or think of it consciously as such. It's merely their personal code: how they measure themselves and others, what they believe and don't believe, what they'd do and wouldn't do. Their standards, criteria, moralities. It's a prescription a person formulates for himself early in life, and either abandons early or retains to the bitter end. Other terms for it are honor, character, integrity—and either you have it or you don't. I think you do, Marcie."

A candle flickered in a blue globe on the table, and their eyes met and held a moment in the glow. "Well, thanks. But don't you think you do?"

"I'm not sure." He drank. "But before this journey ends, I may find out."

"What're you talking about?"

Ben shrugged. "Damned if I know. My father used to say leave the preaching to the preachers and the philosophy to the philosophers—and here I am, neither, indulging in both. Must be high."

"On two bourbons?"

"Double bourbons."

"You'll feel better after dinner."

"Maybe," he said softly. "Then again, I might just feel more philosophical and bore the hell out of you."

"I wouldn't be bored, Ben. I can't speak for you, but I've had an interesting, stimulating day."

"Ditto," Ben said. "And thank God for that. It'd be the devil of a trip if we bored each other, wouldn't it?"

The candlelight threw shadows into Marcie's face, purpled her eyes. She sipped her martini as if she must conserve it. "I may be wrong, but I don't think Eddie would have sent you if there were any danger of that, Ben. You seem to have been—how shall I say it?—hand-picked."

Her intuition was questing again and on the verge of discovery. It was time for another detour. "We can order dinner in here," he said.

"If we can read the menu."

"The light, you mean? They keep it dim purposely, not because it's so romantic but so it's difficult to see the prices."

Marcie laughed, delightful laughter, Ben thought, cool and merry, effervescent as sparkling burgundy. "I believe it. But I see they have pompano, and I love it—though I'm sure it can't compare with Antoine's."

"Antoine's?" Ben raised his brows, formed a silent whistle on his lips. "I'm impressed."

"Don't be. We dined there only once, when Eddie was feeling successful, and 'dined' is the proper word. No one ever 'eats' at Antoine's. The food is gourmet all the way and the service impeccable. All the 'monsieuring' went to Eddie's head. He tipped so lavishly we had to eat hamburgers and hotdogs the rest of the week."

"That sounds like Eddie, all right."

"Yes, poor darling, he's loaded with complexes."

"Not of inferiority," Ben remarked.

"But that's exactly what it is, Ben! He camouflages it with ego."

"Marcie, that's a patent contradiction. A person can't be simultaneously inferior and superior."

"Eddie can. Deep inside, I think he knows he'll never hit the top, but he hasn't admitted it outside yet. If he could afford analysis, that's what they'd discover about Eddie."

"Among other things," Ben said, motioning the waiter. "Shall we order?"

After dinner some couples got up to dance on the few feet of polished floorspace. They watched them. Ben, having another bourbon for dessert, was silent, somber, smoking as if he expected tobacco to be withdrawn from the market momentarily. The shadows darkened his gray eyes to slate and gave his face an artistic cast, all sharp planes and angles, a not unattractive gauntness. But he seemed preoccupied, remote and inaccessible, and Marcie felt suddenly abandoned, as if he had walked away and left her. Did he have these dark brooding moods often, these private and impenetrable reveries?

"I'd like to dance, Ben."

"Don't know if I'm steady enough on my feet."

"Who'll notice, the way they twist and squirm now? Like writhing worms."

"I don't do any of that discothèque stuff, Marcie. Never had the time or the inclination to learn. My style's high school prom, class of '55."

"How old does that make you? Thirty-one, thirty-two?"

"Thirty-one."

"College?"

"Two years at the university in Burlington, Vermont."

"Why didn't you finish?"

"Money. Free education isn't really free, you know, not even at state-supported institutions. I wasn't either brilliant or athletic enough to win a scholarship. I tried working my way, but the part-time jobs didn't pay enough to buy room-and-board in addition to the other expenses, and my folks couldn't help financially. Dad was a small town minister, if you can imagine their income. He's dead now."

"I'm sorry," Marcie said.

"That's life."

"I still want to dance, Ben."

Since it was inevitable, Ben rose to the occasion, glad the floor was too crowded to permit the presently popular gyrations. The other couples were forced to dance conventionally also, holding each other close, gliding in easy rhythmic coordination or remaining stationary, immobile, except for glandular response. And in this position, pressed against Ben, the warmth of her body releasing its fragrance, Marcie knew it had been a mistake to insist on dancing. She didn't want to encourage him.

"You shouldn't, Ben."

"Reflex action," he said. "Happens every time I dance with a pretty girl."

"Then we'd better sit down."

"Maybe we'd better shut down for the night." He guided her back to the table and signaled for the check.

"I didn't mean to spoil anything," Marcie said, walking back to the motel. "The floor was just too crowded."

"Marcie, it was a normal, natural reaction. I'd rather not analyze it. Have the desk wake you at 6 A.M."

"Leave your call, too."

"I will."

"I had fun, Ben. I enjoyed the evening."

"Me, too."

They said good night at her door. Ben proceeded to his room and directly to the telephone. He gave the motel operator the number of Eddie's apartment in the Village. No answer. Ben suggested that she try another number, and this time Miss Haddington answered. Ben asked if Eddie Eden was there.

"Who's calling?" she inquired.

"Ben Hale."

"Oh," she said with cordial recognition. "Yes, he's here, Mr. Hale. Wait a minute, please."

Waiting, Ben heard talk, laughter, music in the background. Soon Eddie was on the line. The noises were less audible, and Ben knew Eddie was taking the call in a quieter room, one of twelve in the penthouse.

"Hi, man!" he greeted Ben. "I hope it's bonanza!" He sounded jubilantly drunk, high on liquor or something else. "We're celebrating. Big bash."

"Celebrating what?" Ben asked.

"I'm going to marry the lady, Ben. I'm going to propose tonight, and she's going to accept."

"That's impossible, Eddie. Bigamy is illegal. You already have a wife, in the room next door to me now."

"Next door? What's she doing next door?"

"I'm on an assignment, Eddie, not an affair. My job is to deliver Mrs. Eden safe and sound in Manhattan. That's what you contracted for, and that's what you're going to get. Nothing more, nothing less, nothing else. So you might as well cancel your celebration, man. It's premature."

"Mrs. Eden," Eddie scoffed. "You mean you're still at that stage? Don't she appeal to you?"

"You wouldn't understand," Ben said.

"No, I wouldn't. But you'd better understand, Ben. You know damned well why I exposed you to Marcie, and I'm expecting something to develop between here and there. Don't give me any blank negatives."

"Get off my back, Eddie."

"Not until you get Marcie on hers."

"What're you, some kind of pervert? You get a charge thinking of your wife with another guy?"

"Cram the analysis, writer, and cut the phony ethics. I'm in a bind with Silver. If I don't shuck Marcie, she'll shuck me—and I don't intend for that to happen. No need to make a project of it, Ben. You some kind of monk or fag? You impotent or castrated? What's so difficult about bedding a babe?"

"She's not that type, Eddie."

"They're all that type, Ben, with the proper approach. She's no virgin and she's fun, I promise you."

"Shut up," Ben said grimly.

"Hey now! You sound downright chivalrous, Man. The Ole South get to you? Moonlight and magnolias and all that storybook shit? You got a glow for Marcie? That's great. Terrif! Should cinch it."

"Just shut your goddamn mouth, Eddie."

Eddie laughed. "You're tense, man. You dance with the doll tonight, maybe? Rub her up a little? Get a whiff of that sweet jasmine stuff she wears? Subtle, that scent, but effective. Potent as Spanish fly on the sex glands. I was real hooked on it, once. Stop fighting it, Ben. Relieve your tensions. She'll be insulted if you don't at least try."

"Look, you wild sonofabitch! I'm trying to tell you something, and you'd better listen. I don't care what you think was implied or understood, there was no deal to that effect. And I don't give a goddamn if Silver Haddington has you skewered with ultimatums and roasting on a spit, that's your fire and you fight it."

"Okay, I heard you, Ben. Now you hear me. I've got the chance of a lifetime with this woman, and you're not going to foul it up with your chicken conscience or soul or whatever the hell has suddenly possessed and obsessed you! You had your chance to pull out and didn't, so stop this jazz. You're going through with it, or you'll wish you had."

"You've blown your brain, man. What kind of party is that? A freak-out with pot and acid on the menu? Maybe you just went to Rome and think you're Caesar, but you're still a punk to me, and I don't take orders from punks!"

Static punctuated the hum on the wire, and then Eddie's voice came on again, ominously low. "You shouldn't have said that, Ben. You shouldn't have called me a punk. I don't take insults from nobody. You got a kid, haven't you, Ben? Be a shame if he had some kind of accident. Kids do, you know. They fall from trikes and tumble down stairs and get real banged up sometimes. I know. I was a kid once."

Ben was incensed. He gripped the receiver hard enough to imprint the plastic. "You lay a finger on my kid, Eddie, and you've sung your swan song."

"Me? Touch your brat? Take such a risk with all I got going for me now? Don't be flaky, man. But accidents do happen, and I'm just warning you to be careful, that's all. You dig, man?"

"I dig, man. And screw you."

Eddie laughed again, in high spirits. "No, Benny Boy. You screw Marcie." The receiver clicked, the line was dead.

Ben sat down on the bed, staring at the telephone, tempted to call Harvey Dobbs and let him straighten out his cuckoo client. Eddie was turned on tonight, no doubt about that. He was bellicose, belligerant, irrational, yet making a crazy kind of sense. If Silver Haddington was pressuring him, he had to give her promises and reassurances, and pressure Ben into making them materialize. And even in his drugged desperation, he knew Ben's biggest vulnerability was his son. The threat to harm Timmy was spontaneous and probably a bluff that Eddie wouldn't have the guts to carry out himself, but he knew the kind of creeps who would for a pittance, or even the sheer sadistic pleasure of it. You met that ilk in the places Eddie had frequented before fate had sent Silver Haddington and some of her swinging sycophants to the Amber Alley in East Village, where the Jet Set shopped for curiosities and carried on its extra-curricular social activities.

Ben doubled his fist and smashed it into the pillow; it made a muffled sound, an impotent dent. He could take Marcie into his confidence, try to explain and hope she'd understand. Understand what? He had no proof of this conversation. Eddie could deny it, and why should she accept his word against her husband's? Or she might blow an emotional fuse, get Eddie on the phone—and precipitate whatever insane action he contemplated in his hallucinations.

Take it apart, he told himself. Break it down, study it, examine it. Exactly what did Eddie Eden want him to do? Nothing much. Nothing cosmic. Just take his wife to bed. Make love to Marcie. Seduce a woman. Reduced to simple terms it was a simple endeavor and shouldn't require a complicated procedure or cause him consternation. He'd done it before, hadn't he? Drunk, sober, in love, out of love, for love, for lust, for hate, for revenge—he'd done it before. Since Dale it had been sex for the sake of sex. Relief, gratification, a function of life as natural and normal as eating, sleeping, evacuating. So what was the mental block now? Would his continence in this instance change the sexual habits of humanity? Hell, right now, in this very establishment, there was probably a couple thumping away in every other bed without benefit of clergy. Adultery was nothing these days. Even some highly esteemed ministers condoned it, as long as it wasn't practiced too often, whatever that meant. How often was too often? And he was in the somewhat unique position of having not only the husband's consent and approval, his blessing as it were, but his threat and demand.

It wasn't that he didn't want her. He had almost from the moment he'd seen her, that delightful barefoot girl in the backyard, with the sun in her hair and the female provocations under the boyish apparel. For a few wonderful moments he'd felt like a youth of twenty again, all eager and intense and turgid with adolescent tumescence, before the image of the dirty old man spoiled it. And this evening, when they'd danced, the desire had returned, as impossible to control as his breathing, but she had diverted it. She wasn't a tease, thank God. A less scrupulous female would have played that scene to the hilt, for the sheer vanity and triumph of it, even if she had no intention of a finale in bed.

Dale, for instance. Dale, who'd used her beauty and body as weapons against men, luring them into defenseless positions, defeating them even in her own surrender, and gloating over her victories, but as incapable of love as she was of loyalty. It hadn't been necessary to resort to any tricks of the trade to trap Dale. All he'd had to do was come home unexpectedly, and there she was in bed with the evidence, a lanky-limbed, pimply-faced boy in his late teens, contributing to the delinquency of a minor. She made no effort to cover herself, although the poor delinquent was shivering and looking pathetic and ridiculous trying to shield himself with a quivering hand like a fluttery fig leaf.

Dale was furious. She screamed at Ben. "You've got a nerve spying on me!"

Spying, because he'd had the temerity to enter his own home unannounced!

Ben thought first of the child, wondering how much of this scene he'd witnessed. "Where's Timmy?" he demanded.

"Well, not here, darling. What kind of mother do you think I am? He's with a neighbor."

"And he's not coming back here, Dale."

"Oh, Christ!" Dale turned to her young lover, who was standing now, naked and petrified except in one area of his anatomy, which had gone limp and might never rise again. "Did you ever see such a jerk, Ronnie? One of the duties of his crummy job is to chase adulterers, but he still believes in marital fidelity. Isn't that a blast? Doesn't it just melt you with mirth?"

Ronnie wasn't melting. He was frozen, tongue-tied, eyes bugged out like a gigged frog's. He was perhaps twenty, and terrified, having never been caught in such a mature predicament before and having no idea how to cope with it. He expected to be shot or beaten to death, if he didn't die of fright.

"I presume you came here dressed," Ben said quietly, feeling sorring for him in spite of himself. "I'd appreciate it if you'd leave the same way."

"Yes, sir," he gulped. "And I didn't know she was married, mister. Honest. I came here selling magazines, working my way through college and—"

"Get out," Ben interrupted in the same even tone. "Get dressed and get out before I kill you."

"Yes, *sir!*" Galvanized into action, he scrambled into his collegiate clothes and fled wildly, forgetting his magazines, grateful for his life.

Ben yanked open the closet door, pulled a suitcase off the shelf, began throwing clothes into it for Timmy and himself, tossing Dale's things aside and on the floor.

"Here, let me help you," she said, donning a black lace negligee, "before you tear the pad apart."

Ben brushed her aside. "A kid, Dale. How low can you get? A snot-nosed kid!"

"But old enough," Dale said. "Pretty well matured in some respects, and I'm not exactly an old woman, you know."

"How many others have there been? Newsboys, milkmen, plumbers, drummers, repairmen?"

Dale shrugged. "Who counts?"

"Bitch," Ben muttered. "Free whore."

"Crap," Dale said.

"That's your answer to everything, isn't it?"

"Why not? Let's face it, darling, it's a crappy world. Life, love, marriage—nothing but crap."

Ben paused in his packing to study her seriously, trying to see the woman beneath the dark sensual gypsylike beauty, to understand her moods and motivations, discover what made her function as she did, what impulse or compulsion or insanity drove her to promiscuity with any available partner. He'd suspected others since their marriage, former lovers, but this debauchery today was a surprise, a shock, a depravity difficult to comprehend.

"Why?" he asked desperately. "In the name of God, Dale, why do you do these things?"

"Well, not in the name of God," she replied. "Oh, you and your goddamn inquisitive mind! Can't you accept facts at face value, Ben? Must you always probe below the surface for motives, detective? And is this true interest or superficial—more research for all those Great American Novels you're going to pen in a pig's eye?"

"I'm trying to understand you, Dale. To *know* you. Can't you help me a little? Cooperate?"

"Shit," Dale sputtered. "The man was never born who could understand a woman, and never will be. You know why, writer? Because he has to be born of woman. Put that in your goddamn notebook for future reference!"

It was useless, hopeless. "I'll talk to a lawyer as soon as possible."

"Talk to the Supreme Court," Dale said. "Who gives a damn? You've got the grounds in this State, and you can get custody of the kid."

"You don't even care about him, do you?"

"If I said I did, would it matter? You'd take him, anyway. You've got to punish me, Ben. You've got to have your revenge and satisfaction. You'll get it through Timmy. Sinners must be condemned—that's the preacher's son in you." She smiled wryly. "But thanks at least for not going through that corny, stupid routine of where and how and why we failed. I never could see the mawkish picking over of a dead marriage like buzzards a carcass, gnawing away the rotten flesh to the bare bones."

"The rotten flesh is yours, Dale."

"Fink," she hissed.

"Fuck you," Ben said.

"Ronnie already did."

Ben swung at her, connecting his fist with her face. Dale spun and reeled backward on the bed. Blood spurted from her cut mouth. Tomorrow her full lips would be swollen fuller, and she'd have a black eye. She glared at him with bitter resentment. "Wife beater."

"Charge me with it," Ben said, snapped the bag shut, picked up his hat and left.

The next time he saw Dale was in court, to pick up an uncontested divorce decree. He hadn't thought seriously about a woman since. Now there was Marcie.

Maybe if he got a little drunker? The package house was still open. He could order a jug. No, if ever he got that far, he wanted to be sober. He wanted to know what he was doing and her to know what she was doing, and each of them to know what the other was doing.

When he heard the knock, he wasn't sure where it came from. He went to the front door. No one was there. It was repeated, and then he knew. Marcie had unlocked her side of the double-doors and was tapping quietly on his. Somewhat stupefied, Ben opened it.

"I'm sorry to bother you," she said, "but I need help. My zipper is stuck. I called a maid, but she couldn't fix it."

"No bother," Ben said. "Come over to the light. These things sometimes require mechanical genius."

It really was stuck and his hands were unusually clumsy, numb at the fingertips, and he worked on it like a novice.

"Were you on the phone a few minutes ago?" she asked.

"Yes."

"Anyone I know?"

"No," Ben said.

"You're lying," she accused softly. "It was Eddie, wasn't it? Why are you lying to me, Ben?"

His fingers fumbled even more. "I can't release this damned device, Marcie. You'll have to sleep in the dress."

"Oh, no! It's a good dress, cost me a whole week's

salary, and I'll need it in New York. Eddie likes me to look nice when I go where he's appearing."

"Call another maid," Ben suggested. "Call the fire department."

"Ben, you must have freed females from hung-up zippers before! Stop trying to brush me off that way. You and Eddie had words on the phone—I heard you raise your voice a few times, and I wasn't eavesdropping, the walls are just thin. Why did you call Eddie, Ben? Were you supposed to? If so, why didn't you tell me? He's my husband, after all. I'd like to have talked with him, too."

"Then call him yourself," Ben told her.

She was affronted. "That's pretty harsh, isn't it? I only meant we could have done it jointly. Was he at work? The Amber Alley?"

Ben nodded. The lies came easier now. "Between acts."

"Why did you quarrel?"

"We had some blunt words, Marcie, that's all. Hot tempers, both of us."

"Ben, be honest with me, please. Did Eddie impose on friendship with this—this escort service? Did you really have business in New Orleans, or was that just a trumped-up thing and you're tired and bored with it?"

"No."

"No what?"

"I did have business in Louisiana, and I'm not tired and bored with you," Ben said. "Far from it. Now stand still, and I'll get you out of this bind."

Finally he managed to free the fastener and lowered it to the tip of her spine. They were standing under an airconditioning vent, and Marcie felt a rush of cold air on her bare back. She shivered and Ben put his arms around her.

"You're trembling," he said.

"I'm cold."

"You're not afraid of me, are you?"

70

"I don't know," she answered. "You're strange sometimes, Ben. Moody and mysterious. I don't know what to think."

"Just don't be afraid, Marcie. I won't hurt you."

He lifted her chin and kissed her mouth gently. Marcie kissed him back, as if seeking a reassurance in his lips that she had not found in his words. His hands caressed her throat and shoulders. Then he unhooked her brassiere, more skillful in releasing this garment, but as he would have fondled her breasts, she broke away.

"Oh, Ben, what're we doing? It's my fault. I shouldn't have come in here. I should have slept in the stupid dress. I'm sorry if I gave you the wrong idea."

"Marcie—"

"No, Ben. I'm sorry. I'll see you in the morning. Good night." She held the back of her dress together and retreated swiftly to her room, closed the door, and locked it.

chapter
6

BEN WAS THINKING. If he could get Timmy and his mother out of town to his uncle's farm in Vermont, they'd be safe from any of Eddie's wild abberations. He didn't know about the farm. Dobbs knew about it but not the exact location and would not tell Eden if he did. Whatever his personal ethics and scruples, Dobbs had a professional code. He was extremely clever in his operations, an expert at tactical conspiracy and coercion, too shrewd to let a far-out punk cross him up. Some of the best private investigators in the business had served with him, and Ben didn't know of a single instance in which Dobbs had allowed one of his men to be a scapegoat or sacrificial lamb to satisfy an impatient or demanding client. When they got hurt, as they occasionally did, it was usually an unavoidable accident, and Dobbs would rant and rave about negligence and stupidity or some other carelessness, justifiable criticism or not, but he never withdrew his support unless he considered the agent derelict in his duty to Dobbs, which he equated with duty to God and country. In fact, if he suspected Eden of any connivance or treachery, if he knew he'd made even a vague or idle threat, he'd drop him immediately and probably clobber him to boot.

But Ben couldn't depend on such contingencies, because Eddie Eden wasn't like ordinary people. His element went on binges and off on tangents. A few puffs of marijuana and he thought he could conquer the world; a drop of LSD in his blood and he went into orbit. He didn't experience moods and emotions as normal human beings; he had blasts and trips and dreams and balls in which logic and rationality were not companions. Silver Haddington was his current obsession, latching on to her legally his present goal—and the lengths to which his determination might carry him were awesome to contemplate. If ever Ben had heard a potential paranoid, it was Eddie Eden last night. In addition to his delusions of grandeur, he was tormented by a persecution complex. Fate, Marcie, Ben, the world, everybody and everything were against Eddie Eden, all in conspiracy to prevent his getting what he wanted and deserved out of life. The idea that his wife would not free him was probably as unrealistic as the one that he could marry Silver Haddington if he were free. Had he ever asked Marcie for a divorce? He didn't need grounds of adultery in Louisiana. Incompatibility, mental cruelty, sufficed in most States, and he could get a quickie in twenty-four hours in Alabama. He must know this. If he were serious about a divorce, he must have had legal counsel on it. There was something more behind this facade for freedom. Oh, the guy was weird, all right, even when he wasn't juiced up!

His hands gripped the steering wheel tighter, his foot pressed harder on the accelerator. The car shot forward. Startled, Marcie glanced up from the map, saw his profile tense and strained.

"You're speeding," she cautioned. "We'll pick up the highway patrol."

Ben slowed down. "What's the next town?"

"Several small ones," Marcie said. "Birmingham's the next big one. Why?"

"I have to make a phone call."

"Eddie?" she asked suspiciously.

"No. My mother. I want to see how she and Timmy are."

"Of course. She'll be happy to hear from you."

Ben nodded. "She worries when I'm away."

"Are you away often?"

"Freelance writers roam."

"I guess all mothers worry about their children, even when they aren't children any more."

"Not all," Ben said, thinking of Dale.

"You mean Timmy's mother doesn't worry about him? Is that why you got custody? Didn't she want him?"

"Not particularly," Ben reflected somberly. "He was just a—a consequence."

"What kind of woman is she?" Marcie asked and realized the question was not just conversation or idle curiosity. She was interested.

Ben shrugged. "A woman who wasn't meant to be a wife or mother. There are some like that, you know. Maybe they can't help it. Maybe the maternal instinct is as alien to them as it is inherent in other women. Marriage and motherhood stifles them, and so they rebel with their most potent weapon."

"And what is that?"

His eyes shifted briefly to her face and back to the road again. "What else? Sex."

"Well, there are some men like that too, Ben. They resent marriage and dread fatherhood and its responsibilities, and so they chase. It gives them a sense of freedom." She paused and then asked tentatively, "How long did it take to get over her, or have you?"

He seemed to brood in his contemplation. "I have, and it took too damned long. But I don't love her any more. I don't even hate her. Just pity her, because I think she's on a collision course with self-destruction."

"'Maybe that's better than being in a blind alley,'" Marcie said quietly. "I think that's where Eddie is now."

"What makes you think so?"

"Just a hunch. Woman's intuition, whatever you want to call it. But I'm afraid Eddie expects too much from life, much more than he deserves or can possibly get."

"That won't prevent his trying," Ben said grimly.

"How well do you know Eddie, Ben?"

She was exploring again, drawing blanks in the conversation and expecting him to fill them. His secrecy about the telephone call last night had obviously upset her. Apparently she sensed that something was not Hoyle about this situation, and she was curious, skeptical, apprehensive, even distressed.

"How well can you know anyone in three months?"

"Well enough to make an appraisal," Marcie said. "Some people can do it in three hours, or three minutes, and a writer ought to have a keen perception and ability to judge character. We've known each other less than three days, and I think I know you fairly well. At least I hope I do, although I'll admit you puzzle me at times." She waited, drawing another blank, disappointed by his silence, his lack of cooperation. "How did you meet Eddie?"

"At the club. A friend of mine knows the owner of the Amber Alley. He introduced us."

"Then you've heard Eddie sing? Does he draw good crowds? Is the audience receptive, responsive?"

"Average, I guess. He doesn't get standing ovations, exactly. Women seem to like him better than men."

"Naturally," Marcie said. "He's handsome in a brutish sort of way, and mature women seem to fancy him. I used to eavesdrop on the table conversation, and some of them would get doe-eyed and others giggly and giddy as teenagers over their idols. But it's screaming youth that puts entertainers over nowadays, and somehow Eddie just can't attract that crowd. I guess he's a little too old, or a bit too conventional in his appearance. He tried the beard and the long hair bit, but on him it was ridiculous, laughable, and somehow detracted from his greatest asset, which is his masculinity. He tried teaming up too, first with a couple of boys, then a girl folk-singer, but that didn't click, either. He Frenched up his act, putting *amour* and *chérie* in the love songs, a male Geneviève, but that flopped like a fallen soufflé. And he's sort of stymied now."

"Tough," Ben said.

"No, I'm rationalizing, and you know it," Marcie said. "Frank Sinatra's no kid any more, nor Dean Martin, Tony Bennett, Andy Williams, nor even Elvis Presley, plus a dozen others who can electrify an audience. They all have their style, their individual charm and fascination, their special rapport with the audience, their loyal fans and cults. But they've also got something else, that magic ingredient that can't be acquired or accomplished. You know what I mean?"

Ben nodded. "Charisma, though it's an overworked word nowadays, becoming a cliché."

"But still accurate. A commercial commodity, eminently salable to the public, and if you could buy it in bottles or boxes, Eddie'd be an instant success. But you can't convince him of that, because he thinks he has it in abundance."

Traffic increased as they approached Birmingham, and Ben was occupied with the task of driving. The car was low on gas, and he looked for a station with a telephone booth outside. There was one within a mile. He pulled into it, told the attendant to fill the tank and check everything else. Marcie went to the restroom.

Ben called home. His mother wanted to know everything at once, where he was, how he was, why she hadn't heard from him before, and when he would be back.

Ben answered the questions in that order. "I'm in Birmingham, Alabama. I'm fine, I couldn't call before, I'll be home late tomorrow, barring car trouble. What I called about now, Mom, I know it's getting hot in town and it'd be nice for you and Timmy to go to the country. Uncle Avery's farm. Yes, Mom, I *know* you don't go to the farm until August, but there's no reason why you can't go in July, is there? It's almost August, anyway. Just a few more days. Get some clothes together and take the bus to Vermont. Timmy'll love it."

"Of course, dear. But Timmy's a little under the weather right now."

"What?" Ben shouted unconsciously. If that lunatic had already gotten to Timmy ...

"Now, don't get excited, Ben. It's just tonsillitis again. We got caught in a little shower in the Park yesterday, and you know how his throat flares up when he gets wet or takes cold. I've already had the doctor and he's on antibiotics, and there's nothing to worry about. He just has to stay in bed until his temperature's down, and a week or so afterwards. To prevent any possible complications of rheumatic fever, you know. I wasn't going to mention anything about it to you, dear, but when you mentioned the farm—"

"Okay, Mom. Forget it. Have I had any calls?"

"A couple of girls," Mrs. Hale replied but couldn't remember their names. "And Mr. Dobbs. That's all, I think. Now you'd better ring off, son. Long distance is expensive, you know."

"I'll put it on the expense account," Ben said. "Tell Timmy hello for me, and take care of him. 'Bye, Mom."

The attendant was wiping off the windshield. Marcie was back in the car, map unfolded on her lap. "Everything okay at home?"

"Not quite. Timmy's sick."

"Oh, I'm sorry, Ben. Nothing serious, I hope?"

"Could be if neglected. Tonsillitis. He's sort of subject to it. Guess his tonsils will have to be yanked one of these days."

"Don't worry, Ben. I'm sure your mother will take good care of him. Most grandmothers are natural nurses."

"I know that, Marcie. That doesn't worry me."

"You want to talk?" she prompted. "I'm a good listener."

"Five-fifty even, sir," the attendant said, holding out his hand.

Ben opened his wallet. Marcie glimpsed some kind of official identification card in the first plastic window. It wasn't a driver's license, unless they were completely different in New York from Louisiana. What was it? she wondered and tried to read the lettering before he closed his wallet again. Did he sense her curiosity and foil her purposely? Was it something he didn't want her to see, to know about?

"It's noon," he said, leaving the station. "We might as well eat lunch here."

"I'm not hungry," Marcie said.

"Me neither."

"Want to see Vulcan?"

"Who?"

Marcie smiled. Obviously he'd never been in Birmingham before; she'd spent two weeks there while Eddie played one of the small nightclubs, and had had plenty of time to see the town and environs. Sightseeing was her principal and often only diversion when on tour with Eddie. "Vulcan, the Roman god of fire. The largest cast iron statue in the world, and he overlooks the city from Red Mountain. He's quite famous here, on all the local postcards."

"I'll see him on a postcard, then," Ben said.

"That's not much of a writer's instinct," Marcie chided. "Aren't writers supposed to see and experience things for themselves? Well, Tennessee is next, and it's a very historic State. Civil War battlefields and monuments, all marked on the map. Scenic, too. The Great Smoky Mountains."

"I know," Ben said. "I've been there. It's not much out of our way. Want to go the scenic route?"

"We're not tourists on vacation."

"What are we?"

Marcie looked at him. "You tell me, Ben. You tell me exactly what we are, you and I. What's our real relationship? I'm Eddie Eden's wife and you're his friend, and you're doing us a favor. Is that the extent of it, Ben Hale? Is that it and all of it?"

Ben thought of Timmy, sick and helpless, and his mother not sick but almost as helpless. "Yes," he said. "That's it and all of it." He reached for a cigarette. "Marcie, would you like me to drive you to the Birmingham airport and put you on a plane to New York? I can take the car on myself." He fired the cigarette and smoked rapidly, wondering what he'd do if she agreed.

She appeared to consider it. "No," she said finally. "I'm sorry if I sound dubious, Ben. I guess I'm just tired. I didn't get much sleep last night."

"That makes two of us," Ben said. "I started to knock on your door more than once."

Marcie was reflective. "You know the funny thing about that, Ben? I don't think Eddie would have minded. I don't think he'd have cared at all."

"Why did you run away from me, then?"

"Because of myself, I suppose. Me and the way I am. I couldn't take anything like that lightly, Ben. Shrug it off, forget it. I'm not built that way. Remember that personal code we discussed over cocktails last night? Character, integrity—and you said you thought I had it?"

Ben remembered. "I was right."

"Maybe," she murmured. "But I don't want to be tested again, Ben. I don't want any more connecting rooms."

"As you wish, Marcie. But the same room wouldn't matter unless it was mutual. I've got a code, too. I've never raped a woman yet, and it's impossible to rape a man."

Marcie smiled, though she wasn't amused. "I reckon I'm being silly, Ben. Making a drama out of something most people today regard as a charade. Fun and games."

She sighed. "Let's forget it, shall we? I really am bushed. Mind if I catch forty winks?"

Ben patted his shoulder. "Be my guest."

"Thanks, but I'll try to manage over here."

Ben grinned at her, trying to inject humor into an unhumorous situation. "Coward. What could happen in the car?"

"Plenty," Marcie said. "What do you think keeps drive-in theaters in business?"

"That's kid stuff, and we're not kids, Marcie."

"I know, Ben. There's a lot involved here. That's why we have to keep our heads. We were in danger of losing them last night."

"Go to sleep," Ben said brusquely.

chapter
7

WHEN SHE WOKE, several hours later, rain was falling. The sky was dismal, almost black, and a summer storm was raging in the mountains ahead. Marcie could see flashes of lightning, like cannonade, but the peaks were obscured in mist and haze. "Where are we?" she asked.

"Near Chattanooga. That's Lookout Mountain ahead, where one of your Civil War battles was fought."

"It wasn't my Civil War," Marcie said.

"Okay. Truce."

The rain pelting the steel top sounded like hailstones. The wipers slapped rhythmically at the flooded windshield. Wind rippled long gray sheets of water across the highway. It was moist and steamy in the car, and Marcie wondered how long she had slept.

"Quite awhile," Ben said. "I'm surprised the thunder didn't wake you."

"Gabriel's horn couldn't wake me, Ben. I was beat. Dead to the world. Gee, this is dreary."

"And dangerous," Ben said. "Slow, tedious driving. There was a bad wreck about twenty miles back. I started to wake you."

"I'm glad you didn't. Accidents unnerve me."

"I was afraid it might, that's why I didn't disturb you. Besides, you look cute asleep. Curled up like a kitten. Purring like one, too."

Marcie was shocked. "Snoring?"

Ben laughed. "No, mewing a little occasionally. What were you dreaming?"

"I don't remember."

That wasn't true. Why was she lying? She did remember, for it was a familiar recurring dream, and in the manner of dreams it assumed haunting reality. She was stranded in a strange town, bewildered, bereft of funds and friends, and she couldn't find Eddie. She went to his last place of employment and saw a big canceled banner pasted diagonally across his poster, and she asked the management what happened and where he had gone, and they stared at her blankly. They never spoke or showed signs of recognition or understanding. In fact, no one ever spoke to her in these dreadful dreams, or answered any of her questions, as if they were all deaf mutes, and she'd walk away wondering what had become of Eddie and what was to become of her? Ironically, when finally she awoke, she usually was in a strange place, and Eddie was rarely beside her. For the first time in her marriage another man was, and she was almost as embarrassed as if she were in bed with him.

"It's not fair to watch someone sleep," she admonished him. "Suppose you let me drive now and watch you?"

"I have a better suggestion. Let's stop early today, check in somewhere. We're not on a schedule, so there's no great hurry, and driving in this kind of weather is risky. I've practically got the shakes. I need a drink."

Marcie was amenable, amiable. "I'm sure it's the sensible thing to do, Ben. And what I said about the rooms before—don't argue. Take whatever is available."

Other travelers had the same sensible idea, and No Vacancy signs were out all over town. Accommodations were limited to expensive suites, which they were lucky to get in the height of the tourist season. It was a cozy, attractive arrangement of bedroom, sitting room, bath—precisely what Eddie would have ordered for them. The sitting room had a studio couch, which could double as a bed for Ben.

The bellboy helped them get settled in. Ben tipped him generously, perhaps too generously. When he had gone, Marcie asked, "How did you register?"

"The only way I could," he answered. "This is a respectable establishment."

Marcie frowned. "How'll I explain that to Eddie?"

"Why should you have to? Anyway, didn't you say he wouldn't care?"

"I said I didn't think he would."

"Same difference," Ben said, a little impatient with her feminine whims. "Marcie, you told me to take what they had, and this isn't the kind of weather to shop in!"

"It's just the record, Ben."

"Records aren't necessarily facts, Marcie. Statistics. Shall we go out to dinner, or have it sent here?"

"Have it sent," Marcie decided. "But let's dress, anyway. Look in the desk drawer. The house menu is usually there."

"I know, dear. I've been in hotel suites before."

"Oh? I didn't think poor writers could afford them?"

But rich clients could. Why didn't he say that? Insert the wedge of truth, get this whole business out in the open, regardless of the consequences?

"I happen to know some people who can," he said. "What shall I order for you?"

Marcie was on her way to the bedroom. "The same as for yourself."

"Then it's steak and salad. How do you like your meat?"

"Rare," Marcie flung over her shoulder. "But not bloody."

"Medium rare," he said. "Salad dressing?"

"Blue cheese."

"Vodka martini?"

"Not mint julep or planter's punch, suh."

Taking her robe from her luggage, Marcie disappeared into the bathroom. Ben heard the shower running. She emerged in a short white terrycloth coat, feet bare, hair curling in damp ringlets about her face and neck, looking like a child again, dimpled knees and all. Ben had just finished with room service. "Next," she said, "shall I get your robe for you?"

"No," he said, remembering the gun in his luggage. "I need other things, too."

By the time Marcie was ready, slender and chic in a sleeveless white knit shift, dark hair smooth and mouth pale pink, the drinks had arrived. The food would be along later, the bellboy said, at whatever time Mr. Hale had requested it.

Ben, in his dark dacron suit again, fresh white shirt and different tie, handed Marcie her martini. "Maybe we should have ordered champagne?"

"Champagne? Mercy, no! We're blowing enough on this suite. Thirty-six dollars a night! It's posted right there on the door."

"This was the cheapest one," Ben said. "They had one at forty-two, one at fifty, and the bridal number at sixty-five." Hell, why hadn't he taken the sixty-five job? Silver Haddington could afford it. "Well, skol or something."

They touched glasses. "Skol," Marcie said.

A plateglass window in the living area overlooked the swimming pool and gardens. They stood watching it rain on the pool and the striped umbrellas and the white lawn furniture. Varicolored lights glowed in the shrubbery, which appeared artificial in the wetness. He ought to call Eddie again, Ben thought, just to make sure the kook wouldn't jump the gun in his eagerness and desperation. But how could he do it with Marcie around? Perhaps later, when she was asleep—or he'd have to find some excuse to go out. It was going to be a long night.

Marcie abandoned the window abruptly for the

couch. Ben lit another cigarette, his third since they had arrived. "You do have the habit, don't you?" she scolded, sounding like his mother. "Don't you know it's bad for your health? Don't you read the warnings on the package?"

"Nobody lives forever," Ben said. "Wonder what's on the big ugly eye?"

"Summer reruns."

"Should be bloodshot at these rates. Color."

"It is," Marcie said. "I can read it from here. RCA Victor Color TV. That's living."

"Yeah."

"I wish it'd stop raining," Marcie sighed, "so we could go somewhere."

"We can, anyway. You won't melt if you get wet, will you?" He drained his glass. "I've got to order another drink. This was just a teaser."

"Order me another, too."

"What's your limit, Marcie? Your capacity?"

"I don't know, Ben. I've never tried to find out."

"Well, don't try tonight."

She gazed at him curiously. "I wasn't going to, Ben. What made you say that?"

Ben swirled the dregs of his drink into a miniature whirlpool. "Because I know how this evening is going to end, and I don't want either of us smashed."

"You're wrong, Ben. It's not going to end like that. I'm going to call Eddie after dinner."

"For what? Moral support? Reassurance?"

"Don't joke about it, Ben. It's not funny to me."

"You think it is to me? Am I laughing?"

"No, you're tense and restless and even angry. This has all been a terrible strain on you, I know, and I'm sorry, Ben. But I didn't create the storm. Why don't you just forget it, try to relax?"

Two white-jacketed waiters delivered the dinner, complete with portable table, white cloth, silver, flowers, and candle. They went about their business swiftly and skill-

85

fully, lighting the candle ceremoniously at the last. Immediately they left, Marcie extinguished the flame, saying, "Temptation, courtesy of the management, which we can do without."

"Right," Ben agreed. "All we need is nourishment and the chimeras will disappear."

"What chimeras?"

"Marcie, must you take everything I say literally?"

"Sorry. I keep forgetting you're a writer, and fantasy and vagary just come naturally, don't they? Does all this food and folly strike you as a bacchanalia or what?"

"Shut up and eat," Ben said.

At 9:30 room service returned to remove the remains, and Marcie went into the bedroom to telephone Eddie. Minutes later she came out with a perplexed face.

"He's not there, Ben. Eddie's not at the Amber Alley."

"Stepped out?"

"No, they said he didn't work there any more. They have a new attraction, some girl folk singer from Arkansas—Ozark Annie, or some such person. I tried Eddie's apartment in the Village, but there was no answer."

Ben pondered the tip of his cigarette. "Well, that's simple enough, Marcie. He probably got a better offer somewhere else, and the Amber Alley released him."

She sighed forlornly. "More likely he was canceled again—and here I am on the way to New York! I should have stayed in Rainbow and worked. We'll need the money."

"Marcie, don't jump to conclusions. Things may not be as you imagine at all. Wait and see."

"Did he say anything to you about this last night, Ben?"

"No, but Eddie doesn't have to tell me his business, Marcie. I'm not his agent or business manager."

"If he was scratched again, he won't have an agent or manager much longer," Marcie worried.

"Well, isn't that what you really want? Wouldn't you rather have him in some other kind of work?"

"It doesn't matter what I want, Ben. It's Eddie's life. He has a dream and he has to follow it. He'd be utterly miserable if he didn't, and eventually ill."

Ben pitied her, wasting so much sympathy on a man so unworthy of it. He tried to distract her. "Hey, the rain's slacking off! Let's go out on the town?"

"No."

"Marcie, we'd better go out to a movie or something. We can't retire at ten o'clock."

"I want to try to call Eddie again, later."

Ben sighed heavily, more of a groan. "It's no use, Marcie. He won't be at his apartment."

"Why won't he?"

"How can he if he's working somewhere?"

Marcie went to stand before him, confronting, demanding. "Where did you find him last night?" No answer. "Is there a girl, Ben? Is that where he was last night? Is that where you think he is now? Does Eddie have a girl in New York?"

Ben turned away from her, back to the glass expanse, to stare glumly at darkness and the mist-fuzzed lights. He set his chin firmly. "Marcie, don't grill me."

"I don't have to," she said, returning to the couch and lowering herself on it. "I know there's someone, Ben. There's someone in every town Eddie plays. What I don't know is why he sent for me. What does he need with me?"

"You're his wife, Marcie."

"Sure, I've got a paper to prove it. But I've been his wife for seven years, Ben, and he's never needed me when he had someone else." There was a convulsive sob in her throat. "Will you order some more drinks, or should I?"

"No, Marcie. I meant what I said a while ago."

"About how the evening would end? So you're psychic, prophetic. I won't run tonight, Ben. Drunk or sober, I won't run."

Ben came and sat beside her and took her hands in his. "Do you need the words, Marcie? Would it help?"

"No, you don't have to say them, Ben."

"I want to say them. I love you, Marcie."

"Thanks," she murmured. "I guess maybe it does help. Oh, Ben, don't let me cry! I've cried so much over Eddie I don't know how I could have any tears left, but somehow I always manage to squeeze a few more. . . ."

His eyes indicated the bedroom. "Go in there with me, Marcie, I can carry you dramatically if you prefer, but it'd mean more to me if you walked."

She went passively, neither eager nor reluctant, but apparently aware of her action. Ben could not have pursued this otherwise. But it would have been easier last night, he thought, during the zipper episode, when she had shown some passionate abandon, however brief and remorseful. She would require stimulation now, and reassurance. In the bedroom he asked about precautions. It wasn't necessary, she replied, she took the pill, Eddie insisted on it.

"Promise me something," Ben said.

"What?"

"You won't mention Eddie's name again tonight."

"I'll try," she said. "Do you want everything off?"

"Please."

"Turn out the light."

"After I see you."

"I'm just like any other woman."

"Every woman is different in some way, Marcie. Every man, too. I hope you like the difference."

Undressed, Marcie stood before him. His eyes surveyed her nude body with carnal pleasure and anticipation, completely honest in his desire. He was still fully clothed, including coat and tie. Marcie tensed under his scrutiny, shied a little in embarrassment.

"Are you just going to look?" Maybe he was some kind of odd-ball and leering would be the extent of it.

He smiled and removed his coat.

The bed was oversize, with a padded headboard and a foam rubber mattress. Marcie had never slept in anything quite so luxurious. She was glad they had splurged. A cheap, dingy room would have been sordid, appalling. When Ben joined her, she said, "I feel wicked wallowing in all this luxury. Positively wanton."

"That's good." He kissed her. "Tell me what to do."

If he wasn't teasing, then he was a strange one. "Don't you know?"

"How would I know? I told you, every woman is different. I've never been with you before. Tell me. Take my hand and show me."

"Oh, Ben—"

"Marcie, if it takes all night, you're going to get something out of this, too."

That had never particularly concerned Eddie, but she had promised him she wouldn't think of Eddie. "Kiss me first," she said. "Your best French. You knew how last night."

He still knew how, but her response wasn't exactly erotic. She hadn't blanked Eddie out of her mind yet. He'd think she was frigid, and somehow it seemed important to convince him she wasn't. She took his hand and guided it over her body, hesitantly at first, then with more assurance. The sensitivity of his touch was surprising, considering the size and strength of his hands. It produced some stimulation, rapture; she wanted, needed more. She whispered to him. He pretended not to understand her, but she knew he did.

"Say it aloud," he said.

"Leave me some pride," she murmured.

"There's no pleasure in pride, Marcie."

He practiced a form of subtle, exquisite torture. He was determined to explore every emotion of which she was capable, evoke every sensation, release every inhibition, and in this determination he was ruthless and relentless. A few times Marcie thought she would scream for consummation.

"Finish it," she implored.

"This way?"

"Any way. Only finish it. Please."

"I thought you'd never ask, darling."

He moved over her and waited. Marcie knew what he wanted, what he expected, and it vanquished the last vestige of her pride, but as she had discovered, as he had just taught her, there really wasn't any pleasure in pride.

She didn't know how long they lay together afterwards, for time seemed in suspension, and she wished it might stay there, with his arm curved around her shoulders, his hand resting lightly on her breast.

"What time is it?" she asked.

Ben consulted the luminous dial of his watch. "Midnight."

"Did you mean what you said earlier, about loving me?"

"You know I did."

"And now?"

"More, if that's possible. There are many great emotions in life, Marcie, but few great moments. I'll cherish this as one of my great moments."

Marcie was touched. "I can't say it so beautifully, but I feel the same way, Ben. I'm glad it happened."

His lips brushed her cheek. "I'm glad you're glad, darling. And it'll happen again, you know."

"Yes," she said. "I'm going to divorce Eddie, Ben. I have to, now. There's no alternative."

"Don't make any irrevocable decisions tonight, Marcie."

"I already made one, Ben, when I walked in here with you."

Eddie had not been mistaken about that, Ben thought grimly. There was much he didn't know about his wife, but he had not miscalculated her reaction to adultery. She might condone her husband's but not her own. How

90

simple it all seemed now that it was done, an accomplished fact. Except for one thing: he was in love with her, and she still didn't know the whole truth, and only he could tell her.

chapter
8

THE NEXT MORNING Ben excused himself to go for cigarettes and used the telephone in the lobby. This time the rat was in his hole in the Village, which meant he had not succeeded in moving completely into the coveted tower yet, and his chagrin reflected in his voice. He growled into the receiver, angry at being disturbed at that ridiculous hour.

"You again? Don't you ever sleep, man?"

"Just keeping you informed, Eddie."

"Well, I hope it's glad tidings," Eddie mumbled.

Ben had to placate him without delivering the news Eddie expected. "I'm making some progress, but not much. She's not vulnerable to my approach—rather implacable, in fact, just like you predicted, Eddie. Might take a while to reach New York. We're taking the scenic route."

"Got to make a production of it, eh? Okay, if that's what it takes to make the scene. Build her up, hearts and flowers, the full treatment. Southern dolls are romantic, you know."

"I'm learning," Ben said. "You alone?"

"Except for the rats and roaches," Eddie drawled.

"Well, I just wanted to tell you we'll be delayed, Eddie, so don't get impatient, hear?"

"I hear," Eddie said, yawning. "And it'll be worth it to you, Ben. She's a firecracker if you can ever get the fuse lit. But do me a favor, pal. Don't call again until after the explosion."

Ben twisted the wire in his hand, as if it were around Eddie's neck. "She tried to call you herself last night."

"Jeez! Why'd you let her do that?"

"Couldn't stop her. She called the Amber Alley. They told her you'd left. I smoothed it over with lies about a better offer elsewhere."

Eddie chuckled. "That's no lie, man. I got a better offer, all right. Marcie fall for that writer stuff?"

"I think so. It's partly true, you know."

"Yeah, well she would, anyway. Naive kitten, that kid. You'll have to be an aggressive cat, Ben. Use all your sexual prowess. Too bad you're no James Bond."

"Any more advice, Eddie?"

"No, I think you've got the idea finally," Eddie said and hung up.

Ben picked up a pack of cigarettes at the counter before returning to the suite. He caught Marcie in his arms as she stepped out of the shower.

"How do you feel?"

"Wet," she laughed.

"Not wet and wild?"

"Defenseless. Vulnerable."

"Anything else?"

"Ben, it hasn't been an hour ago! You're oversexed."

"Okay. Forget it."

"I'm sorry, darling. It's all right, if you want to."

"Don't you?"

"Do we have time?"

"You in a hurry to get to New York?"

Marcie averted her eyes. "Not any more."

Somehow the moment had passed. "Get dressed," Ben

told her. "I'll call Mom and see how Timmy is. If all's well, we can proceed leisurely. Do you like mountains?"

"There aren't any around Louisiana," Marcie said. "But yes, I like mountains."

"We're near the Great Smokies," Ben said. "I've done some hunting and fishing there, wrote some articles and stories about the region. A sports editor I know has a cabin in the hills, and he wouldn't mind if I borrowed it."

Marcie smiled wistfully. "You proposing a honeymoon?"

"Yes. I just wish it could be the real thing."

Marcie was slipping into some lime-colored slacks and a floral print blouse. "Is that chivalry or conscience speaking, Mr. Hale?"

"Love," Ben said.

"What happened to love a moment ago?"

"I didn't think you were much in the mood."

He was too perceptive, and sensitive perhaps. "Just a little surprised and overwhelmed by your ardor," Marcie said.

"Love," Ben said again.

"Of course, darling. Call your mother."

Timmy was progressing. His throat was still sore but he insisted on talking to his father. Ben told him to be a good boy, mind Grandma, and stay in the house until he was well. Mrs. Hale came back on the line and wanted to know if Ben was eating and sleeping enough and not smoking too much.

"I'm fine, Mom," Ben assured her. "Everything's fine."

"Are you carrying your gun, son?"

"Good-bye, Mom," Ben said, his back to Marcie.

"Ben?" Marcie said.

He turned and smiled at her. "It's all set."

"It'll be fun," Marcie said.

Ben nodded. But God, how was he going to tell her, and when, and what if she hated him afterwards?

Once they left the main highway through the mountains, the road became a tortuous trail barely wide enough to accommodate the car and requiring the instincts of a bloodhound to follow. Spruce and hemlock mingled with hardwoods in the forests. As they went deeper, the land became an unchartered wilderness of savage peaks, and sheer gorges, rushing streams and foaming rapids, dense groves and bramble thickets. Not even in the swamps had Marcie felt such remoteness and isolation. You couldn't get lost in the Teche if you followed the Bayou, for eventually it led to a town or landing on its banks. But in twenty miles of travel in this country a mountaineer's shack and pigpen were the only signs of human life or domestic animal, and she knew she could not have found her way out with a map and compass.

Precarious shelves of rock, hazardous gaps and gulches, steep climbs and swift descents. In places the road was chiseled into the mountainside; one swift pull of the wheels in the wrong direction would plunge them into a ravine and almost certain death, perhaps never to be found, since no one would know where to look for them. The realization made her tense and nervous.

"How much farther?" she asked breathlessly.

"Few miles," Ben answered. "We'd do better with a jeep or horse, but we'll make it." The car hugged another curve and he had to veer sharply to avoid a rockslide. Marcie screamed her fear, and the outburst angered Ben.

"Don't do that, Marcie!"

"I thought we were going over the cliff."

"Distract me enough and we will."

Her throat had swollen shut. She swallowed to open it, a dry gulp. One word croaked out. "Sorry."

"It's all right, darling. I shouldn't have shouted at you that way, but this is rugged country."

"Yes," Marcie said and thought it rather neatly fitted the adventure writer image he had projected of himself.

He looked hard as flint and lean as a panther, competent and capable and alert to any contingency, and his presence should have comforted and reassured her. Instead and incongruously, she felt an increasing apprehension and even awe of him which puzzled her. She had thought she knew him well last night, now he seemed like a stranger again. You could become lovers in one night, but not necessarily friends. Love occurred, friendship must be cultivated. How hurt he would be if he could read her mind! Or would he? Somehow she could not overcome the conviction that he had not been completely honest with her, even in love; that there was still much about him she did not know, and might have to learn the hard way in this wilderness.

Low gear grinding, motor straining to brake the wheels, the car made its final descent into a deep valley embraced by mist-shrouded mountains. There, in a clearing partially reclaimed by nature, stood an old settler's cabin, built in the dawn of American civilization.

"Disappointed?" Ben asked, watching her face which did not show the hoped-for reaction.

"Surprised," Marcie said. "It's not quite what I expected."

"What did you expect? A fancy lodge with a Man Friday? A tax deduction for the magazine?"

"Something like that," Marcie admitted. "Surely nothing this primitive. What about food?"

"Jack keeps an ample supply of staples," Ben said. "But you have to forage for fuel and water. No electricity, no gas, no telephone, no television. This is truly God's country, as He made it. A hunter's paradise and a hermit's refuge." He looked at her. "And a lover's idyll."

"Have you brought many lovers here?"

"None," Ben said. "I can't vouch for the other guys, but you're my first here."

"I'm glad," Marcie said. "How do you get out when it snows? Dog sled, or wait for the spring thaw?"

Ben laughed. "You stay awhile, but that's the beauty

of it. Bad weather on the ridges drives the game below for food and shelter. It's just a matter of being prepared with necessities of your own. But isolation wouldn't last long, in any case. There's always a quick thaw—the elevations are not high enough for perpetual snow like the western ranges." He smiled at her seriousness. "Cheer up, darling. There's no danger of being snowbound with me. This is summer."

"That doesn't worry me, Ben."

"What, then? You look anxious."

"It's just that I keep finding myself in strange places and situations with you," Marcie said. "First a swamp, then a hotel suite, now a rustic cabin. A few days ago I didn't know you, had never even heard of you! How did it happen, Ben?"

"A fatalist would call it destiny," Ben said.

"Are you a fatalist?"

"In some ways, I guess. Shall we go in? The key is over the door, but the lock is to keep out animals, not people. Come, darling."

The ceiling was open-beamed, the chink-filled log walls bare except for a few hunting and fishing trophies: the heads of a snarling black bear and many antlered deer, and a large bass vainly attempting to leap from a varnished plaque over the stone mantel. Wooden shelves held a kerosene lamp and lantern and candles in brass holders, pipe rack and tobacco humidor, books and magazines. A woven rug lay on the unpainted board floor, but no shades or curtains covered the windows since they were not needed for privacy. Plumbing facilities consisted of a wash-basin and outdoor privy. Primitive as a cave compared to the hotel suite in Chattanooga, Marcie thought. Eddie, who loved city atmosphere and conveniences, who would not even go on a picnic in the country, would have hated it. But bucolic Ben, raised in the Vermont hills, was in his element; and of course it was an ideal place to write. Still, she had difficulty feeling that she belonged there and forgetting the circuitous route by which she had arrived.

"I have to chop some wood," Ben said. "You can get the water. There's a fine spring at the base of this mountain, about fifty yards away. Just follow the trail behind the cabin. You can't miss it."

He removed his shirt and was swinging the ax when Marcie left, an empty pail in each hand like a country milkmaid, and was swinging it when she returned, the muscles in his shoulders and back rippling in strain, the woodpile steadily growing. She paused to watch him, smiling.

"Shades of Lincoln."

"Log-splitting's the mountaineer's physical therapy, good for body and soul."

Marcie carried the full buckets into the cabin, trying not to splash the water as she put them on the pine table in the lean-to kitchen. What would she fix for supper? The pantry was well-stocked, if you liked canned goods and instant food products; obviously the guests were expected to supplement the staples with game and fish, and the sportsman feasted or famined according to his skills and luck.

Ben brought in wood for the range and the bedroom fireplace. "The nights get cool here, even in summer."

"That's nice. I like open fires."

"We'll have one tonight. Do you like to hike?"

"Well, I'm not exactly equipped for mountain climbing," Marcie said. "These are flats I'm wearing, not boots."

"We won't go far, and I'll help if you get tired."

"All right, put it on tomorrow's schedule. Right now, I'd better relax. That precarious journey sort of wound me up." She glanced about. "I forgot, no TV to unwind with."

Ben laughed. "That's really roughing it, isn't it? We'll just have to find other diversions."

"Which reminds me to take my pill."

"Science has sure simplified sex."

"And sin."

"Why not think of it as love?"

"You're always saying that, Ben. What is love, really? For some people it's just a four-letter word. That's all it was to Eddie."

"To Dale, too," Ben said. "But it won't be with us, Marcie, because we won't let it be."

"We're different?" she said wryly. "We're going to sanctify it with marriage."

"Yes. As soon as you're free."

"You don't have to marry me, Ben."

"Damn it, Marcie! I *want* to marry you. What do you think this is all about?"

"I wish I knew, Ben." She shook her head vaguely, biting her lower lip. "The way things developed, it's hard to believe it was just coincidence—or destiny, as you call it. It's more like it was supposed to happen. Planned."

Now, Ben thought. There's your chance. Take it, follow through. Get it off your chest.

Instead he bent to lay the fire. "You're tired, Marcie. Lie down and rest. I won't disturb you."

"Not even if I want you to disturb me?"

"Only if you want me to."

"Won't Eddie wonder about us, Ben? Why it's taking so long on the road?"

"I don't think so, Marcie."

"No, I reckon not. Especially not if his new love is interesting enough. Do you know her, Ben?"

"We've met," Ben admitted.

"What's she like? Beautiful, naturally?"

"She has her charms."

"Blonde, brunette, redhead?"

"Silver-blonde."

Marcie nodded. "Eddie's partial to blondes. His affairs with fair-hairs outnumber the others two to one. Maybe blondes not only have more fun but are more fun. I've considered bleaching my hair."

"Don't you dare," Ben said. "Some men prefer brunettes. As for who has more fun, too bad you can't ask Elizabeth Taylor. Richard Burton ought to have some opinions on that subject, too. Don't change your hair, Marcie. It's lovely."

"If you think so," she said. "I hope you like Spam, pork and beans, and instant potatoes, because that's what we're having for supper."

"Not exactly cordon bleu," Ben said, "but nourishing. I'll make the fire for you. Ever cooked on a wood range?"

"No, but I learn easy."

"Just be careful, Marcie. Don't burn youself."

"No," Marcie said. "I wouldn't want to get burned, Ben."

chapter
9

AT DUSK THE COOL DAMPNESS came down from the hills and settled on the valleys and chilled the land. The fire felt good in the cabin and they sat before the hearth a long while, talking. A hunter's moon rose beyond the windows, a big yellow disc, the kind of moon hounds bay at. Outside, some animal or fowl was scratching in the leaves—a forager, probably, lured by the scent and promise of food. The captive bear snarled from his mount, teeth bared, glass eyes gleaming in the firelight.

Marcie wanted to know what kind of stories Ben had written about these mountains. He told her they were standard adventure yarns for which he'd received eight hundred dollars apiece. "You don't find much love and sex in the men's mags, except *Playboy*."

"Why don't you write a novel?"

"I have," Ben said. "Several. No sale."

"You weren't in any wars, were you?"

"Domestic," Ben said wryly. "Not military. That's what makes it tough for material. I did my hitch in the Service, but except for boot camp, where I had a sadistic sergeant, it was completely uneventful—after Korea and before Vietnam. The successful novels of this generation written by men are war epics. Women penned the others."

"I guess that's right," Marcie said. "But I'm sure you'll come up with something and succeed, Ben."

"Thanks for the vote of confidence." It was more than Dale had ever given him. Ridicule and scorn were the spurs with which she tried to drive him to success. It was too bad, according to Dale, that the pulps were out of business, because that was his natural market. She had constantly interrupted his work, seeming to take a vicious delight in her snide sarcasms. "Will the Mighty Muse please take out the garbage?" And, "Could the Great Scribe spare a few moments from posterity's portfolio to fix the leak in the toilet?" And, "Hey, Writer, the kid's got crap in his pants, and I'm too busy to change him!"

"Thanks," he said again.

Marcie moved into his embrace. "Are you happy, Ben?"

"Now? Yes."

"How long are we going to stay here?"

"A few days. I wish it could be longer, but I don't know how to manage it."

"It's like a dream," Marcie said. "And New York is reality, and I don't want to face reality, Ben."

"Maybe you won't have to, Marcie. Maybe something will happen, and you won't have to face it."

"What could happen?"

"I don't know. It's just a thought."

"Wishful thinking?"

"Yes."

"It's getting late, darling."

"Want to go to bed?"

"If you do."

"I do," Ben said.

A certain mystique had developed between them, encompassing the esoteric essentials of a truly close and compassionate relationship, of which neither was yet fully aware, although Ben was more conscious of it than Marcie. There were still too many other intrusions into Marcie's consciousness for her to appreciate what was happening to her.

They lay in bed watching the shadows on the naked rafters, quiet and pensive, and then Ben made love to her with a kind of desperation, as if he feared he might never have another opportunity. The leisurely lover of last night was now intense, urgent, bringing her swiftly to climax but repeatedly delaying his own, reluctant to end the intimacy and break the physical contact, so that Marcie marveled at his control.

"How can you do that?" she asked.

"What?"

"Rare up and then rein yourself."

"Concentration. Sublimation. An art the yogis mastered centuries ago."

"But you don't have to practice it now, darling. There's always tomorrow."

"Am I tiring you?"

"No, of course not."

"Why don't you try for another thrill? A woman doesn't have to settle for one, you know."

"Could you teach me the yoga trick?"

"No, you have to teach yourself. It's largely a matter of discipline and restraint. Takes years of practice to perfect. You couldn't possibly accomplish it tonight."

Marcie smiled, rubbing her fingers in the hair at the back of his head. "I know what you should write."

"What?"

"A sex novel. You know about sex, all right, every phase and angle. It'd sell."

He laughed. "It might come to that."

She thought he must also have learned some Hindu secrets for revitalizing himself, for though he never slept or rested as much as she, he always seemed to have more vitality. He was awake first in the morning and standing before the open door, breathing the fresh, crisp air, while she was still yawning and stretching in bed.

"Hi!" he greeted her cheerfully. "It's going to be a great day for hiking. Tumble out of there, Sleepyhead. We'll walk before breakfast."

"Why not run?"

"Get up, darling—or I'll get back in bed."

"You're oversexed."

"I didn't hear any complaints last night."

Marcie threw a pillow at him. He caught it and tossed it back, suggesting a pillow fight.

Marcie declined. "Where do you get all that animal zest and energy?"

"Clean living," Ben said.

"Hah!" She wrapped her arms about her bare shoulders. "There're some coals on the grate. Stir up a fire, Ben. It's cold in here."

"The mountaineers say brisk, darling."

"I'm a flatlander, remember. Swamp country."

"I can't wait to show you Vermont," Ben said. "The Green Mountains. My uncle's farm is in a broad valley in the foothills. I used to hike between the farm and the village where we lived. I told you about my family, didn't I?"

"Yes, dear."

"Well, they're all old now. Aunt Mae and Uncle Avery are in their seventies and have to hire most of the farmwork done, but they wouldn't be happy living anywhere else, and in that respect I take after them more than my parents."

He had two love affairs going, Marcie thought, one with the country. But if he felt so keenly about it, had such a rapport with the land, why didn't he live there, help the old folks and write in his spare time? Why did he struggle in New York if he had a haven in Vermont?

"Then that's where they belong," Marcie said. "People should live where they're happy. There should be a constitutional Amendment guaranteeing the right."

"There is," Ben said. "The pursuit of happiness."

"But it doesn't allow for preference of location."

"Okay. I'll write to my Congressman about it."

Marcie put on slacks and a long-sleeved blouse, but she was still cold. Ben went outside to get more wood from the pile he'd chopped yesterday. Marcie wished she'd brought a sweater along—but you didn't think of sweaters when it was ninety-nine degrees in the shade. She wondered if Ben had one in his luggage and decided to see. She opened the bag and rummaged through the garments and flinched as her hands touched cold steel. Startled, she stared at the object as if she'd never seen one before: a snub-nosed revolver, but she had no idea what make or caliber. Her heart raced wildly, pushing her swollen lungs and breasts tight against her blouse.

Why did he carry a gun?

Writers didn't need guns, not even Mickey Spillane!

Law-abiding citizens didn't carry guns. Ben was breaking the law. Why? Oh, dear God, *why*?

Travelers sometimes carried guns, she rationalized, and he had known he was going on an automobile trip. But he had carried that thing on the plane to New Orleans! How had he managed that? A deadly weapon, probably loaded, no doubt loaded, since what good was an empty gun? Didn't they check luggage even routinely, unless they'd had a bomb scare? A nut could hijack a plane, terrorize the passengers, shoot them! And other nuts went around assassinating people.

Maybe he had a legal right to carry a weapon? Then why hadn't he told her? Of course he didn't expect her to rifle his luggage. But maybe there was a simple explanation. She stiffened and almost gasped aloud in sudden horror. Simple explanation indeed, and she'd been too simple to realize it!

She heard Ben returning and closed the bag quickly.

"This ought to do it," he said, filling the wood-box beside the hearth. "You know, it *is* brisk out there."

Marcie had to summon her voice. "More like frosty."

Ben was building the fire, humming happily. "Want to help?" He stood and offered her a stick of wood.

It looked like a club to Marcie. She stepped back, cringing involuntarily. "I was never a campfire girl."

Her imagination ran rampant. Intuition had told her all along there was something peculiar about this setup, but she had gone along with it blindly, naively; and no doubt Eddie had counted on her naiveté. Did he need money? Eddie liked to gamble. Was he in debt over his head and under pressure to pay? Was his new love too expensive and demanding? His wife had a ten thousand dollar life insurance policy, double indemnity, and some other insurance through the Rainbow Sugar Mills. Was she supposed to have an accident? Mother of God! Eddie wouldn't do *that* to her, would he? He didn't love her, but he didn't *hate* her that much, did he?

And surely Ben wasn't one of those desperate characters you read about in the newspapers, some sort of underworld hood and hired gun? Surely he couldn't . . . not after the things he'd said and done . . . or could he? What did she know about him, after all? A stranger she'd met four days ago, and two of the nights she'd been in bed with him. And she thought she had character, honor, integrity!

The fire was blazing now, crackling invitingly. Ben beckoned her. "Come warm yourself, darling."

Boy, he was a clever one! Cool and crafty. Maybe he wasn't really Eddie's friend but a paid accomplice? Had they planned this caper together? And was her seduction part of the plan, or something he'd decided on his own? A little bonus for Ben. Why not have some fun and games with her first? "Do you need the words, Marcie?" Sure, he'd say them. Solace for the condemned. Anything, just get in bed, baby. What would he have done if she hadn't walked willingly into that hotel room with him? Wrestled her on the floor. Raped her? And what if she'd been fat and ugly and undesirable—would she be dead already?

"Marcie?"

"I'm warm now, Ben." She was freezing with fear, quaking like a leaf in a strong wind.

Ben crossed the floor and put his arms around her. She stood like a statue. "You don't have to pretend, darling. We'll take this thing by degrees."

What thing? her mind questioned frantically.

"What thing?" she murmured through chattering teeth.

"The countrifying of Marcie Eden." He paused, frowned. "I don't like that last name. What was your maiden name?"

"Landers."

"Well, it'll be Hale soon as we can change it. Mrs. Benjamin Franklin Hale. That's quite a handle, isn't it? Obviously my folks didn't expect a failure when they hung it on me. Or maybe they did and hoped to shame or coerce me into living up to it. Could have been worse, though. Ezekiel or Isaiah or Jeremiah, since Pop was hooked on the Bible."

Marcie heard his voice but the words didn't register. Her mind was reaching in other directions. When does it happen? Where? How? And what could she do to prevent it?

Get in the car and leave! But he had the keys in his pocket, kept them on him for some reason. How could she get the keys without alerting him? Tonight, when he was asleep—no, she'd never get in bed with him again! And maybe she wouldn't have to, because she might not be around that long. Accidents could happen easily in a place like this. Of course! That's why he had brought her to this wilderness known only to him, the cabin proprietor and the Creator! A slip, a fall, a push over a cliff—how many other victims had he brought here? Maybe this was his official disposal, and the woods were full of skeletons and ghosts. Inaccessible, no telephone, some of the advantages of the place, he'd said. Sure, it had a lot of advantages!

"I'm hungry," she said, though the thought of food repelled her. "Let's have breakfast first." The condemned was entitled to a last meal. . . .

"It's better to hike on an empty stomach, Marcie. You don't tire so easily, and the exercise increases the appetite. You'll enjoy your food much more afterwards."

"Can't we even have coffee?"

"All right," he relented. "Coffee, but that's all. I'll make it."

He poked up the coals in the stove, added kindling and kerosene, and soon the pot was boiling, spilling aromatically onto the hot lids. There was canned milk in the pantry, but he drank his brew black, sipping from a steaming pottery mug and smoking between sips.

"It's too strong for me," Marcie said. "I have to dilute mine and we're out of water. Will you go to the spring for some?"

"Add more milk," Ben said.

He was ahead of her, seeming to anticipate her every move and thought. "Shouldn't you call home again?" she asked hopefully. "See how Timmy is?"

Timmy, she thought ruefully. Was there such a person, or was it just a code he and Eddie had worked out to keep Eddie informed? When Timmy was sick, things weren't going well; when Timmy was better, things were improving. Sure, and now she knew the reason for his call to New York that night, but why had they quarreled? Ben wasn't moving fast enough for Eddie? Ben wanted more money, perhaps? Why hadn't he done it in the swamp? He'd recognized the possibilities there, all right. "Ideal spot for a murder," he'd said, apparently contemplating it even then. Was it too close to her home, therefore risky, or had he just decided that he wanted more time with her?

"No, I'm sure he's doing fine. Besides, there's no telephone around for twenty miles or more, remember?"

Marcie nodded, swallowing hard. Another of those advantages, she thought grimly.

"Do you have a picture of Timmy? I'd like to see him." She'd also like to see inside his wallet again. Maybe that was some kind of official badge she'd glimpsed, a permit to carry a gun, and he wrote for the Police Gazette . . . and that still would not explain his association with Eddie, nor his presence with her now. She was just rationalizing, grasping at nebulous straws. The pieces of this puzzle had to be fitted together somehow to reveal the complete pattern, even though some of the important ones were missing. . . .

"No," Ben said, gazing into the mug. "I don't happen to have one with me." In his business, you didn't carry pictures of your family or your home address. You didn't make such information readily available to the twisted, the thwarted, the vengeful, the desperate.

There is no Timmy! she wanted to cry. There's no dependent mother. No farm in Vermont. No writer.

"Too bad," she murmured. "I wanted to see him."

"You'll meet him in person, when we get to New York. My mother, too."

"Sure."

"Now you've stalled long enough, darling. We're going for a walk."

Did he take his victims for walks rather than rides? And did she dare refuse? Could she count on his lust to keep her alive another day, another night? And wasn't she helpless, anyway? If he was a professional killer, this surely wasn't his first effort. He'd probably had plenty of experience; they wouldn't send a novice on such a job. Even if he was only Eddie's tool, he was alert and clever, and she couldn't hope to outwit him. The only slight advantage she had now was that she was wise to him, whereas he was still apparently unaware of her knowledge and suspicions.

She forced a tremulous smile. "All right, darling. But I'm still cold, and I saw an old hunting jacket in the closet. I'm going to borrow it. Wait for me outside, will you?"

chapter
10

THE HOT COFFEE which had scalded Marcie's insides earlier had cooled in her stomach, and fear and apprehension increased her chill. Every fifty feet or so she paused and scanned the landscape, trying to maintain her bearings enough to find her way back to the cabin alone if she had to. Leaves and evergreen needles, brittle with cold, crackled underfoot. The pungency of spruce and hemlock sharpened the air. Dew glistened on the trees and bushes and the long tenuous spider-webs strung intricately between them. A wild turkey gobbler made a sound like a barking dog, startling her, and the lighter cry of a hen answered him. A small flock had recently passed that way, their tracks and droppings were still fresh. Ben told her that in spring their lovesick mating calls trumpeted a shrill reveille in the valley, echoing off the ridges, and while Marcie pretended interest in the conversation, her mind continued to mark the trail, noting certain trees, bushes, rocks. Then a rabbit scurried across their path, disappearing into a convenient burrow, and she screamed and jumped backwards, brushing against Ben and hoping he had not felt the hard object in the right-hand pocket of the baggy hunting jacket.

Apparently not, for her fright amused him. He caught her, laughing. "Brace yourself, darling. That was only a bunny. We might meet a bear. They live in these mountains, you know. Big black wild ones. They scavenge around the cabins at night, but they rarely attack human beings. They're vegetarians mostly, and only the deviates are dangerous."

"How do you tell which is which?"

"If they eat you, they're carniverous. Of course, it's a different situation with grizzlies and polars, they're all formidable, but there's none around here."

"I guess bears are pretty much like people," Marcie said tentatively. "Some are dangerous and some are not. Some so-called civilized men are basically cannibalistic head-hunters, if not actual flesh-eaters."

"That's a weird observation," Ben said. "I trust it's not comparative?"

"Why?" Marcie asked with a false levity. "Could it be? Are you dangerous, Ben?"

He grinned. "Terribly. I eat pretty girls alive."

Marcie's step faltered. He was enjoying himself. He was some kind of pervert deriving sadistic pleasure from his macabre anticipations. She should have realized it last night, when he practiced that strange yoga on himself: a masochist's self-amusement. Now he was playing cat-and-mouse with her, prolonging the gory climax, and having another perverted thrill. . . .

"Let's go back now," she suggested during another pause for reconnaissance.

"Darling, we've hardly started. You can't be that much of a tenderfoot. Look around you, Marcie. Isn't this magnificent country? Pristine, unspoiled, uninhabited. It hasn't changed since Genesis."

"Genesis?"

"The dawn of time. The creation of the world."

"I know, Ben. I've read the Bible. I'm just a little surprised that you have."

"Why, for God's sake?" He was affronted. "Why

should that surprise you? I'm not an atheist, Marcie, nor even an agnostic. An iconoclast in some respects, perhaps, but not irreverent. Didn't I tell you my father was a minister?"

He had, but Marcie did not believe that any more, either, although she let him continue as if she did.

"Dad loved the Green Mountains. We used to take spring and autumn hikes there and have summer picnics by the lakes and streams, and we always went after our Christmas tree in the snow, because Dad thought it lessened the spirit to buy a commercially grown tree in the market. The mountains made him pensive and philosophical; he said no man could feel big or important or immortal in the mountains, that they reduced even giants to insignificance. When he needed inspiration for a sermon, he went alone to meditate on his private Mount and returned humming *Rock of Ages* and *Nearer My God to Thee*. Those granite hills were his Paradise and Mecca and Promised Land and Shangri-La all rolled into one, and I guess I inherited his feeling and fondness for them. It was my legacy from him."

How could anyone lie so sincerely? Marcie wondered. So lyrically, convincingly, even poignantly?

"Sorry, Ben. I'm just tired, I guess."

"Okay," he said. "Rest period."

They sat on the ground in contemplative silence, and Marcie thought it was a little like being in church; a great open-air shrine with a blue-sky dome and misty green spires. She could imagine a mighty organ thundering and reverberating in the valley, and a choir singing the hymns he'd mentioned. She felt as if she were suspended in infinity, hovering on the brink of eternity.

Ben picked up a fallen twig and idly snapped it in pieces. Marcie watched his hands, even more conscious of the long-fingered strength than the first time they had touched her. A sudden vision of those sensuous fingers fastened around her throat sent a new shudder through her body.

"I killed a big buck not far from here," Ben was saying. "Those are his antlers in the cabin. And about a hundred yards farther on, near a brook, I shot a huge bear. He was eating some berries when I spotted him. The big black devil challenged me, and I blasted him right between the eyes. His hide's now a rug before my uncle's hearth in Vermont."

"Do you enjoy killing, Ben?"

"I enjoy hunting, Marcie."

"Defenseless animals?"

"Few game animals are defenseless, darling. A buck deer can rip a man to pieces, ditto the bull moose and elk, and they'll attack without provocation during rutting season. A grizzly is one of the most ferocious animals in the world, including those of the jungles. I have qualms but no compunction about hunting them."

"How about people?" she probed. "Would you have any compunction about hunting human beings?"

He looked at her. "What put that in your head?"

"Oh, I don't know. Just a vagary, I guess. But sometimes men do have to hunt and kill other men, don't they, in war and self-defense? And for other reasons. Have you ever stalked a person, Ben?"

He had, of course. Tailing criminals and suspects was part of his job, and locating missing persons was a frequently employed service of Dobbs Agency. But he didn't like her intuitive questioning; it was too uncanny for comfort.

"There are different kinds of professional hunters," he hedged, "and some perform necessary and essential human services. Detectives are often people-hunters; sometimes forced to track them like animals, and there are allied occupations requiring the same skills and tactics. Unfortunately, our highly civilized society hasn't made them extinct yet."

But his expression more than his dissembling betrayed him to Marcie, who saw only that her question had struck a responsive chord. She thought that he looked

113

guilty as Cain. He *had* hunted people! And probably killed them. For money. A bounty hunter!

"That wasn't my question," she said.

"It's as near as I can answer it," he said.

He reached for her hand, a diverting tactic, but Marcie let him hold it. She let him kiss and caress her, make love to her. It was her life insurance, she thought. As long as he desired her, as long as his lust lived, she would live. At first she only pretended to respond, then she met him eagerly and ardently and wondered what was wrong with her, that she could enjoy him and herself under the circumstances. Like animals, both of them, surrendering to the sexual urge whenever and wherever it prompted them, wallowing on the ground in carnal passion, heedless of the consequences. . . .

"I know what you're thinking," Ben said afterwards.

She sat up, dusting the debris from her tumbled hair, buttoning her blouse. reaching for the hunting jacket she had sensibly removed. "Really?"

"Yes, you look disgusted with yourself and me. I can't seem to leave you alone, Marcie—ravishing you on impulse in the bushes. I'm sorry, darling."

"You didn't ravish me." She stood, brushed off her clothes, donned the jacket again, the concealed weapon weighing her right side. Didn't he notice the bulge, the sag? Surely his instincts were trained to observe such things? How could she beguile him so easily?

"Now can we go back to the cabin?"

Ben was on his feet, temporarily naked emotions guarded again in a saturnine mask. "That wasn't why I brought you out here, Marcie."

"I'm not blaming you, Ben. I'm easy, that's all. The male animal takes advantage of the female at every opportunity, doesn't he? That's the law of nature. Why shouldn't you?"

"Take advantage? Is that what you consider it? I had a different impression. I thought it was mutual—that you met me half way. Am I wrong, Marcie?"

"No," she murmured. "I know I'm wanton with you, Ben, but I can't help myself. Somehow your touch puts me in instant heat." She sighed helplessly. "I love you, God help me, in spite of everything. And I guess I'll want you till—till I die."

"That'll be a long time, then."

"Will it?"

"Don't you think so?"

"I don't know," she said wistfully.

"You're full of vagaries and caprice today, aren't you?"

"Am I, Ben? Is that all it is?"

"Yes, but don't apologize. I'm pleased and flattered."

He smiled and put his arms around her and slid his hands up to her shoulders to stroke her throat, but as he would have done so, Marcie tensed and screamed shrilly, "No, don't, Ben! Please don't!" and wrenched herself free and ran.

Physical violence couldn't have surprised Ben more than these sudden mental aberrations. "Marcie, wait! You're going in the wrong direction! The cabin's the other way! You'll get lost!"

Marcie ignored him, convinced that he had intended to strangle her, possibly during an embrace. The kiss of death. That would be the final touch of a killer with literary aspirations. Merciful God, she was trapped in a wilderness with some kind of intellectual fiend!

She discovered a hunter's trail, one of many that traversed the forest. The woods enveloped and shielded her, but she could not feel safe, for surely he was familiar with the immediate territory. She ran faster, stumbled, retrieved herself and continued at a gallop without the vaguest idea where she was headed. She heard Ben calling to her, his voice echoing off the cliffs, shouting pleas and cautions. Panic seized her, she was frantic to escape. Trees towered everywhere, surrounding her, arching above and ahead of her, and in the near distance, the misty mountains, formidable, impregnable.

She tripped on a berry vine, fell again, skinned her legs and arms, and the red juice of crushed ripe berries stained her clothes. She lay on the ground panting, terrified, helpless with fear and frustration.

Ben was approaching, and he was angry and impatient. She could hear him swearing to himself, feel the earth vibrating under his restless feet. She eased herself into a thicket and pressed her fist into her mouth to stifle an impulsive cry.

"Marcie!" he shouted impatiently. "Where are you? Stop playing this crazy game—it's dangerous! Answer me, or I'll have to leave you here and go to the nearest town and organize a search party! You hear me, Marcie? There're some caves in the mountains! Don't go in them! Bear dens. You'll get mauled!"

Marcie clamped her fist harder on her mouth, bruising her lips against her teeth. She had a hysterical urge to laughter. She'd already been mauled! Nausea stirred in her stomach, convulsed its way to her throat; if she vomited, he'd know her position. Somehow she contained the impulse and remained motionless, peering from her vantage. Fallen leaves were thick here, swept in by winds and drifts and held by brambles, difficult not to rustle, like trying to walk on ice without making a sound. She wished she possessed the abilities of the chameleon to camouflage herself. She felt of the pocket of the jacket, where she had put the pistol before leaving the cabin, but it offered little aid and comfort. She knew nothing about guns, had never even fired a pistol. She had shot a rifle a few times, at a shooting gallery during the Mardi Gras, but she hadn't won any prizes for accuracy. Nevertheless, if he came any closer, if he tried anything, she would defend herself.

Her heart fluttered like a captive bird in her breast, beating its wings against her rib-cage. Survival, self-preservation absorbed her every sense and instinct. She watched her enemy with a kind of hypnotic fascination, her eyes fastened on his crimson sport shirt.

Sweat drained from her armpits, though her extremities were cold and clammy. Ben's approach routed several grouse from the brush, flushing them to flight with a startling whir, and a pair of bluejays scolded him for disturbing their summer solitude. An opossum waddled by, bloated in pregnancy. A squirrel skittered up a tree. The distractions unnerved Marcie. Her hands trembled so she could hardly hold the gun, and she feared she would never be able to aim accurately and fire it. The damn thing was too heavy for her weak wrist; she must hold it with both hands and try to sight her target down the stubby barrel.

Ben was stationary now, almost rigid, in an attitude of listening. The hunter's instincts, Marcie thought. Silence, wariness. Was he trying to scent his quarry on the wind, get a whiff of her perfume? Or was he aware of her location and her intentions and offering her a challenge, making it more interesting for himself by giving his prey a sporting chance? If so, that was foolish of him, risky, daring. His whole chest was a red knit target, a bright bull's eye, a bleeding heart. She had only to squeeze the trigger. . . .

Her nose began to itch and run. She had nothing to wipe it on and let it drip like a leaky tap. The moisture formed first in her eyes, trickled over her cheeks, out her nostrils, down her throat. She could not swallow the saliva fast enough and soon it was choking her. She coughed, muffling it as best she could, and the bluejays fussed again. Her vision blurred. Ben's shirt looked like wet blood.

Now her stomach rebelled, adding to her misery, cramping, churning as if she had ptomaine, and she knew she was going to be sick. She tasted the bitterness of regurgitated bile in her mouth. Her head was spinning, she was too dizzy to remain on her feet. She knelt down, slipped the pistol back into her jacket, held her aching belly with both hands. Then she sprawled on the earth, violently and desperately ill, retching, clawing the leaves in an acute spasm.

She never knew how long she lay there, vomiting the pain and pressure and poison out of her system. It seemed forever and she thought she might die there, alone in the leaves and the dirt, and she did not care.

"My God," Ben said, kneeling beside her. "My God, darling, what happened to you? What came over you?"

Marcie couldn't speak. She thrashed on the ground, moaning, sobbing, murmuring incoherently, hysterical, sure she was in her final agony before she slipped into blissful oblivion.

Ben picked her up and carried her to a nearby brook. He placed her on the bank, in the shade of an oak, then wet his handkerchief and wiped her face. Her scratches had yielded some blood on her clothes, but most of the stains were berry juice. She was limp as a ragdoll. Ben continued to bathe her face with cool water, and finally she revived and seemed to recover her senses.

"Feeling better?" he asked.

"Get it over with," she said. "Don't torture me, Ben. Don't drag it out, get it over and done . . ."

He dipped his handkerchief in the brook again, wrung it out, mopped her face. Obviously she was still in shock, delirious from whatever had brought this on, if it wasn't an epileptic seizure. "Hush, Marcie. You're hysterical. No one's going to hurt you."

"Who hired you, Ben?"

"Hired me?"

"It's no use, Ben. The pretense. I found the gun. I was looking for a sweater in your luggage this morning. I have it with me. I was going to use it on you awhile ago, but I couldn't. I couldn't kill you, even if you have to kill me. Who sent you? Murder Incorporated? The Mafia? How much is Eddie paying to get rid of me?"

"Marcie, for God's sake! It's nothing like that!"

"Oh, don't lie, Ben! You've lied enough already! I know why you brought me here. What's the modus operandi? A rock on the head, a fall from a cliff, a bullet, strangling? And how do you dispose of the body? Shallow grave, cremation in that cozy fireplace, quicklime from the privy, or just let the buzzards and wild animals take care of it? You can't prove murder without a corpus delicti, can you, and there's little danger of finding one here. . . ."

"Good Lord," Ben moaned. "Is that what you think? Is that what caused all this? Well, you're wrong, Marcie. Completely wrong. I should have told you before. Will you listen now, and not interrupt until I explain everything? Every lousy rotten goddamn thing?"

She gazed at him mutely, as if she had lapsed into unconscious indifference again. And Ben, agonizing over his confession, realized he had waited too long.

"The El Dorado Eddie's been seeking all his life," she said when he'd concluded. "So he's finally found it in Manhattan?"

"Or thinks he has," Ben said.

Either way, it didn't seem to matter much to Marcie any more. She sat up enough to rest her back against the tree trunk. She tossed an acorn into the water, watched it drift awhile, then trailed her hand listlessly in the stream. It was clear and shallow, sparkling in the sunlight, gurgling over a rocky bed, but slimy in the isolated little pools where it had stagnated, and wriggling with tadpoles.

"I didn't know Eddie wanted a divorce, Ben. I don't know what he told you, but all he had to do was ask me. I couldn't leave him when he was down and out, which was most of the time. But if I'd known how he really felt, that he wanted out, I'd have vacated his life immediately. If he'd only been honest enough to tell me!"

"The sonofabitch," Ben muttered. "He handed my boss and me a different story, pictured you as a clinging vine who was stifling him and his career. Somehow I knew he was lying, especially when he hired protection for you."

"But still you accepted the assignment?"

"On orders, Marcie."

"And the love-making—was that on orders, too?"

"In a way, yes. But from Eddie, not Dobbs. That's what the quarrel was about that night you heard me on the phone. Eddie was hopped up on something, talking wild and crazy. I tried to reason with him, and he ended up threatening Timmy."

"Then you really do have a son?"

"Of course! A mother, too. I wasn't lying about my family, Marcie. I'm sorry I had to lie to you about anything at all, but everything I'm saying now is true. What could I do when he threatened my kid?"

"He's lost his mind," Marcie said.

Ben acknowledged that possibility. "This whole crazy thing is the scheme and delusion of a madman."

Marcie began to cry again. Ben tried to comfort her. She pushed him away vehemently. "Let me alone, Ben Hale! You're as bad as Eddie. Worse. You've been lying to me all along, too, for your own cruel and selfish reasons. You let me think you loved me. Oh, God!" She wept freely, as if tears could wash away the memory, dissolve the shame. "When were you going to tell me the truth, Ben? After how many more 'acts of love'?"

"I don't know, Marcie. I guess I was hoping I'd never have to tell you, because I was afraid of the consequences. Afraid of losing you."

"All the beautiful lies," she wept.

"They weren't all lies, Marcie. You know that."

"Even so, do you think I could believe you now? That I could ever believe you again?" Her tone was bitter, derisive. "Did Eddie tell you I wasn't bad in bed? Was that part of the inducement?"

"Marcie, please."

"I already pleased, Ben. You must have got some kicks planning the seduction. But it was easier than you imagined, wasn't it? 'Walk in there with me, Marcie.' And dumb little Marcie did." She turned her face aside, brushed new tears from her eyes. "Put that in your report, Mr. Detective. Subject willing. Subject gullible. Subject stupid."

"Stop it," Ben pleaded. "You're killing me, tearing my heart out."

"What heart?" she mocked. "You and Eddie, heartless, both of you. Two of a kind."

"I guess I can't blame you for thinking that, and I don't know what I can say or do to convince you otherwise." The woods were quiet except for the sounds of the water and the wild life. "What do you want to do now, Marcie? Go back to Louisiana?"

"I should, of course, because there can't possibly be anything for me in New York."

"There can be if you want it, Marcie."

"That's over, Ben."

"It's not over, Marcie. Even if you hate my guts now, I still love you."

She shrugged, as if it were unworthy of debate. "Obviously Eddie is in a hurry for his freedom? Am I supposed to get a quickie divorce in Nevada or Mexico, or where?"

"I don't know."

"You mean he didn't discuss that with you?"

"No, and I don't think he's discussed it with his girl friend, either," Ben said.

"If she's financing the whole show—"

"I'm not sure that she is, Marcie. Eddie may just be dreaming about marrying her, as he's dreaming about becoming a star. He has a lot of dreams."

"Who is she?" Marcie asked and when he hesitated, "I think you owe me that much, Ben."

"Silver Haddington."

"*The* Silver Haddington? The one who's always jetting around the world and headlining the gossip columns? The one who's been married a dozen times?"

"Five times," Ben said.

"And she wants to marry Eddie?" That seemed the most preposterous, incredible part of all.

"So he thinks."

Her face was grimly wry. "Well, I reckon I have to find out, don't I? I have to go to New York and try to find out what this is all about. . . ."

She tried to rise but couldn't. Her left foot was hurt, possibly sprained. She winced with pain to stand on it. "I don't think I can walk, Ben. I twisted my ankle when I fell. It hurts awfully."

"I'll carry you," Ben said. "We'll find a doctor."

"Maybe if I just stay off it awhile—"

"Don't argue," Ben said, lifting her in his arms. "We'll find a medic if I have to beat the bushes. But first, do me a favor and put that damn gun in the other pocket of the jacket. It's poking my ribs."

"You knew I had it all along?"

He nodded. "I saw you take it through the window."

"Spying on me?"

"Certainly not. There're no shades, remember. But surveillance is habitual with any detective, and he does it automatically and unconsciously."

"Why didn't you stop me?"

"I was curious to see what you'd do," he said. "I thought you wanted the pistol for protection in the woods, against animals. I was waiting for you to give it to me. I knew differently when you pulled that wild stunt and tried to escape and hide. You really frightened me, then."

"You took a chance hunting me, Ben."

"Not much," he said. "I didn't think you could actually kill me, even if you thought I was a hood. It's not always true, that every person kills the thing he loves. Besides, you never took the weapon off safety. You can't fire a gun on safety, Marcie. Remember that, in case you have to use it in earnest."

"How did you manage to take it on the flight to New Orleans?" she asked.

"Showed the authorities my credentials, naturally. The badge you tried so hard to see whenever I opened my wallet."

"Nothing much gets past you, does it? You're a good detective, Ben, and you could have spared me so much pain and anguish just by telling me the truth."

"I know, darling, and I'm sorry."

More apologies, Marcie thought. The whole affair was an Odessey of contrition.

He paused, shifting her weight to better balance it. "But I wonder if our relationship would have developed as interestingly as it did if I'd been honest in every respect from the beginning? I'm not sorry about that part of it, Marcie, and I never will be. I wish you could feel the same."

Marcie dropped her head on his shoulder and closed her eyes; she was tired, and her eyes still burned with spent and unspent tears. She wished she could feel the same about it, too. But it was too late. Surely his powers of detection were keen enough to realize that?

chapter
11

AT THE CABIN Ben put Marcie carefully in the car. Then he went inside and collected the luggage and brought it out and stowed it in the trunk. The sight of Eddie's guitar enraged him; he barely restrained an impulse to grab it and bash it against a tree.

Somehow the exit from the valley seemed even longer and more hazardous than the entry to Marcie, perhaps because of her eagerness to leave it. She sat so close against the door on her side that Ben reached across her to lock it, and as he did so she tensed and retreated even farther away.

Chagrined, Ben said, "We've got eight hundred miles and more to go, Marcie. If you're going to wince and squirm every time I make a move toward you—"

"Just don't make any moves toward me, Ben."

"You hate me that much?"

"What's hate, Ben? A four-letter word, like love, and sometimes I think they're synonymous. I don't know what I feel or think any more. How should I know after what happened? I'm still nervous, I guess. And exhausted. I never knew fear could be so exhausting."

Ben was concentrating on the erratic road; removing his eyes for an instant could be disastrous. "It's mental exhaustion, Marcie, not physical. You worked yourself into a feverish pitch. Now you have to calm yourself back to rationality. Do you have any pain?"

"Some," she nodded, suspecting that too was more of the mind than the body. The scratches and the bruises and the twisted ankle hurt, sure, but they weren't the true traumas.

"A doctor will help that," Ben said. "There has to be one out here somewhere."

There was, at the crossroads. Doctor Harold Thorpe, an old man in his seventies, with a weathered shingle over his residence door. In mountain country, his practice survived on such cases as Marcie's: bruises, sprains, wounds, bones broken in falls from rocks and horses, fish-hooks caught in human flesh; and at least half of his summer patients were tourists. He instructed Ben to carry this one into his office and place her on the examining table. Ben introduced Marcie as his wife, and Doctor Thorpe said, "She oughtn't to be in those tight pants, can't bind the ankle properly. Help her out of them, Mr. Hale."

"I can manage myself, Doctor," Marcie said.

"Now, darling," Ben said, "you know you always have trouble with your zippers."

Marcie suffered his assistance. And while the doctor, satisfied that there were no broken bones, wound a length of elastic bandage around her foot and ankle, Ben went out to the car to get more appropriate apparel from her luggage: a candy-striped cotton dress, sheer and cool, easy to slip in and out of, with a front closing to the hemline.

"No real damage done," Doctor Thorpe said. "Just rest and take it easy, ma'am. You'll be good as new in no time."

"Can I travel, Doctor?"

"I don't see why not, long's you don't do it on foot," he replied with rustic humor. "I'll give you some pills for pain. Aspirin's good, too. That'll be ten dollars please, Mr. Hale."

Ben paid him and carried Marcie back to the car, though she could have walked with assistance. "I wonder if we can buy a pillow somewhere," he said.

"Why?"

"So you can sleep. I'm going to drive straight through to New York, Marcie. Think you can take it?"

"I'll try," Marcie said, grimacing with a sudden twinge of pain.

"Take a pill," Ben advised.

"No, it'll pass."

"That's silly, Marcie. Why suffer needlessly?"

"It's not unbearable, Ben. I can stand it."

"You want to play martyr?"

"I don't want to be knocked out."

"Oh, I see. You think I'm *that* kind of bastard?"

"I'm not sure what kind of bastard you are, Ben."

"Marcie, use your head! You're no safer awake than you'd be under sedation. How fast and far could you run with that leg? You're hobbled and helpless, and you know it. I could do any damn thing I wanted, and you couldn't stop me."

There was some logic in that; there was some maddening, frustrating logic in everything he said and did. "I guess not," she murmured. "I'm at your mercy."

"Does it bother you, being dependent on me?"

"Maybe. I've never been dependent on a man."

"It was vice versa with Eddie, wasn't it? Is that how you wanted it, Marcie?"

"No, but there didn't seem to be much choice. When he needed me, I considered it my duty to help. Sometimes I longed desperately to be the cared-for instead of the caretaker. ..." Her voice broke and receded, as another paroxysm of pain crossed her face.

"Take a pill and rest, Marcie. Things will be different from now on. I'll take care of you."

Marcie said nothing, but her resolve did weaken enough to take a pill.

Ben drove day and night, stopping only for gasoline, food, and bodily functions. Sedated, Marcie slept most of the time, all the way through North Carolina, waking at sunrise in the Blue Ridge Mountains, ignoring Ben's good morning.

"Where are we?" she asked drowsily.

"Virginia. The Skyline Drive in the Shenandoah."

"More mountains," Marcie groaned. Her unhappy experience in the Smokies had soured her on all such country, and Ben regretted this as much as anything else, for he had wanted her to feel and share his rapport with the hills.

"I'm sorry there's no way for the car to sprout wings and fly over them," he said, "But this is some of the most beautiful scenery in America, Marcie. Try to enjoy and appreciate it."

"I'd enjoy and appreciate a cup of hot coffee more," she said petulantly. "Turn the heater up, Ben. Why does it always have to be cold in the mountains?"

"It's not always. But don't worry, you'll feel at home in New York in summer."

"I doubt that," Marcie said. "I doubt if I could ever feel at home in New York. You'll have to find a cheap hotel for me, Ben. I don't have much money."

"You're going home with me," Ben said.

"Oh, no I'm not, Ben Hale!"

"Oh, yes you are, Marcie Eden. And you'll find it just as I represented it to you, not fancy but fairly comfortable. With a little boy and a gray-haired mother—a capable chaperone, if that's troubling you."

Her smile was sheer whimsy. "It's a little late for chaperones."

"Marcie, it's not the end of the world."

"Isn't it? Everybody's world ends sometime, Ben. Mine ended yesterday. I just haven't gone through the formality of burial. Eddie can inter me in New York, and you can be my pallbearer."

"You're dramatizing, Marcie. How's your foot?"

"Numb. A little swollen."

"The elastic bandage is probably too tight, interferring with circulation. Put your legs up on the seat."

"There's not enough room."

"Use my lap."

"No, thanks. I'll just take another pill."

"You're determined to be tragic about this, aren't you?"

"Should I be comic? Flippant?" She turned toward the window, to gaze across green valleys to blue ridges blending with the sky, cresting in the clouds. "What happened between us is probably routine with your female clients, but I thought it was special with me. That 'great moment' you talked about. I believed you, Ben, because it was a great moment for me, too." She swallowed the throb in her throat, but the ache remained. "Yes, I guess maybe it is tragic to me. And you *did* kill the thing you love—or claimed to love, Ben. That loved you, too."

"Come over here, Marcie."

"Why? So you can kill me some more?"

"You and Mohamet," Ben muttered.

"Don't they have restaurants up here? I hope you won't consider this too dramatic, but I have to go to the john."

Ben laughed, easing some of the tension. "There's a relief station coming up. I saw the notice a couple of miles back. Uncle Sam is considerate that way. This is a national park, you know, the Shenandoah—and that's the famous valley down there, the one your General Lee called the cornucopia of the Confederacy."

"He wasn't my general," Marcie said. "And that was over a hundred years ago."

"You mean the South has finally conceded the loss of the Civil War?"

"The South conceded at Appomattox," Marcie retorted. "But you and I can fight another civil war, Ben."

"We're fighting one now, Marcie, and it's stupid, because we should be allies. We need each other now, and even more in New York."

"How much farther is it?"

"New York?"

"The relief station."

"Just ahead. You're not listening to me, Marcie."

"Listening, Ben. Just not believing, ever again."

In the vast valley below, the crops were being harvested, the fruit picked—only the apples were still green in the orchards. And the orchards were everywhere, stretching alongside the roads, crisscrossing and intersecting the grain fields in patterns like patchwork quilts. Horses grazed in blue grass meadows. Old mansions sat back from the road, half-hidden by trees and shrubbery; here and there an entrance gate was open, affording a glimpse of tall white columns and boxwood garden. Green, peaceful country, with markers to commemorate past violence.

"The Shenandoah must smell like a perfume factory in spring," Marcie said, "when all those fruit trees are in bloom."

"I'd rather smell the ripe-apple scent in fall," Ben said. "My uncle has a small orchard in Vermont. The apples you buy in stores don't taste like the freshly-picked ones. When I was a kid, I could hardly wait for Uncle Avery's MacIntoshes to get ripe. Sometimes I got impatient and ate them green and got a helluva bellyache."

"I guess green apples are one of the temptations of childhood," Marcie said. "And that damn apple Eve ate in that garden must have been green too, because love can sure give you a big bellyache. I thought it would go away if I went to the bathroom, but it didn't. It still hurts." She dug in her purse for the bottle of pain pills.

"What still hurts, Marcie? Your foot, your stomach?"

"For lack of a better diagnosis, my heart."

"Let's stop somewhere and fix it."

"It hurts, Ben. It's not broken. And your kind of fixing would only make it hurt more."

"You're punishing me," Ben said. "Why do women always think that's the way to punish a man?"

"Why do men always consider it punishment? Is that all they want out of life, and if they don't or can't get it, it's punishment?"

"I can't argue that, you win."

"Win what, Ben? I've never won anything in my life, not even an argument. I'm one of those people born to lose."

"Now you're being melodramatic."

"You and your literary observations."

"Marcie, I know you're tired and your foot is no fun. We'll be near Washington this evening. Would you like to spend the night there, yes or no?"

"No."

"Then it's straight through to the Jersey Turnpike. We should draw rein in Manhattan by midnight."

"And then what?"

"This coach turns into a pumpkin, I guess."

"It was a pumpkin all along," Marcie said.

part **2**

chapter
12

EDDIE WASN'T AT THE PENTHOUSE. One of the servants admitted Ben. The household staff, consisting of two maids and a cook, had been a part of Count de Martinique's retinue and had formerly included a butler and a valet, the majordomo hired when the master had discovered in the interview that a freak accident in his youth had impaired his manhood, thus rendering him ideal in the nobleman's estimation for employment in the household of a potential Lady Chatterley. After the Count's departure from the Regal Towers, Silver had kept the female domestics who did not speak enough English to engage in backstairs gossip, but promptly dismissed the Count's personal entourage, having no need for the services of a valet and considering the butler a pathetic eunuch.

Miss Haddington, wearing bell-bottomed silver lamé pajamas and sipping a cocktail, greeted Ben Hale warmly when the maid ushered him into her presence. Although she was voluptuous by nature, there was nothing in her appearance to suggest sensuality, indeed the opposite. She was tall and slender, of delicate bone structure and supple grace, her facial features as finely worked as an ivory intaglio. Silver Haddington was thirty-five and looked her age, but her dissipations did not show to disadvantage; conversely, they enhanced her rather gaunt beauty, adding the patina of maturity to her sophistication and creating a look of exotic emaciation currently popular in the world of high fashion.

She had long since willingly abdicated her throne in conventional society (rather than risk exile, her envious enemies said) and become the pacer for the International Jet Set, known as Café Society a generation ago. Her excapades, marital and otherwise, kept her name perennially in print. Her weakness for titles had twice stuck her with insolvent European nobles and exhorbitant divorce settlements. One of her five husbands was a British actor, whom she found insufferable after two years of wedlock and shed in Mexico. Two were professional athletes, a boxer and a football player, because brute strength fascinated the frail lady. Her friends and lovers were a clique of avant-garde sophisticates, pseudo-dilettantes and sedulous sycophants, both foreign and domestic, whom she discarded when they began to bore or depress her.

Silver never forgot an interesting male, however, and her past association with Ben Hale put him in that category. She was happy to see him but surprised that he should be seeking Eddie Eden there. Evidently the news of her new affair was getting around, despite her discretion and precautions about appearing in public with him, and naturally a detective would be among the first to know.

"Ben Hale, how nice to see you again! It's been a year or more, hasn't it?"

"Yes," Ben said. "How are you, Miss Haddington?"

"Oh, skip the formality! I'm in my prime, darling. And you?"

"The same, I hope. When do you expect Eddie Eden?"

"Why, I don't know, Ben. He happened to be here when you called the other night, but I was having a party and he was entertaining my guests. He's a singer, you know."

Ben nodded and repeated his question. "When do you expect him?"

No use pretending with this man, Silver thought. He knew too much about her, past and present, and it was highly likely that she would need his services again in the future. "So you know, Hawkshaw? Well, he's not on a time schedule. Neither am I. We don't report to each other on the hour." Her smile revealed beautifully capped teeth. "As you know, I allow my pets a lot of freedom."

"I think Eddie Eden considers himself more than that."

"More than a pet?" She shrugged elegantly, the way girls were taught in expensive finishing schools. "I don't keep poodles or parakeets, Ben. I keep men, which is no secret, and I keep them as pets. That's what Eddie Eden is, and all he'll ever be."

"Have you told him that?"

"Not in words. But he's not stupid or naive. Surely he realizes it."

"He expects to marry you, Silver."

She was drinking a gimlet; she smiled over the platinum-rimmed glass. "You've got to be kidding, Ben. Eddie Eden's fun and games, nothing more. When I get tired or bored—" She made a gesture of flicking a fly off her pajamas. "Shoo fly shoo." She smiled again, shaking her head, as if the prospect were incongruously amusing. "Have a drink, Ben. Sorry I didn't offer you one before. Forgot my manners, I'm afraid—your unexpected visit so excited me." An exquisitely groomed hand adorned with a square-cut emerald, which Silver believed matched her eyes, indicated the well-stocked bar. "Help yourself, dear. There's everything an alocholic heart could desire."

"Mine's not in that category yet," Ben said, "but I do need a buffer." He fixed himself a tall cool one, and then relaxed in the air-conditioned comfort. "If Eddie's just for kicks, Silver, why do you want him to divorce his wife?"

"Divorce his wife?" Her oblique green eyes slanted under dark-winged brows. "Where'd you get that drivel?"

"From the horse's mouth."

"Horse's ass, if he thinks that." Her vocabulary, while eloquent, was not always as elegant as her person; and she seemed to delight in surprising and even shocking her audience, as if shattering an illusion of grandeur and perfection about herself which she found distorting and irritating.

Ben had suspected as much. Eddie had lied about this as everything else. But he wanted to arouse Silver's ire against him. "The plan was devised and the arrangements made right here in your tower, Countess. You were out but Eden implied it was with your knowledge, consent, encouragement, and blessing, not to mention your money."

Silver rose from the jade velvet sofa and strutted about the room like the thoroughbreds she rode on the Haddington Horse Farm in Connecticut. "What plans, what arrangements?"

"Nothing much," Ben said. "Just tried to frame his wife, that's all. Get her involved in a compromising situation, so he could force a divorce and marry you."

"What're you talking about?" Silver demanded.

Ben explained.

"Why, that lying sonofabitch! He told me he wanted to borrow this place to rehearse a new act, along with a few thousand dollars to buy some new duds and clear his debts. I knew he'd never repay the loan, but I've lost much more on men. I had some appointments, and a cocktail party and dinner on the agenda, so I made myself scarce. But anything else is pure conjecture on Eddie's part. I don't care what he implied, Ben, that's not the case at all. Why, I wouldn't lash up legally with that Cajun cat for all the sugarcane and rice in Louisianal My family are Boston Brahmins, aristocrats, and his are Teche swamp rats. That Southerner ought to know that while quality folks sometimes bed with white trash, they don't often wed them. He's out of his tree."

Ben had an uncontrollable urge to laughter and had to indulge it. There was some poetic justice in this world, after all, if not much of any other kind. Just retribution, and Mr. Eden was about to get his.

"It's funny," he said, laughing. "But somehow I don't think Eddie's going to see the humor in it."

Silver fitted a cigarette into a long jade holder and Ben flipped his lighter for her. She nodded her thanks, inhaled and exhaled as if she were doing a TV commercial for the product. "That supercilious egomaniac," she said, marveling at the man's arrogance and presumption. "Damned if he isn't even more conceited and cocksure than that actor I married. And you believed him, Ben? A smart guy like you?"

Ben sobered, frowned. "I was on a job," he said. "And that part wasn't funny. I got my licks, too."

"You mean it boomeranged? Oh, that's beautiful, baby! Classic. I had a Puritan ancestor who believed religiously in divine retribution."

"So did I," Ben said, thinking of his father.

"She must be something to shake you? That's more than I could do. I'd like to meet her, congratulate her."

Ben swirled his drink in that habit he had. "What're you babbling about?"

"Oh, come off it, Ben. I wasn't that subtle, surely, nor you that dense. Remember when the agency was chasing that fag count of mine, trying to catch him in the act? I made some passes at you, Sherlock, but for some reason you chose to ignore them. I thought you were still hung on your ex?"

"Maybe I was," Ben said. "But why me, Silver? Why Eddie? Why anybody? You've got everything on earth going for you, why do you tangle up with so many different guys?"

Cynicism pervaded her smile. "You want the story of my life, Ben? I know you scribble on the side! You want to research Silver Haddington? I thought the rags had related my tale so often it was common knowledge."

"Sure. The poor little rich girl. The old clichés."

"No, they don't call me that any more," Silver said. "I'm not a girl, I'm a woman now. A jaded rich bitch they'd like to label me, but they're afraid of libel. Hell, I wouldn't sue anybody, because no matter what they printed it could be proved one way or another. I've been everywhere and done just about everything. I don't know why my family hasn't disowned me, but I wouldn't care as long as they didn't disinherit me. My psychiatrist says I'm a compulsive hedonist, self-destructive, a potential suicide, among other things, but he's muttering in his beard, because I enjoy life too much. I delight in burning my candle at both ends, it gives a psychedelic glow, and I have no intention of snuffing the lovely thing until it's all used up, or melted with age." She enjoyed his quizzical expression. "You look surprised and puzzled. Did you expect to hear a somewhat different tale? About a sad lonely child with Mommy too busy with her social activities to pay me any mind, and Daddy too busy making millions to bother, either. Shit, the poor souls worshiped me, smothered me with affection and attention. I'm not rebelling against background, family, society, money, or anything else. This is just my element, my bag, and I like it."

"And that explains Eddie Eden?"

"Adequately, I trust. He's an interesting playmate. He knows tricks. I like men who know tricks. I bet you know a few yourself, Hawkshaw."

Ben rose to make himself another drink. Silver's eyes followed and measured him as if she were judging a stallion in a horse show. No phenomenal physique, he nevertheless fulfilled most of her specifications, for she had discovered that masculinity was not necessarily commensurate with the appearance of it. She had known

138

some muscular marvels, a couple of her mates included, who were deficient in the most significant male function. Ben Hale's sinewy sparseness suggested strength and agility and endurance, and his features were as rugged and solid as if they were hewn out of his native Vermont granite. Furthermore, his apparent indifference to her charms, his total disregard for what she could do for or to him if she chose, increased his attractions. He was unique in this respect, like no other man in her acquaintance, most of whom fawned and acquiesced and even groveled before her monetary power; she was intrigued and determined to break down his defenses. It was a matter of pride as much as interest. She was not accustomed to his kind of detachment.

"Are you going to wait for Eddie?" she asked.

Ben was dropping ice-cubes into his glass with his fingers, ignoring the silver tongs. She liked that. "Any objections?"

"None whatever. Tell me, what's Mrs. Eden like?"

Ben returned with a full glass, sat opposite her. "Young. Lovely. A wonderful person."

"That serious, huh?"

"You don't expect me to answer that?"

"No, but you really don't have to. Your face is sphinx-like most of the time, but it was unmasked when you spoke of her just now. I've seen such expressions on visitors to shrines. Veneration." She waited for his reaction. She had touched a nerve, she saw it flicker about his mouth, but he wore the stoical mask again. "She must be some chittlin, that little magnolia puss. But evidently not enough for Eddie. Did he sic you on her, Ben, with all those nasty ulterior motives he's capable of? I hope you cuckolded that cunning Cajun? But of course you did! It sticks out on you like a pair of phallus-horns. Well, maybe I can help you in your cause with honey chile, play cupid and fairy godmother rolled into one."

"Stop fishing, Silver. You won't catch anything."

"I know, dear—you've already been caught. What kind

139

of hook did she use, and bait?" Her discreet laughter, like her well-modulated voice, was also refined in the mills of exclusive schools. "Seriously, Ben, what do you expect to do with the lady's husband? He may not step conveniently aside when he learns I'm not interested in making an honest man of him."

"She has sufficient grounds for divorce," Ben said.

"No doubt. But Eddie's going to get something for himself out of this, Ben. You can bet on it."

"I know he wants to marry you, Silver."

"And in lieu of matrimony and money, what else could I give him? Publicity, right? His career is on the skids."

"What career?" Ben asked grimly.

"But that's exactly my point, Ben! What does he need now more than a *cause célèbre* on two continents? And who could better provide one than I? He was never famous, but he's in a professional eclipse now, in danger of demise. A transfusion of notoriety might save him. If he could splash this affair with me over the front pages, he could possibly revive, survive, and even prosper. People would want to know who Eddie Eden is, how he got involved with Silver Haddington, and all the other juicy details. There'd be pictures and interviews, he'd be hot copy. He has a passion to make *Variety* headlines. And it's happened before, you know. Publicity, good or bad, has rescued many a falling star from oblivion and elevated many an obscure artist from obscurity. Eddie has nothing to lose and everything to gain. The odds are in his favor, and he's gambler enough to realize his chances of winning. You, I, his wife would be the losers. He used us, Ben. He'll use anybody he can to get what and where he wants."

"Granted—but what's the alternative?"

"Well, I'm not going to marry him," Silver said emphatically. "That's too great a sacrifice to save even myself. Not that I think he could actually destroy me. I'm no stranger to the front page, you know. I'll survive.

If you have enough money, you can survive anything but death and taxes."

And if you haven't? Ben thought. Where did that leave him and Marcie? He stared into his glass, as if he might find the answer there. "I'm not in that league, Silver."

"That's unfortunate, darling." Her silver thongs glided across the white carpet. Ben felt her hand on his shoulder, smelled her scent. "Want some comfort?"

"Thanks, but I'm not in the mood."

"I can change that."

"Cool it, Silver."

She smiled. "Just commiserating, darling. I'm sympathetic by nature. How about some snacks while you keep your virtuous vigil? Maybe I can tempt you with my domesticity and culinary arts. Believe it or not, my talents aren't limited to the boudoir. I'm a whiz in the kitchen, too."

She was preparing canapés when Eddie came in, using his pass key. He was surprised to see Ben there, sitting moodily at the bar. He crossed the room with an outstretched hand, which Ben ignored. "Hey, man! When did you arrive?" His head swiveled around the room, as if he expected to find his wife. "Where is she?"

"With my mother. She has a sprained ankle."

Eddie grinned appreciatively. "Must have been some chase. You won, though? You caught her?"

Silver emerged from the kitchen carrying a tray of caviar, cheeses, crackers, olives, stuffed celery. Her eyes barely flicked Eddie. "Where've you been, lover? Another card game?"

"Yeah."

"Don't tell me. You lost again."

"Not much. Two grand."

"Not much! That's a heap of sturgeon! I own mills and mines, Eddie, but no mints."

"Now, doll—that's small change to you, and you know it. You spend more on one evening gown."

"That's my business, Buster!" Silver set the tray on the bar with a clatter. "And while we're discussing finances, Eddie, just what sort of deal did you make with Dobbs Detective Agency concerning your wife? Surely you don't imagine you're prominent or successful enough to have to hire a security guard for her?"

Eddie shot Ben a glance. "How much did you tell her?"

"Everything. I thought she knew it all and concurred. Isn't that what you led Dobbs and me to believe?"

"No, you fool! That was confidential. Between client and agency."

"Client, hell," Ben said. "You tried to con and coerce me from the beginning, Eddie. There won't be any fee for service. Consider it good will."

Rage flushed Eddie's face. "You mean to tell me you didn't accomplish anything?"

"Nothing. Not a goddamned thing. But you'll get your divorce, man. That I can promise you. You could have had it for the asking, Eddie. Why did you hand me that cock-and-bull story about the clinging vine and the millstone? You were the clinger, Eddie, the yoke when you were broke. She'd work and carry the load when your act folded, which it did with accordion regularity. Well, I hope you've got it made elsewhere, man, because it's all over with Marcie."

Silver stood tapping her thonged toe soundlessly on the carpet, smiling at Eddie's chagrin and discomfit. He turned to her, exercising his charm as if it were an irresistible magnet. "I don't know what this goon told you, baby, but don't believe a word of it. He's a liar."

"I'm not going to marry you, Eddie. I never had any such intention, and I can't help it if you did. What's more, your assets, such as they are, don't outweigh or even balance your liabilities. I can't afford you, lover."

"You mean the gambling? I'll quit. I'll never touch another card or pair of dice. On my honor."

"What honor?" Silver mocked. "And it's not just the

gambling, Eddie. You've got other expensive vices and habits."

"A little pot now and then, an occasional trip?"

"Heroin's next, Eddie."

"No, baby, no. I've seen too many bums thrown from horse. That's one ride Eddie Eden'll never take, you can make book on it."

"No, thanks," Silver declined. "I never won on a man yet, and the odds should have been in my favor. I can pick horses fairly well, but I'm a born loser with men. You're a born loser too, Eddie. It's time you realized it."

"Don't count me out, Silver, I'm not down the tube yet. As Paul Revere said, 'I've just begun to fight.'"

"That wasn't Paul Revere."

"Whoever the hell it was, I'm not licked yet, Silver. And I'm not bowing out on your wishes or orders. I'll have you begging tonight, baby, because I got a whole bagful of tricks I ain't used yet. Been saving 'em as a surprise."

Silver smiled musingly. "Really? That's what the actor and the count and the baron and the athletes said when I canceled their credit cards. And you know what, Singer? They couldn't deliver, because nobody knows that many tricks, and neither do you. I'll have to bounce you, baby—only this time it won't cost me a million."

Eddie didn't say anything, but his smile sent shivers up Silver's spine. Then he whirled on Ben. "What're you grinning at, you bastard? This is all your fault. You and your big stupid mouth! Dobbs will sack you when I tell him how you muffed this job!"

He swung at Ben. Ben ducked and swung back and Eddie crashed to the floor and lay a few seconds, stunned, spread-eagle. Then he got up and rammed his head into Ben's belly like a football tackle, knocked him off balance, and the two of them wrestled in earnest until Silver broke it up.

"Stop it, you studs, before somebody bleeds on my white carpet!"

"You and your goddamn white carpet," Eddie muttered, scrambling to his feet. "You got a fetish about that thing—you know that, Silver? One of these days I'm going to dump ashes and blood and crap all over it."

"You do, Buster, and it'll be your blood and ashes and crap," Silver warned him and turned to Ben. "Why didn't you break his neck? Dobbs told me you can use your hand like an ax. Why didn't you chop this worm up in pieces?"

"I was tempted," Ben admitted, straightening his tie and combing his hand through his hair, "but I thought you might like that pleasure, ma'am."

Eddie followed him to the door. "What kind of stupe do you take me for, Ben? You got to Marcie, all right. Your trouble is, she also got to you. Well, I warned you that might happen, remember? Did you have fun?"

Ben doubled his fist again, but Eddie backed off, taunting, as if he had the advantage now. "Yeah, man, you're hooked on her, deep. She's in your blood like a transfusion. *You* want the divorce now, right? Well, hear this, Detective. If you queered me with Silver, you'll have a long wait for Marcie. A goddamn long wait."

"You sonofabitch," Ben muttered.

"Aren't we all?"

"I ought to kill you, Eddie."

"Man, you got a violent streak. I thought you were a preacher's seed?" He laughed, enjoying the situation as if it were made to order for him. "Now take off, will you, so I can try to repair the damage you did here. . . ."

chapter
13

MRS. HALE WAS PREPARING chicken curry. Ben smelled the savory herbs and spices the moment he entered the brownstone house. Marcie was sitting on the divan, turning the pages of a picture-book for Timmy, who was still confined indoors. The child had taken to her immediately, and she to him. This pleased Ben enormously, although it didn't seem to affect Marcie's attitude toward him, nor change any of her recent resolutions concerning their relationship. She wouldn't allow him to touch her, except to help her move about on her aching ankle, and Ben thought she was letting her pride punish him and herself.

"Hi, Daddy!" Timmy greeted him.

"Hi, son."

"Miss Marcie is reading to me."

"So I see." Ben lifted the child in his arms, hugged him, set him on his feet. "But now Daddy wants to talk to Miss Marcie. You go to your room until supper, Timmy."

"Okay. Granny's cooking."

"Yes. I smell it. Curry. Delicious. Run along now."

When Timmy was gone, Marcie asked, "Did you see Eddie?"

"Yes."

"Well?"

"We had a brawl."

"What did that solve?"

"Nothing. He started it."

"And you were spoiling for a fight, weren't you? When am I going to see Eddie? Talk about the divorce."

Ben frowned. "I don't know, Marcie."

She stared at him. "I thought he was in such an almighty hurry for his freedom? What's the delay now?"

"Things aren't progressing as he hoped with Silver."

"How does that affect me?"

Ben sat down beside her. "Marcie, you might as well realize this right now. The divorce, if there is one, will probably be messy. Eddie wants the publicity. He wants his name linked with Silver Haddington's in the news, one way or another. If he can't marry her without any fuss or fury, he'll create some. He'll use her, or make you use her. She knows that herself."

"And she'd let him use her that way?"

"Money would be the alternative," Ben said. "She'd have to buy Eddie off, and it'd be expensive, as expensive as any of her divorces. She doesn't intend to pay him, says she's not afraid of adverse publicity. She's a battle-scarred veteran of the press wars."

Marcie dropped her eyes. "Did you tell Edlie about us?"

"Good God, Marcie! Of course not."

"But he can find out, can't he? That hotel in Chattanooga—he could hire another detective and find out?"

"Yes, he could," Ben said. "And he suspects the truth, Marcie. He's not stupid. He made some nasty cracks. That's the reason we fought."

Marcie considered the prospect and the ramifications of public exposure. She'd look worse than Silver Haddington, because she had a husband supposedly waiting for her in New York. Aunt Beth would be scandalized, the Rainbow gossips would have a picnic, she could never return there to live in any kind of peace or seclusion. Eddie's family would be dragged into the mess, and Ben's. Mrs. Hale had been kind to her from the moment she had arrived, limping on Ben's arm, trying to apologize for her intrusion at that late hour, while Ben hushed her and explained her injury and the necessity of her staying there. His mother had accepted the situation graciously and assigned the guest to her son's room, relegating Ben to the living room divan. The next morning she'd brought a breakfast tray to the bed, but Marcie'd decided she couldn't allow that and hobbled to the kitchen table. Though she was obviously curious, Mrs. Hale contained her curiosity admirably, evidently restrained by her son's frequent edict of no interference in agency business. But Marcie felt like an impostor in her home and was afraid that, if Mrs. Hale knew the truth, she would not want her around, and Marcie would never earn her confidence and respect and friendship as she hoped.

"Ben, I can't stay here any longer. You've got to find a room for me some place."

"Don't be ridiculous, Marcie. You can't get around on your foot well enough yet."

"I'll manage," Marcie insisted. "And I can get money for living expenses by selling the car. The title's in my name, I bought and paid for it myself, and it's no use to me here. I can ride the bus or subway when I get a job. I'm a good secretary." She paused. "But I want to see Eddie, Ben. I want to know where I stand. I want this thing settled."

"He can't come here, Marcie."

"Then I'll go to his place in the Village," Marcie said. "He still has it?"

Ben nodded. "He hasn't succeeded in changing his address to the Regal Towers yet."

"But he's there now?"

"He was when I left," Ben said.

Marcie glanced away. The knowledge hurt. Maybe it

shouldn't but it did, and she couldn't help it. Seven years washed out. Had it ever been love for Eddie? Had he ever been happy or content with her, even briefly, between affairs?

"Marcie, let's go out tonight, if only for a ride? I'll show you some of the sights."

"No, thanks, Ben. I'll take a Greyline Tour."

"You're being childish," Ben accused. "You can't just sit here and sulk and brood. You can't seal yourself in a vacuum and live, Marcie."

Marcie pushed the damp hair off her forehead. The swamps had nothing on New York's weather in summer. The brownstone house was like a huge Dutch oven, baking her all day long. But still she didn't want to leave it, for it represented some quiet and peace and security. She had traveled fifteen hundred miles with Ben Hale and left bits and pieces of herself scattered along the way. To be whole again, a complete and solid and functioning person, she'd have to retrace that course and pick up the fragments, glue them back together like a shattered vessel, and she didn't think this was possible. She lacked the heart even to try for fear of failure. How did you make broken people whole again? And if somehow you succeeded, how long would the mended product endure?

"I can," she said listlessly, "because I'm accustomed to vacuums, Ben. Most of my life has been a void."

"You're being tragic again."

"So I'm a tragic figure," Marcie said. "But are we any better than they, actually, Ben? Any more honest, decent, moral, any less guilty? Eddie put us to the test, and we proved to be made of the same clay. We're in a glass house throwing stones."

"Marcie, what's done is done. There's no way to undo it. We can't retreat, we have to go forward."

"To what, Ben? What's ahead?"

"What do you want, Marcie?"

148

She sighed, shrugged. "I don't know, Ben. I just want it over with, as quickly and painlessly as possible."

"It won't be that way, Marcie. Divorce is not like a tooth extraction—a shot of novocaine and it's easy and painless. Somebody gets hurt. Somebody suffers."

"It'll be me, then. It's usually the wife."

"Not necessarily," Ben said, remembering his own experience. "Marcie, what about us—you and me?"

"Isn't there something you stamp on cases before you file them away, Ben? CLOSED."

"I haven't closed this case yet, Marcie." Exasperation edged his voice; there was a limit to his patience with temperament and caprice. "You want me to beg, crawl—what?"

"Supper's ready," Mrs. Hale announced, standing on the threshold. "I guess I should say dinner, but somehow I've always felt that one eats dinner in dining rooms and supper in kitchens."

"I feel that way, too," Marcie said. "So does my Aunt Beth, in Louisiana. Your son liked her kitchen and her cooking. Didn't you, Ben?"

"Yes," Ben said.

"Help her, son," Mrs. Hale said, as Marcie tried to rise. "She can't walk alone."

"I know that," Ben said. "Trouble is, she doesn't."

chapter
14

"LET'S HAVE DINNER on the terrace this evening," Eddie said. "I like to dine out there."

"Dinner, dine." Silver's laugh was mockery. "Trying to impress me with your refinements, Eddie? How about Voisin or Le Pavillon, so you can show me how you can order in Cajun French?"

"Well, I could, you know. My grand'mère was French-Canadian, never spoke anything but her native tongue, and I learned at her knee. Not pidgin French or finishing school French like yours, Silver, but the real article. Grand'mère taught me to sing, too—I cut my teeth on *Allons a Lafayette* and dozens of other folk-songs. They don't print a menu in New Orleans, Manhattan, Montreal, or Paris that I couldn't read, *chérie.*"

"You fool," Silver scoffed. "Do you think I give a damn about that? And do you honestly think you could acquire enough savoir-faire to counterbalance your other faults and shortcomings? Do you imagine I saw the possibility of playing Pygmalion in reverse when I picked you up at the Amber Alley? That I might want to mold you into the kind of gentleman I'd take home to Boston to meet my family?"

She was moving around, nervous and angry in a way

Eddie had never seen her before, losing her cool and using her tongue like a whiplash.

"Now that we're on the subject, Countess, just what did you see in me? What appealed to your highness? My lowness?"

"Your muscles, vagabond lover."

"Which one, *bébé?*"

"Not those in your head, *mon ami.*"

"Okay, since this is the honest hour, what do you think I saw in you, Madame?"

"That's easy, *chanteur.*"

"If you know that, *ma petite nymphée*, then you should know it's not going to be easy to dump me."

"Threats, Monsieur? Blackmail?"

Eddie feigned pain. *"Chérie,* you wound me. I love you, I adore you. You seduced me, alienated my affections from my wife, broke up my marriage. You promised to marry me."

"Lies," Silver muttered, enraged now, yet regal in her hauteur, as if she were dealing with an insubordinate servant whom she had befriended out of kindness and pity and who was now attempting to repay her compassion by involving her in a sordid backstairs intrigue. "Lies, lies, lies!"

"Maybe, but I'll give the papers permission to quote me. Then it's your word against mine, and you know the rags, *Comtesse.* Front page headlines, back page retractions, and nobody reads the retractions."

He was sprawled on the velvet sofa, observing her through hooded eyes, his supercilious nonchalance provoking Silver's ire to greater intensity. At that moment she longed passionately to destroy him.

"What kinds of snakes breed in your swamps, Eddie?"

"Rattlers, moccasins, many kinds. Poisonous, some. Others harmless."

"But not the wandering troubadour species. Someday somebody's going to cut your glottis out, Eddie. But maybe they'd be doing you a favor—the operation might improve your voice if not your personality."

"Boy, you really know how to hurt a guy! But seriously, Silver, and all this French froth aside, you married a boxer and a football player, why not me?"

"The boxer was a champion and the football player a national hero," Silver replied caustically. "You don't qualify in those categories, Eddie. You certainly aren't the show biz success the actor was, and you lack the title of the defunct nobility. Any more questions, Singer?"

"Just one. Were any of 'em better in bed?"

"No," Silver reluctantly admitted. "None was even as good. You had no competition there, Eddie, no peer."

"Thanks for that," he said dryly. "Crumbs, milady, but thanks."

"Oh, Eddie." Her voice softened almost to a coo. "I don't want to quarrel with you. It's been fun, and it could have gone on longer. Why did you try to change it? And in such a nasty way, involving your poor wife."

His hand made a negligible gesture. "Marcie involved herself. She insisted on coming up here on her vacation, and since I couldn't stop her, I tried to make it easier for her. I threw Ben Hale at her as an alternative—a kind of shock-absorber. I hoped they'd hit it off, so she wouldn't be alone in New York. Dobbs has other agents who might have been more effective escorts and lovers—a couple of real James Bond wolves—but I picked Hale for a reason. He's the kind of guy who wouldn't abandon a babe in this jungle if she'd touched him at all, and apparently Marcie did. Notice his protective attitude toward her? Even has his old lady looking after her, and I've got a clear conscience."

"Clear conscience?" cried Silver in astonishment. "What would it take to muddy the water on your brain, Eddie?"

"Flattery, flattery." Eddie grinned wryly. "You're gonna kill me with compliments, baby. But whether you believe it or not, I care enough for Marcie not to want to hurt her any more than necessary. I thought Hale would be a satisfactory replacement for me. I'm glad she went for him, but to tell the truth I'm also surprised. She wasn't as wild about me as I thought."

"I'm sure you're crushed," Silver mocked. "Or at least your ego is—that's what you're made of, you know, muscles and sinew glued together with ego."

"Is that such a bad combination?"

"There're better ones, Eddie—but not for my purpose."

"If you feel that way, why—?"

Silver interrupted, "Eddie, we've been that route. Don't come unglued and beg now. I hate beggars."

"I reckon most millionaires do."

"I give my share to charity, Buster."

"Sure, Miss Haddington. You never miss a charity ball or horse show, do you? You figure a check absolves all your other sins? Is that how rich folks figure their charitable contributions, as conscience soothers?"

"I wouldn't know about the others," Silver quipped. "I figure mine as tax deductions."

"And how do you plan to write me off, ma'am?"

"Not on a bank draft, mister."

"How then?"

Silver paused under her portrait, one hand on the white marble mantel, with the same condescending attitude of nobility that she had affected for the artist and he had managed to capture effectively. "I don't know, *chéri*. I haven't decided yet."

Eddie sat up abruptly, angrily. "Don't look at me as if I were your lackey, Countess, and guilty of lèse-majesté! I'll make that decision."

"If you bluff this much at cards, no wonder you lose," Silver said, her expression unchanged. "You're transparent, Eddie. People can see through your bluffs and call them. I'm calling you now."

"Very well. We've been playing stud and I've got an ace in the hole, but literally. You know your Polaroid camera and how you like to sleep raw, and some of the acrobatic positions you get in? Well, I've recorded them for posterity."

"You're lying," Silver challenged, gazing at him steadily, the nerves about her mouth flickering imperceptibly.

"You want to bet on it?"

"You scum, you slime, you swamp swine!"

"Oh, cut it, Silver. Sanctimony doesn't become you. You know you wouldn't care if I used them for my own titillation, which was my real reason for snapping them. But I could peddle them as pornography if you force me."

"I'd sue the sawdust stuffing out of you, Eddie."

He laughed, pleased as a tomcat with a cornered mouse. "You'd have to admit it was you first, sweetheart. And with your past, it might be difficult to convince the public that you didn't willingly pose for them."

Silver's fingers tapped the mantel. "So the bartering begins," she conceded. "What's your price, Eddie?"

"The same as it's always been, dear. Marriage."

He must not see her revulsion, or he would raise the ante. She turned to one of the etagères, appraising her curios, touching and even caressing those of particular beauty or interest or significance, as if they were capable of physical response to her appreciation: a Chantilly vase, a Grecian bronze of Socrates lifting the fatal cup to his lips, a cloisonné urn intricately veined in turquoise and gold, a crackled-crystal stag, a golden Aphrodite rising out of a seashell, a jade Buddha, a naked Nubian slave, his muscular torso carved in every minute detail in polished ebony, a slender silver Circe with her magic wand and several prostrate men at her feet in various stages of transformation into swine. The collection was priceless, and the thought of sharing it with this greedy grubber was revolting, sacrilegious.

"I won't pay it, Eddie."

"Suit yourself."

"Let me think about it," she relented.

"Sure, darling. There's no hurry. Meanwhile, up in the tower, we continue our romance."

"Orgy, you mean."

"You said it, *chérie*, not I."

Silver fondled the Circe. "It's true, Eddie. It doesn't even deserve the dubious dignity of an *affaire d'amour*."

"Did any of your others?"

"Perhaps not." She, above all, had no illusions about herself and her cup of tea.

"But it's your bag, baby, your thing, and you love it," Eddie said with a perception that was somehow incongruous with his callousness. "Let's forget it for awhile, Sil, and think of others things. Got any steaks in the freezer? I'll fire up the hibachi and charcoal 'em. You can toss a Caesar's salad. We'll imbibe some booze while we're waiting—and later on, I'll treat you to some of the tricks I promised, for dessert. One day I'm going to take you on a trip with me, Silver. If you think your Jet Set flies, wait'll you go by LSD. Oh, God, the exotic scenery, the erotic sensations!"

"Eddie—"

"Thaw the beef, baby. I'm famished, and I still want to dine on the terrace. . . ."

The sirloins sizzled over the hot coals, and Eddie inhaled the smoke appreciatively. In a family of ten children, he'd been raised on Mississippi River catfish and swamp crawdads—fried, broiled, in bisque and bouillabaisse and creoled dishes of one variety or another. When they had meat, it was usually ground, and he had not seen Châteaubriand until he was twenty-five and ordered it on his one grand experience at Antoine's. Even in youth he had resented his poverty and brooded about it and promised himself gastronomic delights, while he burned the family refuse in the rusty oil drum incinerator or buried it in the swamp, and while he tended the rows of common vegetables in the garden. He would kick at the trees and beat his fists on the bark and

155

cry out his rage and humiliation and despair, curse the fate that spawned him in such dismal gloom and doom and vow that he would not die there. He would not live with the stench of smoldering garbage in his nostrils, decaying and rotting in the dampness like his unfortunate ancestors, while the mosquitoes sucked the blood out of him. He would get out! One way or another.

Now he stood tending the steaks like a master chef, leaving his post occasionally to survey the world around him like a king surveying his rightful realm. He belonged on a pinacle, and he was contemptuous of the plebeians in the pits. Through some horrible mistake of birth, he had begun life in a swamp, but that did not mean it was his natural habitat, his heritage. No man of wit and talent had to settle for a peasant's existence. Success was only a destination, and there were many routes by which to achieve it. Security was the ultimate goal, and a person ought to be reasonably secure by the age of thirty. He'd reached and passed his peak and had no time to lose. He'd served his apprenticeship in poverty and despair and defeat, but no one seemed to realize how deserving he was of promotion to bounty, how driven toward it, or even that desperation was his spur. Ego was only a buoy to keep him afloat in the treacherous currents that kept trying to drag him down and under, drown him, and a few times almost had. Recently he'd tried to escape through pot and acid, but even these were not entirely satisfactory and terribly temporary, and the return to reality was more and more dreadful and harrowing and frustrating.

Silver brought out the salad and set the bowl on the glass-topped table. She had crisped the lettuce and water cress in ice water. She returned to the kitchen for a cruet of olive oil and garlic, a tiny handmill to grind the whole black pepper kernels, a warmer of sautéed croutons, fresh eggs, lemon juice, anchovies. Eddie observed the procedure with interest. She knew what she was about.

"You have a way with greens," he said.

"Like emeralds, jade, greenbacks? That's your real *pièce de resistance*, Eddie."

"Touché," Eddie bowed. "But let's not draw swords and fight again, Silver. Let's sheathe them for the rest of the night. And don't give me any more of your *noblesse oblige*, either. This evening we're equals, peers—and before all's said and done you're going to realize and admit it."

"The only peerless. thing about you, Eddie, is your conceit," Silver said. "I've put some sparkling burgundy on ice. It should be ready when the steaks are. Braise the meat, Eddie, don't burn it."

"Escoffier couldn't do better," Eddie said, forming a circle with thumb and forefinger and touching it to his lips.

There were times when silence mocked more than sarcasm, and Silver knew when to employ which most effectively.

Eddie gazed across the semi-dark expanse of Central Park, to the lighted towers surrounding it. It was an Arabian night like one he'd experienced on a good trip, flying on his LSD carpet; he was Aladdin, and Silver Haddington was his magic lamp; if he rubbed her right, his life would glow. The fact that he had managed to find the lamp at all was a miracle, but to have it seek him out was surely destiny. Kismet had come to the Amber Alley in search of Eddie Eden. . . .

Grease and juices trickled from the searing meat onto the hot coals, causing them to flare and flame. Eddie picked up the tongs, cast a last glance over the parapet. "It's a long way down there," he said.

Silver cracked a raw egg over the salad. "And a hard fall, Humpty-Dumpty."

Eddie disliked the decor of Silver's bedroom; it smacked too much of its last legal male occupant, but it suited Silver, who was definitely the boudoir-type. The furniture had come from France, handcrafted pieces of a workmanship extinct in mass-produced America, and the hangings of platinum gray chiffon were delicate, dainty, feminine. Eddie enjoyed disturbing the perfection of the room, tossing his clothes about and soiling the ashtrays—gestures of juvenile defiance and contempt which Silver tolerated. But now he befouled the perfumed air with the odor of strong tea, and this habit she was less inclined to indulge.

"I wish you wouldn't burn that damn weed in here, Eddie. It stinks."

"It's incense, baby. Fit for the gods. Light up," he urged. "Turn on. Try it."

"I did, Eddie, long ago. I didn't like it. It didn't do anything for me. Just made me dizzy and drowsy. I woke up with a headache worse than any hangover."

"That's because you weren't used to it," Eddie said. "It takes a little time, more than once or twice."

Silver sat at her dressing table, which covered an entire wall and was skirted as frilly as a ballerina's tutu, brushing her hair ritually. Styled in an intricate French twist, her hair was surprisingly long when released, falling in a slivery cascade over her shoulders. On formal occasions she wore it in a coronet, with a string of pearls or diamonds braided into it, or simply crowned by an elegant jeweled tiara. Her slender arms described graceful arcs as she wielded the brush.

"Where are the pictures, Eddie?"

He smiled blandly. So that's what was on her mind? Good. Showed she was worried. "What a leading question." He moved toward her, offered her his reefer. "Take a puff, darling. Inhale. It's the one air pollution you can enjoy. And it's not narcotic you know. You can't get hooked."

"I know that, Eddie. I just don't dig the stuff. It's not my bag."

"You think you've been around, Sil? There're a million thrills you haven't had, a million sensations you're yet to experience. Why don't you aim for the big joys? Shoot for the moon."

"And eventual eclipse?" Silver said. "You're on the dark side of the earth right now, Eddie. You just don't know it."

"Maybe I do, Silver. But you're my bright spot, the force that's going to prevent my total eclipse."

The ivory-backed brush completed an arc, began another. "You're real smooth when you're on the weed, Eddie. Suave, even poetic. Too bad the pot polish has to wear off and reveal the bent tin. Did you take your wife on your excursions? Did she freak-out with you?"

"Marcie? You kidding? I wouldn't dare suggest it. She'd get hysterical and panic. She doesn't even know about my bad habits yet—I don't practice them around her. She's provincial. God, is she ever provincial!"

"Why did you marry her?"

"I guess because I was pretty provincial myself at the time," Eddie reflected. "Provincial parents, living in a provincial parish. A provincial fool."

"And what do you consider yourself now? A sophisticate? A *bon vivant?*"

She watched him in the mirror. Eddie filled his lungs with smoke, expanding his chest, and his eyes had a dilated stare, the pupils enlarged and intent on nothing if not himself. He was absorbed in self-contemplation, transfixed by his own charismatic charm. "Your master, *bébé,* and don't you forget it." He waved the magic wand again, touching it to her lips, but Silver pushed his hand away, affronting him. "Take that goddamn tent off and get in bed, and I'll prove it."

"It's a peignoir," Silver said.

"Who designed it? That French fag?"

"Don't be vulgar."

"Vulgar? That's a corker, coming from you. You might be Boston aristocracy, Silver, but you're the most common creature I've ever known—and I've known several. Marcie's a grand lady beside you. My grand'mère would call you a bourgeois trollop, and worse."

"Shove your grand'mère," Silver muttered.

"See what I mean? Would a lady say that? Now practice your true vocation, *bébé*. Take it off and get in the trough. Wallow in it."

As Silver shed the peignoir, Eddie shook his head wonderingly. "I don't know how you can affect me with that body. You're thin, skinny, almost boyish—which was probably your appeal to the Count. You don't need a girdle or a bra, Silver. Why don't you go on a high calorie diet and round up a bit? That's an inadequate figure."

"The one in the bank supplements it," Silver said grimly. "How much for the pictures, Eddie?"

His arm shot out and pushed her back on the bed. "We're not discussing pictures, Silver. We're discussing you and your licentious libido. I think that's what keeps you thin. Your sexual appetite is ravenous, practically insatiable, and you starve the rest of your body to feed it. Do you have one of those unique Venetian glass phalluses in your objets d'arts collection for when there's no real live flesh one handy? You're not only a vulgar tramp, Miss Haddington, you're a pitiful nymph."

"Nymph is passé in psychiatry now. Eddie. It's a compulsive sex drive. Some people are compulsive eaters, drinkers, smokers, gamblers. It's a glandular affliction."

"You ever tried to cure it?"

"It's incurable and usually uncontrollable—only age and ill-health diminish it. I've been in analysis. Two years and ten thousand dollars worth. I knew my problem before my first visit. I continued for the couch sessions, which were precisely that. You see, the doctor had a bit of a sexual problem himself. Like you, he was a satyr."

"Must have been torture, married to that homo?"

"He was bisexual. Trouble was, he tried to spread himself too thin. When he started favoring young boys over me, that was too much. It got so his touch was repulsive, made my flesh crawl. I had to shuck him, whatever the cost."

Eddie crushed out his cigarette, sat down beside her. "What happened to him?"

"The last I heard he was living happily ever after in his drafty old chateau on the Loire, with his young protégé, on the generous divorce settlement."

"I remember the trial," Eddie said. "Sensational. Dobbs Agency got the goods on him, didn't they?"

Silver nodded. "Their fee was thirty thousand, but it was worth it. Ben Hale was the agent."

Eddie touched her thigh, felt the flesh tense and quiver with anticipation in spite of herself. "Marry me, Silver. You'd never have that problem with me. Whatever else you may think about our relationship, it's right in one respect. You can't deny that. I can send Marcie somewhere for a quickie divorce, and we'll take a trip on our honeymoon. Go into orbit. You'll love it, I promise."

"I told you I'd think about it, Eddie." She closed her eyes, clutched her hands at her sides in a futile effort to restrain and contain her emotions, then dug her long silver-lacquered nails into the bed-linens. "I won't beg, Eddie. This time I won't beg."

"Yes, you will, doll. You're on fire, and I'm the fireman. You'll beg, or burn."

She sent her arms around him in a kind of helpless desperation, as much despair as desire. "Maybe it would work, Eddie, if life were only this."

"What more is it for you?"

"Oh, I don't want to talk about it any more," she cried, writhing against him. "You're such a cruel bastard, Eddie, and you know you have the advantage now. Don't torture me."

"A little pain won't hurt you, Silver. Makes it better. Agony intensifies anticipation and pleasure."

"Don't you understand?"

"Sure, baby. You're pushing the panic button; you

can't keep your finger off it when I touch you. You want action. Well, this won't last all night, *chérie*, with pot it'll only seem that way. You got to learn to tolerate it, Silver—it's made for babes like you."

chapter
15

SOME KIND OF DEMONSTRATION was in progress on the east side of Washington Square, before the University, when Ben and Marcie arrived in the Village. Center of attention was a long-haired, bearded youth wearing a white robe and monk's sandals on his bare grimy feet, apparently convinced that he was Christ incarnate sent once more to redeem the world, his somewhat lethargic disciples clustered around him in the grotesque garb which had become the international hippie habit. They all looked doped, dazed, dirty—disorganized even in organization. Some displayed posters indicting society for its many "crimes and grievances" against them: END THE WAR, END THE DRAFT, END POVERTY, END COMFORMITY, END POLICE BRUTALITY, END THE ESTABLISHMENT, CURE VIRGINITY, LEGALIZE POT AND LSD, VENERATE FREE LOVE. Some milled about restively, as if they were lost and confused and bewildered—scattered sheep seeking a shepherd to lead them. Others lounged against any convenient support, including one another. It was difficult to distinguish male from female, and Marcie thought they looked like mutations from another planet.

"The flower people," Ben said contemptuously.

"They stink," Marcie said. "I can smell them from here. Wonder what they're protesting today?"

"Everything," Ben said, giving the scene a wide berth, driving directly to the alley where Eddie still kept a flat. "Law, order, decency, cleanliness, society, the world in general, and life in particular. Read the signs. That's their litany; they chant it like parrots. Fight conformity. Look at 'em, listen to 'em! They look alike, sound alike, act alike. Beads and beards, wild hair and wild clothes. Did you ever see so much conformity in one gathering? It's ironic, incredible, that they don't seem to realize it themselves. As for being non-violent—I'd hate to be the poor cop on this Bohemian beat."

Marcie wondered if Eddie knew any of them, suspected that he did. But Eddie would never be found in their midst, disporting himself publicly in such ridiculous regalia, nor openly supporting their causes. He had no interest in their philosophies or ideologies, and the only social injustices and calamities he recognized were those which personally affected Eddie Eden. The things he wanted from life could not be obtained through mass assembly, collective bargaining, or ballots. In this respect, at least, he was an individual and a noncomformist; if he had a creed, it was hedonism, and he was actually antisocial in that he lacked the herd instinct and would beat no drums, wave no banners, march in no parade but his own.

Ben stopped the car before a white stucco house with a vermilion door and fake window-shutters also painted vermilion, one of a row of converted nineteenth-century stables which the tenants considered groovy and inspirational in one sense or another. Garbage cans buzzing with flies lined the cul-de-sac on both sides, and the whole neighborhood seemed to be a haven for homeless cats. Ailanthus trees grew out of the cracks in the concrete and pavement and flourished like the proverbial green bay; no one knew on what this tenacious tree thrived so lustily, since there was little soil, water, or light, but it provided most of the summer shade and greenery in the Village. Some years ago a woman had written a nostalgic and highly successful novel around that tree, which didn't only grow in Brooklyn, and Ben had thought it odd that the author had never actually named it anywhere in the book.

Ben helped Marcie out of the car and up the stairs to Eddie's quarters. There was no answer to their knock, and he employed a pass-key. It was one of those improvisations called studios in the Village and efficiencies elsewhere, a garret-coop with a living-bedroom combination, closet-sized kitchen, and bath with medieval plumbing. Shabbily and sparsely furnished but surprisingly clean, mute testimony that the occupant spent little time in residence.

Marcie's ankle ached. She sat down in a wooden chair garishly painted by the color-blind artist who had previously lived there. "He's not here," she said superfluously.

Ben had not wanted to come at all, but Marcie had insisted, saying that she refused to wait around for Eddie to see her at his convenience. "Did you really expect him to be, Marcie?"

"No," she answered. "But can you blame him, Ben? Who'd stay here if they had a penthouse?"

"Eddie doesn't have a penthouse, Marcie. He merely has a temporary lease with the mistress of one, and there're good indications that his lease is about to expire. If he doesn't vacate peacefully, he'll probably be forcibly evicted."

"Then why hasn't he seen me? Why isn't he trying to get this show on the road?"

"Because so far it's just a rehearsal, my dear, and he doesn't have the backing he counted on. His angel is reluctant, ready to pull out, in fact."

"That would kill him," Marcie said.

"I'll weep at his funeral."

"How cruel and bitter that sounds, Ben."

"Marcie, let's get out of here. Maybe you want to hold

a wake for a dead marriage, but I don't. I'm slighting my job. I'm supposed to be on another case."

"Don't let me keep you, Ben."

"You intend to stay here?" he asked incredulously.

She shrugged. "Why not? It's Eddie's home, however humble, and I'm his wife, however humiliated. I can't go on living with you, Ben." At his look, she amended, "With you and your mother. And I doubt if Eddie's here enough to make any difference, if that bothers you. But it's one way of seeing him, confronting him. He must come here occasionally, if only to pick up his mail."

"Bills, you mean. I don't imagine his fans put much strain on the postal department."

Above their heads a skylight, dirty with accumulated debris, filtered in some sunlight and shadow. Marcie's face was in shadow and Ben couldn't see her wistful resignation. "Go to work, Ben, before you lose your job," she said.

"I'm not leaving you here alone, Marcie."

"Eddie won't hurt me, Ben. I've been married to him seven years, and he's slapped me around some, but he's never actually beat me. He has more subtle ways of hurting."

"Even when he's on pot and LSD?"

She stared at him. "He's not on that stuff."

"He is, Marcie. Maybe he wasn't when he left you the last time, but he is now."

"I don't believe that, Ben."

"It's true, Marcie. He admitted it before Silver Haddington and me yesterday. She chewed him out about his vices, said she wouldn't support his habits, and he promised to reform—to swear off gambling, at least. But that doesn't mean anything. He's hooked in more ways than one."

"Then he's sick and needs help."

Ben gestured in despair. "God, you *are* naive, just like Eddie said! He doesn't want help, Marcie—not the kind you can give. He's on his way to the gutter, and if you hang around long enough, he'll take you with him. He'll drive you to drink, or worse."

"You're an alarmist, Ben."

"Realist," he corrected. "Eddie's the dreamer, only most of his dreams are nightmares, Marcie, and I don't want you involved in them." He stationed himself by the door, leaning against the wall, arms folded over his chest. "I'm not going to argue this with you, Marcie. I'm just not leaving. I'll spend the night if necessary."

Marcie glanced away. "That's all he'd need, Ben, to find us here together, in bed."

"Bed?"

"If you spend the night, we'll be in bed."

"I hope so," Ben said. "And while that might have been all Eddie needed and wanted before, Marcie, now I think it'd take considerably more provocation. You can sue him for divorce but he can contest it, with charges and countercharges, and the Haddington name brandished about, no matter how it's introduced. Do you have any idea how vicious and nasty a divorce trial can get, Marcie? Murder can be dull fare by comparison. You've got to realize that Eddie is desperate for money, fame, and success, and Silver Haddington represents all of them to him. You're expendable, Marcie, and so is everyone else to Eddie Eden."

"But if I refused to name Miss Haddington as co-respondent?"

"Oh, Marcie—you're a babe in this Babylon! He'd *force* you to name her by naming her himself."

Marcie sighed, clutching the arms of the gaudy red-and-yellow chair. "I should never have come to New York. If I'd stayed in Rainbow, this couldn't have happened. I'd have been the innocent party, no matter what Eddie did. Now I'm as guilty as he."

"And I'm responsible for your guilt," Ben brooded. "So maybe that makes me a worse dog than Eddie, because I corrupted innocence. But recrimination won't solve anything now, Marcie. Eddie's cunning and devious, and you can bet he has an alternative, a counterplan if this one fails."

That would be natural and instinctive for Eddie, Marcie thought. He had lived in a world of cunning and deviousness most of his life, employing every maneuver and manipulation in his bid for recognition, and his failure thus far was not due to any lack of effort or stratagem. The creatures of the swamp managed to survive under conditions that would have defeated and destroyed those outside it, and Eddie possessed many of their characteristics, either inherent or acquired. Marcie knew she would be no match for him in any game of intrigue and chicanery, and she doubted if Ben Hale or Silver Haddington would, either.

"So what do we do, Ben? Sit and wait for him to use us like pawns on his chessboard?"

"He's already made a move with the queen," Ben said. "It might be wise to wait and see how it develops, before devising one of our own."

Minutes later they heard footsteps on the stairs, and Eddie entered the studio. If he was surprised to find them there, he concealed it adequately.

"Thought I'd locked that door," he said. "But I reckon lock-picking is a part of your professional training, eh, Mr. Hale?" He crossed the room, bent to kiss Marcie's cheek. "Welcome, wife. Did you enjoy the trip? What took so long? Problems? Stagecoach break down? Indians attack?"

Smooth as glass. Nonchalant, even innocent, as if he had no knowledge of the events preceding her arrival, nor his own responsibility in them.

"Save it, Eddie," Ben said. "She knows."

"Knows what?"

"The whole story."

"I don't dig your dialogue," Eddie said.

"You dig, all right. Tell her the truth, Eddie, or I'll beat your brains out."

Eddie's grin was satanic. "You're a violent man, Ben.

You know that? A desperate character. I don't think I realized it before. Reckon I took a chance sending you after my wife."

Marcie's eyes went to Ben and back to Eddie. Her head whirled, her foot throbbed painfully, she felt confused and bewildered. It was like walking into a theater in the middle of a play and waiting for someone to tell her what she had missed.

"Cut the act, Eddie. It's no use. I told her everything. You, Miss Haddington, the whole bit."

For a moment Eddie looked trapped, but he was facile in freeing himself from intricacies. "I don't know what kind of pap this hack has been feeding you, honey, but I hope you weren't impressed. Some writers have terrific imaginations."

"I showed her my credentials, Eddie."

Eddie mulled this information, retaliated abruptly. "What kind of detective are you, that can't keep a case confidential? I reckon you told her about the threats on my life too, and on hers? Scared the poor kid stiff. I hired you in good faith, and you go and blow the whole deal! Dobbs has a dud on his staff and if the rest of his agents are as flaky, I'll have to look elsewhere for protection."

"I've had enough," Ben said, seizing Eddie by his turtlenecked throat, threatening to throttle him. "Level with her, you slimy sonofabitch, or I'll choke it out of you!"

With equal strength, Eddie wrenched himself free. "Jeez, you *are* violent! Marcie, call Dobbs Detective Agency, on Madison Avenue, ask Harvey Dobbs why I hired Ben Hale. He'll tell you it was an escort job, and if anything else happened on that trip it was beyond the call of duty." He extended his hand. "Give me the dossier, Ben."

"I didn't keep one."

"Why not? It was a case, wasn't it? You must've kept some sort of record, if only an expense account? How could you report to the agency? Or were you moonlighting on Dobbs' time, researching my wife for another of your corny who-done-its that don't sell?"

Ben saw Marcie's bewilderment change to despair. Eddie's points were so logical, his accusations and arguments so convincing, it was difficult to negate or refute them. And Ben couldn't comprehend his strategy, either, unless Eddie wanted to hang on to Marcie as a meal ticket until he was sure of Silver Haddington's bread basket. . . .

"Do you deny knowing Silver Haddington?"

"Certainly not. Who would deny knowing Miss Haddington? She's a fan of mine. She caught my act at the Amber Alley, enjoyed it enough to invite me to entertain at a bash she was throwing, and several since. She paid me well. Where do you think I got the dough I paid Dobbs Agency for your lousy services?"

Ben had difficulty restraining himself. "It was money borrowed from the Haddington mint to gamble, Eddie, and you know it! Dobbs didn't get anything but my traveling expenses out of it. What're you trying to pull, Eden?"

"What're *you* trying to pull, Hale?" Eddie jerked his thumb toward the door. "Split out of here, will you? I want to be alone with my wife. You took long enough getting her here, and if you don't mind I'll take over now."

"Marcie, do you believe all this?" Ben asked.

She was sitting in a kind of stupor, as if she weren't sure where she was or with whom, what she was hearing or thinking or believing. "Please go," she said tremulously.

"Then you *do* believe it?"

"Just go," she repeated.

Ben gazed at her, started to protest, shrugged, and left, trodding the stairs heavily.

"Talk about flat feet," Eddie muttered, listening to the echoes in the stairwell. "It'd take more than gum soles for him to sneak up on a suspect. What's the tape on your foot, sugar? Hurt yourself."

"Didn't Ben tell you?"

"Tell me what?"

"I fell," Marcie explained dully.

"Running from him?"

"I just fell," she repeated in the same vague tone.

"That bastard give you any trouble?"

"No," Marcie answered, her eyes on her hands lying flaccidly in her lap.

"Look at me and say that, Marcie. You can't, can you? It's okay, baby. I understand. You were together a long time. Male, female—it was bound to happen. But you don't have to admit anything now. You're not in court, on a witness stand." Marcie raised her head and met his lascivious smile. "How was your first adventure in adultery, Mrs. Eden? Interesting?"

"You're disgusting, Eddie."

"Why? Because I'm curious about your infidelity? I think that's natural enough for a husband. If I were the violent type, like your lover, I'd probably beat the hell out of you. Be grateful I'm just curious." He paused. "Or was it your first offense? Maybe I'm naive and ignorant. Maybe you've been laying in the swamps and the canefields with the local yokels while I was on tour?"

"Would you care, Eddie? Would it make the slightest difference to you if I had?"

"No man wants a whore for a wife, baby."

"How about for a mistress?"

"All right, forget it. Let's make a deal. I won't bug you about your extra-marital cheatings, if you won't bug me about mine. Fair enough?"

"When did you ever play fair, Eddie?"

"Marcie, I said forget it! I don't blame you or that double-crossing Peter Gunn. I'd have done the same thing in his position. I screw every woman I can, if she appeals to me at all. Why should Mr. Hale be any different? He's a man, isn't he, equipped with the proper

171

tool and instinct? If he laid you, he was just following his nature. If he didn't, he was a damn fool. You're choice meat, baby, a delicious cut. I always knew that and always enjoyed it. I'm just not a monogamist, that's all. And I bet Ben Hale isn't, either."

Marcie saw through his tactics. He wanted to make her hate Ben, distrust him, turn against him. She shrugged, as if Ben Hale's morals were of no possible concern or consequence to her. "Where're you playing now, Eddie?"

"I'm between engagements."

How often she'd heard that.

"What happens now, Eddie?"

"Don't worry, sugar, we'll manage. We always have, ain't we? The rent's paid on this pad another month, and I've got bread in my pocket. We'll eat."

"I—I thought you were living in a penthouse."

"Does this look like a penthouse?"

"Oh, Eddie, don't lie to me, please! I know you want a divorce, so you can marry Silver Haddington. But why couldn't you just ask me, Eddie? Why did we have to go through this sham, involve so many other people? For publicity?"

"Is that the detective's deduction?"

"Yes. Is it correct?"

"Why do you ask questions, Marcie? You have all the answers. Ben Hale supplied them well in advance."

"Eddie, even if I wanted to hold on to you now, I wouldn't try. I know I'm no competition for a woman like that—"

"Like what?" Eddie prompted when she paused.

Marcie rolled and chewed her lips. "Well, she's rich and glamorous and important. The stories you read about her in the newspapers and magazines, and she's always in the gossip columns. . . ."

"So what harm could that do me? The right kind of exposure can be very beneficial to an entertainer's career. Cheer up, baby! You're here, and we haven't been together in months, and a celebration is in order. I don't have any booze in the pad, I'll have to dash out for some. Not many groceries, either. Been eating at cafeterias and delicatessens."

He started for the door, and Marcie said, "There's a stampede in Washington Square. Don't get trampled."

"The fools," Eddie said. "You see that guy in the Jesus costume?"

"Which one?"

"The Savior, he calls himself, the pariahs' preacher. Wears a white drapery and monk's sandals. Man, he's the most, the wizard of odds! He's preserving his protests for posterity, writing a book called *The Gripes of Wrath*. Isn't that a gasser? He pushes pot on the side."

"How do you know that?"

"The weed flourishes among the flower people."

"I thought they were mostly in California," Marcie said. "Haight-Ashbury and Big Sur and San Mateo."

"You kidding? They were born in this Bohemia, it's the original colony. Frisco, L.A., Boston, Chicago—just extensions of the Village. Pot and protest and free love are a way of life here, the very essence of it, and every night there's a trip in somebody's pad. I don't dig their crusades, but I got to admit they swing when they're not marching."

"Do you have to live here, Eddie? Can't you move? I can sell the car if you're broke."

"Later," Eddie said, patting her cheek almost tenderly. "We'll discuss all those dreary details later. If I don't go for the jug and loaf now, I may not go at all ... and we'll have to live on love alone."

Marcie thought that would be certain starvation for both of them, but she didn't say so. She merely smiled and waved him toward the door. He hadn't changed. He was still the same Eddie. It was she who was different, she who had undergone the metamorphosis of love.

chapter
16

RETURNING TO THE OFFICE, Ben found a message and a telephone number to call, which he recognized as Silver Haddington's private *private* number. He dialed it and waited, listening to the chimes, drumming his fingers on the desk-top, still upset by the scene in the Village and wondering what was happening there now. He should have clobbered Eddie and tried to shake some sense into Marcie. It was fantastic, the way Eddie could beguile her, from the moment he had entered the studio, almost as if he possessed some malevolent power over her; and even more eerie, the way she responded, seeming to become a willing subject.

Silver's voice answered, removing his own spell, and Ben said formally, "Miss Haddington? Ben Hale."

"Oh, Ben—thank heaven you've called!" She sounded a bit breathless, as if she'd run to the phone. "I've got to see you right away. Professionally," she added, when he hesitated. "Get over here as quickly as possible. It's urgent."

She made it sound important to him as well as to herself, and Ben said he'd be there in twenty minutes. Silver welcomed him at the door with a drink and then went to the bar to pour Dubonnet into a chilled glass for herself.

Ben followed her. "What's so urgent, Silver?"

"Eddie," she said without preamble. "He has me in a barrel, Ben. He's got some pictures."

"What kind of pictures."

"Not the kind you put in the family album and gallery."

"How'd he get them?"

"Believe it or not, while I was asleep."

"Is your face visible, recognizable?"

"I don't know." She sipped the Dubonnet from a hollow-stemmed crystal goblet which appeared to be filled with liquid rubies. "I haven't seen them."

"How do you know they exist? He could be lying. He's a facile and plausible liar, Silver. He just handed his wife a string of lies she seemed to swallow."

"I thought of that, Ben, and challenged him to produce them. Naturally, he wasn't that foolish. He could be bluffing, of course, but I can't depend on it."

"Is the goods that damaging?"

"I told you, I haven't seen it. But I sleep nude, and I'm restless. Judge for yourself."

"I can't, without seeing them."

"Use your writer's imagination," Silver suggested.

Ben straddled a white-leather bar stool. "What do you want me to do about it?"

"Get them, naturally. I'll pay you well."

"Have you tried to buy them from Eddie?"

She nodded grimly. "His price is too high. Marriage."

Ben wished this conversation were being tape-recorded for Marcie's benefit. The bourbon was handy. He replenished his glass. "Here's to Jack Daniels," he said. "The best friend a man ever had."

"I thought only Southern men drank bourbon," Silver said. "Did little Honeysuckle Rose convert you?"

He frowned at her description of Marcie, obviously resenting any snide reference to her whatever. "No, I've been a bourbon-and-branch-water boy since I was weaned. It's patriotic, you know. Leave Scotch for the Scotsmen." He paused. "Seriously, Silver. If those pics are that valuable to Eden, he's probably got them in a vault somewhere. I don't see how I or anyone else could get them."

"Don't you understand, Ben? He could ruin me!"

"Didn't you tell me you weren't afraid of publicity?"

"This wouldn't be publicity, it'd be pornography."

"That bad, huh?"

"I take sleeping pills, Ben. He could have posed me in any position he pleased, and he has an incredibly obscene and prurient mind. I bet he was the kind of kid who made four-letter words out of his alphabet soup and cereal. He claims he snapped them for his private collection, but I think now he was planning this caper all along, ever since I met him and was foolish enough to invite him here. You, his wife—we were all a part of it, Ben. Tools, instruments. Patsies."

"It seems that way," Ben agreed. "Turn him over to the police, Silver. Charge him with blackmail, which this definitely is."

"So far he's asking only for marriage, Ben, not money. How can I make a proposal look like blackmail? Most women don't regard it as a crime or coercion."

Ben pondered, drank. "Silver, I'm not a thief. I can't steal the stuff for you. I may be able to find out where he has them stashed, if they're real, but what good would that do? He probably has negatives."

"No, he took them with my Polaroid."

"If you were knocked out, how do you know? He could've had a professional photographer and pornographer in here. No doubt he knows some."

"No doubt," Silver agreed. "You've got to help me, Ben! I'll pay you anything."

"That's not the point."

"Sorry. I keep forgetting that some men aren't for sale. I've bought so many of them."

"And you must have known Eddie Eden wouldn't be free, either. You must have realized he'd cost you something, that you'd have to pay in some way."

"Of course. But I expected it to be my way, not his. I wouldn't marry that—that Neanderthal if he'd recorded our every sexual act on film and was threatening to hold a world premiere."

Ben grinned. "The proceeds would help balance the deficit of payments here and abroad."

"That's funny, dear, but you'll pardon me if I'm not amused." Her eyes beseeched him. "Can't you think of something? The agency must have run into similar situations many times, with letters and other damaging evidence?"

"Legally, I'd need a search warrant to prowl his garret," Ben explained. "Make a formal complaint against him, Silver, and we can get police cooperation."

"I've already banned the bulls, Ben! Eddie has a fiendish mind. I don't want to precipitate anything I might regret. Can't you make an unofficial search of his pad?"

"His wife is there now," Ben said.

Her brows arched. "You mean she moved in with him, after all that's happened?"

"She's there," Ben reiterated.

"Then she must still be hung on the bastard and wants to hang on in spite of everything. But this is incredible! I wonder what he has that I don't know about? In her place, I'd be sacking him right now. In cement, if necessary." She left the bar and began to pace the room nervously. "Are you taboo in her tent now? Forbidden in the flat?"

Ben shrugged.

"I thought you were gone on her?"

"It's a long story," Ben said.

"Well, write a happy ending."

"It's not that easy, Silver."

"Look, Ben. She'll be caught in this web, too. We all

will, like flies for that goddamn tarantula! If she's too blind to see that, you'd better start illuminating and elucidating. Her darkness is dangerous. And her naiveté is nauseating."

"When do you expect to see Eden again?"

Silver grimaced. "Never, I hope. But of course that's wishful hoping. I gave the rat some green cheese and sent him to his Village hole, told him I needed time to think and would give him an answer when I had one."

"The don't-call-me-I'll-call-you routine?"

She nodded. "I've been thinking of packing my bags and jetting off for an extended vacation, letting him simmer. Is it a good idea?"

"Not for a guy with Eddie's emotional temperament," Ben said. "He'd sweat awhile, but then he's liable to blow his cool. Patience and prudence are not among his virtues."

"What virtues? I've never known a more morally bereft bastard, and I've known scores. Mongrels, including the pedigrees that most of my husbands were, they weren't one hundred per cent curs. Each of them had at least one redeeming quality, if only stupidity, and a pat on the pocketbook mollified them. But Eddie Eden is something else. I'd sooner kill myself than marry him."

"Take it easy," Ben soothed. "It may not come to that, Silver." He ruminated the situation a few moments. "Call Eddie, tell him you haven't reached a definite decision yet, but you miss him and want to see him. That'll placate his ego and get him out of the apartment."

"What about his wife?"

"I'll just have to be honest and tell her what I'm looking for," Ben said.

"Oh, Jesus!" cried Silver. "If you found it, she'd have me by the tail, too!"

"She's not that caliber, Silver."

"She's some kind of martyred saint? What would any frau do with such evidence? Christ, Ben! This gets stickier by the minute. International intrigue couldn't be any more involved. I feel as if I'm sitting on a rocket with a lit fuse. Isn't there some way you can get her out of the place, too? Wasn't she with your mother?"

"She left."

Silver drained the goblet, so that only the hollow stem remained red, like a thermometer indicating a high temperature. "She has to work, doesn't she? Send her on a job interview. I have connections. I'll arrange something. Eddie says she's a secretary. They're always in demand. I'll make some calls and set it up."

Ben was skeptical. "Not the Haddington Enterprises, Silver. She wouldn't take it."

"Dear boy, give me more credit than that," Silver laughed. "I can open other doors besides my own." She paused. "How much does she know about Eddie and me?"

"Enough," Ben said.

"She must hate me?"

"Well, she's not happy about it."

"If it's any consolation to her, neither am I. Not with these new developments, anyway."

"That doesn't help much."

"No, nothing helps much." She sighed, her hands shook. "I need a tranquilizer. I had to take several barbs to get any sleep at all last night, even after Eddie exhausted me. I never thought anything could worry me this much. Either I'm getting sensitive about my reputation, or losing my imperviousness to public opinion, because I find myself actually dreading another battle with the press. I have a battery of attorneys, but even they've never been entirely successful in warding off the enemies' barrage."

"Poor little rich girl."

"Don't waste your sympathies or your sarcasm," Silver said wryly. "I concoct my own ragouts, and I deserve to stew in them. Getting back to Mrs. E., I guess I owe her something, and I'd like to make amends. There're other people I can pressure which she can't possibly connect with me. Influence is one of the advantages of affluence. Tell her you heard of an opening in an insurance agency, I'll give you a card before you leave. That can be your open sesame to the abode this evening, if you must justify it."

"Thanks," Ben said. "But don't expect this scavenger hunt to yield any treasure, Silver. Eden's not the type of pirate to bury valuable loot in home harbor."

"Maybe we'd better make it tomorrow night," Silver suggested, testing. "Give him a chance with his wife tonight. After all, he hasn't seen her for some time."

Ben's reaction was precisely what Silver expected. "No, get him over here this evening and keep him here. I'm sure you know how, Countess."

Silver smiled. "It's like that, is it? Then we'd better get that stud out of there, pronto, hadn't we, because a mare is a mare to him, like a stallion's a stallion to me."

"I'm going back to the office," Ben said, standing. "I'll have to acquaint Dobbs with this, so he won't think I'm moonlighting on my own."

"Oh, Lord—that means a retainer."

"Well, Madison Avenue offices have high overheads, ma'am, and you'd be amazed at the cost of some of the equipment. But I won't pad my expense account."

"You'd be the first man I ever knew who didn't," Silver said cynically.

"Much obliged for the drink."

"Not at all, dear. Any time."

Naturally Dobbs had the best office in the organization. Spacious, comfortable furniture, carpeting, air-conditioning, and two windows on the world. Sitting behind the big circular desk, which was cluttered with papers and various electronic devices—the bugs of the business—he looked like anything but the prototype of the private investigator, or even a reasonable caricature. His Simple Simon face gave the impression of a brain to match, and his pudgy hands might have been playing with the toys of the trade. But he hadn't always been bald and paunchy; an exceptionally shrewd and clever mind belied the bloated cupid countenance, aided by a set of keenly developed instincts and senses. When Ben apprised him of the latest developments in the case which Dobbs had considered closed, he shook his head skeptically.

"Eden's a gigolo, not a blackmailer."

"Call it what you like, he's trying to intimidate Silver Haddington, and she's worried."

"Deserves to be, if she's been cavorting in the nude before a candid camera."

"I told you, she claims she was asleep." .

"Claims, the bitch. Probably titillated herself as much as him with her antics. Her and her fucking frolics."

"Harv, will you forget your innate prejudice against womankind for once? She hasn't even seen the pictures."

"You know that's not a blackmailer's MO, Ben. They always show the potential victim at least one deusy, and claim to have a hundred more, plus negatives, in a vault in Chase Manhattan Bank."

"To quote you, Eden's a gigolo, not a professional blackmailer. But he's capable of it, Harv. This is just the first profitable prospect he's had. Could open up a whole new field to him."

Dobbs selected a cigar from the box on his desk, sniffed it appreciatively, fired it up and chewed it pensively. "You have a personal interest in this case, don't you, Ben? Something also developed between you and Eden's spouse? You couldn't just bang her a bit like I advised, you had to go and get emotionally involved— and that's bad in this business. Risky. Clouds the logic. Maybe you weren't wounded in the womb, but you're sure getting your licks outside it."

"Are we back to your prenatal trauma?"

"No female's made a fool of me since," Dobbs declared proudly. "Can you make that statement? I should think, after the shafting you got from Dale—"

Ben groaned. "Okay, Boss, okay! I'm traumatized, too. But it seems to me you're the one with the wandering mind and fuzzy logic now. Granted Eden has the pics, and granted he'll use them if he has to, how'd you stop him?"

"You know the answer to that as well as I, Ben. Let the metropolitan police stop him. Blackmail is against the law. A warrant will lock him up."

"Sure, but I briefed you, Harv. Miss Haddington doesn't want the cops on it. Besides, so far all Eden's proposed is marriage. He can't be arrested for that, and he could and would deny any other motives. She has no proof of his intentions, no witness to his threats."

Dobbs was slowly chomping the tail of his White Owl to pin-feathers. "No doubt Eden's coveting her bankroll, anticipating the magnanimous divorce settlements she's famous for when the marriage sours," he said. "And she'll pay again, one way or another, photos or no. Her type always does. Never thinks of the consequences of her frigging follies until the prick turns on her. If I had a fraction of the money she's been screwed out of by her husbands and lovers, I could retire to my Cape Cod cottage and build boats in bottles for the rest of my days. And you could sit on your ass and pound your portable."

"Yeah—well, it's a sweet dream, Chief, but no more than that. How much you going to clip her for this time?"

"Whatever it's worth to her," Dobbs said. "This isn't a non-profit organization, you know."

"I could do it on my own," Ben offered.

"Not unless you're fixing to set up shop for yourself," Dobbs suggested.

"That's what I like about you, Harv. You're always encouraging me. And you never put a guy down. You know damned well I couldn't afford to hire an answering service, much less anything else."

"You could if your conscience would allow you to rob the Countess's coffers for your services," Dobbs drawled.

"I reckon that would include stud fees, but why should you mind that? You don't have to limit yourself in that area, do you? But don't worry, Ben. I'll call Miss Rich Bitch and settle the ugly monetary details."

"You don't consider that a little unethical, Harv? Last week Eden was our client."

"That was last week," Dobbs said flatly. "You delivered his wife, that ended our connection with Eden—and I don't want anything further to do with the bastard."

"He's the center of this mess, Harv. The hub of it. How can we avoid contact with him?"

"You can't, Ben. I can." The hand he waved in dismissal was pink and plump as a pin-cushion, the nails neatly trimmed and buffed, so that it was difficult to imagine the fingers ever pulling a trigger. "Go ahead, Ben. See if you can get that dumb broad off the hook again. Her anxieties are self-made, you know. She creates her own problems. Fortunately for her she can pay others to try to solve them, the bitch. Not everyone is that lucky."

"Not everyone," Ben agreed. "And Dobbs has made its share off her problems, so take some soda and stop your goddamn bellyaching. You know your real trouble, Boss? You don't get laid regularly enough? Why don't you find some sexpot and get married? When you want it, it's there."

"And when you don't want it, it's still there."

"Okay, simmer in your own juices," Ben said and returned to his office to call the client.

Maybe Dobbs had the right idea, after all, the sensible philosophy. Take all you could get in this world, whatever the product or the source. Where did decency get you? What had principles and scruples ever done for him? Silver Haddington had propositioned him often enough, as agent, bodyguard, lover. He could set up his own agency and prosper on her business alone, not including the elite clientele she could send him. If sex was part of the package deal, why not? She wasn't exactly repulsive. . . .

What the hell was wrong with him? Why couldn't he just grab, root, and growl like the rest of the greedy, selfish sonofabitches in this world, and let the devil take the meek and the timid and the hindmost?

Once a preacher's son, always a preacher's son.

He dialed the private *private* number.

chapter
17

ALL DAY THE STORM had been building. The morning had been unusually hot even for the first week of August. At noon thunderheads began to form on the horizon. Just before dusk the sky turned a lurid sulphurous yellow, and the air smelled of brimstone. An acrid disagreeable odor, like rotten eggs, Ben thought on his way to the Village. He wished the storm would hurry and break and bring cooling showers to the city, which continued to smolder in the summer heat an hour after sundown.

The green Chevy was parked before the white stucco house in MacDougal Alley. Evidently Eddie had answered Silver Haddington's summons in a cab. He wondered what excuse he'd given Marcie, if indeed he'd felt obliged to make any at all. Probably not. Eddie Eden wasn't the type to explain his actions or absences to wife or mistress; as Silver herself had said, he wasn't on a time schedule.

Marcie seemed glad to see him, not happy or eager or excited as he'd hoped, but quietly glad, as if she were lonely and wondering what to do with the long hot evening which would surely culminate in a storm. She was wearing the same sunny yellow dress she had worn the day they had begun the trip together, and Ben could hardly believe it had been only a week ago. In seven days four lives had been disrupted, their courses irrevocably altered, and several private worlds shattered with no imminent hope or promise of reconstruction.

"Hello, Ben. Come in. Eddie's gone. His agent called a couple of hours ago. Some auditions or something. One late one after the club closes."

His eyes brooded over her. Did she believe the story, or only pretend to, because it was easier to accept lies than to challenge truth?

Ben saw that she had already adopted one of the stray cats that swarmed over the Village, either out of loneliness or an innate weakness for strays. The tabby, a long lanky brindled animal of the familiar alley species, lay on the windowsill, watching Ben through slanted green eyes, flicking his ratty tail restlessly, aware of the pending storm.

"My new pet," Marcie introduced him, walking over to scratch the creature behind the ears. "He just climbed up there by himself, scaling the tree outside and jumping onto the roof. I don't know his name. I call him Tramp."

Her suitcases were against the wall on one side of the room. Ben couldn't tell if they'd been unpacked.

"Have you decided to stay here?" he asked.

"I might as well." She shrugged, as emotionally unsettled as the weather. "I've no place else to go."

"We'll find some place, Marcie."

"I have to find a job first."

"That's one of the reasons I came," Ben said, careful to imply that there were others, lest she later accuse him of subterfuge and deception. "I heard of a job open at a large insurance brokerage. Steno. I'm sure you could handle it."

"I was secretary to an executive in a sugar mill, Ben. I don't know anything about insurance."

"Marcie, it's typing and dictation, not underwriting. You write letters and fill in blank spaces in policies.

186

Somebody else supplies the words. Better take it, there's no sugar mills in Manhattan. It pays one hundred ten a week to start, with fringe benefits, and opportunities for advancement."

Marcie almost gasped at such munificence. She'd earned seventy-five in Rainbow after several years. "Where is this bonanza, and why aren't the local girls clamoring for it?"

"They will be, soon as they hear about it," Ben said, handing her the card that Silver Haddington had given him.

"Dibrell, Cantrell, and Larson," Marcie read. "Sounds impressive. I'll see them tomorrow if I have to hobble all the way to Rockefeller Center."

"Foot still bothering you?"

"Well, I can't run, if that's what you mean."

"I don't intend to chase you, if that's what *you* mean."

"Not even a little?" She smiled and gestured toward the liquor and food on the table, the celebration fixings interrupted by the telephone call from the Regal Towers. "Would you like a drink, Ben? A corned beef sandwich or something?"

"No, thanks, Marcie." He'd starve before he'd eat Eden's food or drink his liquor, even if Silver Haddington's bounty had procured it. "I'm not hungry or thirsty."

"Me, either."

She lifted her dark hair off her neck, as if it were a curtain obstructing breeze, let it fall again. She looked tired and disconsolate, Ben thought, with shadows under her eyes, obviously worried and under considerable strain. "It's terribly hot and still even after sundown, isn't it? We get Gulf breezes in Louisiana at night. Doesn't the wind blow off the Atlantic here?"

"On the waterfronts," Ben said. "The buildings tend to impede it elsewhere. And it's worse this evening, because there's a storm brewing."

"Maybe it'll cool down temperatures."

"For tonight," Ben said. "Tomorrow this rockpile will steam like a sauna bath."

"I'd like to see some of the sights," Marcie said. "The Statue of Liberty, for one. Is that square nowadays? For Hicksville tourists only?"

"If so, this country's in bigger trouble than some people think," Ben said. "But you have to catch a ferry to visit the Lady, you know. Let me take you, Marcie."

"I might," she said. "I'm sure Eddie wouldn't mind. He has other diversions."

There was a racket down in the alley, a couple of dogs fighting over the contents of a garbage can, and now the air smelled of rotten fish. Ben thought of Eddie in the Regal Towers. Must be exciting to view a storm from that height, stimulating; maybe up there in the clouds, you were a part of it. Did Eden really have the pictures, or were they just a mythical club to hold over Silver's head, a ficticious passport to the kind of life he coveted?

He said, "I've got to search this place, Marcie."

She was startled. "Search—why, for what?"

Ben told her. The information sickened Marcie, first with shock, then disgust, then incredulity. It was difficult to believe a man she had once loved, respected, trusted, even admired, could sink to such depths. She sat down on the shabby love-seat, avoiding the broken spring at one end.

"That's the real reason you came, isn't it? The job bit was just a ruse."

Ben was chagrined. "Marcie, you've got to stop suspecting my every move and motive. There is a job open, and you can probably get it if you want it. But this other problem is also real, and Dobbs Agency has been hired to try to solve it quietly. I was assigned the duty. It's dirty, and I don't like it—but it's part of my job."

"There's a lot of dirt in your work, isn't there?"

"Only because there're a lot of dirty people around," Ben said.

"Like Eddie, and your—your client?"

"Marcie, this is hard enough for me. Don't make it any harder, please."

"Go ahead," Marcie said, gesturing. "Search every crack and crevice—but don't expect me to help you, Ben."

He was methodic, so efficient Marcie thought a germ would have had difficulty escaping if he'd had a microscope. He turned up unpaid bills, lipsticks, compacts, bobbypins, earrings in unexpected places, plus a tiny pair of black lace bikini panties no bigger than a G-string in the clothes-hamper, and a strapless satin bra of impressive dimensions under the kitchen sink, all of which may or may not have been incriminating, since they could have belonged to a previous tenant; publicity pictures and posters of Eddie Eden, a book of addresses and telephone numbers—a conglomeration of the usual stuff found in the average bachelor's apartment, with the exception of a small package which he kept from Marcie's sight. Without opening it, he'd bet it contained narcotics or drugs of the illegal variety.

Marcie speculated on the owner of the lingerie. "Hers, do you think?"

"Not the bra," Ben said. "She's not built that way."

"How would you know?"

"I'm not blind, Marcie. And she's not dishonest enough to wear falsies. Besides, she'd never come to a dump like this for an assignation. Her lovers go to her."

"I wonder who the lucky girl is, then?"

"Lucky?"

"If happiness is a C-cup, she ought to be ecstatic," Marice said. "That's a D, at least."

"Is it? I've never known a D."

"If there was one around, Eddie'd know her," Marcie said ruefully. "But if the Countess is an A-minus, what's her attraction? Don't answer that."

Ben continued his search, unsuccessfully.

"Maybe he carried the treasure with him," Marcie suggested bitterly, "next to his heart."

"That'd be the wrong place," Ben said. "Or maybe not, considering his heart. But it would be foolhardy to keep it on his person, Marcie. Miss Haddington could hire a dozen strong arms any day in the week to relieve him of it. Eddie couldn't risk that."

"I can't believe she was asleep," Marcie said, reluctant to add the image of a peeping tom to the one which grew more grotesque by the hour. "I bet if ever you find them, she'll have her eyes wide open. Eddie just couldn't be that low, Ben, that perverted—that *sick!* I couldn't live with him seven years and not know him any better than that . . . unless he's a dual personality, some kind of Jekyll and Hyde."

Ben was poking around in the closet again, frisking the pockets of the clothes hanging there, tapping the walls for hollow sounds, investigating the bags and sags in the wallpaper. "Marcie, don't close your own eyes to this," he said. "Don't be a sleeping beauty yourself waiting for some miracle or shock to awaken you. Silver Haddington is no angel, but she's not stupid enough to jeopardize herself with pornography."

"But if that's the case, why can't you find the pictures? And if Eddie uses marijuana and LSD, as you think, where is that evidence? It's not enough to have suspicions and make charges, Ben. You have to support them."

"Would you know pot and acid if you saw it, Marcie?"

"No," she admitted.

"Then maybe it's time you did." He presented her with the small cache he'd located earlier. "These are reefers, Marcie. Sticks, joints, weed, pot—marijuana. They don't look much different from ordinary cigarettes, do they, except the wrapper's not as white and neat, because they're hand-rolled, and of course there's no brand-name. And these litttle vials contain lysergic acid diethylamide,

190

or LSD. The trippers take it on sugar cubes; it also comes in crystal form. There's enough evidence here to have Eddie arrested, tried, and convicted."

"God," Marcie whispered prayerfully. "Dear God."

"Now do you understand why I don't want you living here? If the police were somehow tipped off, if there was a raid, you'd be caught in it, Marcie, and it might not be easy to convince the vice squad of your innocence."

"Destroy the stuff, Ben. Flush it down the commode."

"He'll just get more, Marcie. It's not hard to do here. And this is only the beginning for Eddie. One day he'll be a junkie, a main-liner shooting himself in the veins with heroin and cocaine, and doing God knows what to get the money to support his habit. He won't give a damn about anything but his next fix."

"Maybe he's on it already?"

"No, I haven't found any of the junkie's paraphernalia. Spoons, hypo-needles, tourniquet. But it's next, Marcie. Horse frequently follows the weed."

"Get rid of it, Ben!" Marcie cried somewhat hysterically. "I don't want it around. It makes me nervous."

"It should," Ben said and went into the bathroom. There he dropped the marijuana cigarettes into the commode, emptied the supply of LSD, rinsed the containers and tossed them into the wastepaper basket, where they could pass for unlabeled prescription bottles. Marcie heard the toilet flush. Ben returned. "It's gone out to sea. When he looks for the cache—and he will—he'll think he used it up and just forgot; the mind doesn't function very well under such drugs. But he'll get more, Marcie, because not all the sewers in this town are underground."

"The Jesus man sells it," Marcie murmured.

"Who?"

"Some hippie here who masquerades in Christ's image," Marcie explained. "Eddie admitted that accidently today, although he didn't admit to patronizing him."

"Well, you can bet that's not his only source, nor the only vendor on these streets."

"I wonder how wrong it really is, Ben, how terrible for people to want to escape that way?"

"Moral aspects aside, Marcie, it's a health menace," Ben said. "If you'd ever been to an addicts' ward in a hospital, you wouldn't ask that."

"I guess I'm trying to rationalize and vindicate Eddie," she said wistfully. "This is infinitely harder to accept than his other immoralities, believe me."

"I'm sure it is, Marcie. But you're not really surprised, are you? You suspected it yourself?"

"Yes," she said and fell silent, unable to discuss it further.

A wind blew up, carrying the welcome smell of rain. Lightning streaked across the sky like a comet. Thunder boomed and crashed and rumbled, vibrating the house, rattling the fake shutters. Tramp leaped off the sill, ran to Marcie, and bounded into her lap. She stroked him gently. He purred cozily, as if he'd finally found what he'd been searching the alleys for since birth, a mistress who wouldn't evict him in bad weather.

"I swear the rascal is grinning," Ben said, "and I guess I'd be too, in his position."

Marcie ignored the overture, comforting Tramp when he tensed and trembled at another clap of thunder, sharp as a strike in a bowling alley. And then the storm broke, bursting upon the city in a sulphurous fury, ranting and raving like a vixen in a passionate rage, splashing tears against the windows and the skylight, washing off some of the dust and grime.

Ben lowered the windows and lingered at one, attracted by the sight of a girl in a white blouse, black mini-skirt and knee-high red patent boots, twirling a clear plastic umbrella impatiently, as if she were waiting for someone who was late. She looked about twenty years old, but the rain blurred a misty halo about the street lamp near her, and it was hard to judge either

her age or the color of her long straight hair, which appeared to be reddish-blond. Did he only imagine it, or did she glance expectantly at the vermilion door of this house and the upstairs windows? After some minutes a boy in a black-leather jacket sauntered up to her, seeming to materialize out of the shadows of the alley, and she went off with him, both of their heads ducked under the umbrella. She cast a furtive glance over her shoulder, as if she thought she was being observed or followed, then tossed her mane defiantly, and disappeared into the turbulent night.

"What's so fascinating out there?" Marcie asked.

"Life," Ben answered. "People. Much as I hate this job sometimes, it's seldom dull."

"All the world's a stage?"

Ben nodded, hands in his pockets, still gazing through the wavy wetness of the pane. "And with characters you rarely find in plays."

"What kind of character is Silver Haddington, Ben?"

"The kind of which legends and myths are made."

"I read about her escapades in my teens," Marcie recalled. "The heroine of the tabloids, renowned for her fads and follies and frolics. Why should she be so anxious about a few nude pictures? I don't see how she could be much more maligned no matter what she did."

"Even so, Eddie has no right to threaten and blackmail her, Marcie. Actually, she'd much prefer to keep her private life private, but she was born in a glass house as far as the world is concerned—one of those unfortunate creatures destined to be public curiosities. Her wealth attracts men like a magnet. She creates some scandals herself, sure, but others are inflicted on her. She's raw meat on the chopping blocks of the newsbutchers, and the female of the species is always more vicious in her hacking. One columnist in particular, Melissa Stone, a bit of a bitch herself, can't keep the verdigris of envy out of her stuff, and her pen is as destructive as if it were filled with nitric acid. Her victims get no sympathy, however, because the general public prefers to believe it's reading gospel. And in Miss Haddington's case, there's usually enough truth to preclude libel and slander actions. She's rich and glamorous and fabled, even though not young or especially beautiful any more. She lives her life as if it were one long sensational drama, and the irony of it is that we're characters in this episode, Marcie."

"What parts are we supposed to play, Ben? Silver Haddington's the siren, Eddie's the philanderer. I guess I'm the ingenue. What are you, Ben?"

"What do you want me to be, Marcie?"

"Yourself," she said. "Hunt for the pictures some more, Mr. Detective. Find them!"

"There's no place else to look, Marcie, except under the floor, and I can't see any place where the boards have been tampered with. This is an attic, so there's only the roof above, and there's no indication that the ceiling's concealing anything, either."

"Where could they be, then?"

"Many places. A locker in a bus or railroad station or athletic club. A safe deposit box in a bank. With some trusted friend. Lots of places. The only way to narrow the possibilities is through the process of elimination. That could take a long time and be a wild goose chase."

"You mean the pictures might not exist?"

"Yes, they may be only an ingenious invention of an ingenious extortionist," Ben said. "But if so, he'll have to be a genius to succeed in his game without producing them. Our client's not buying illusions."

"He might just succeed then," Marcie predicted sadly, "because if Eddie has a genius for anything, it's evil."

"I'm afraid you're right," Ben agreed, glad that she had finally realized this herself.

chapter
18

BEN LEFT THE STUDIO at eleven o'clock. Marcie had refused to go home with him, insisting that she would be all right now the drugs had been found and destroyed, and would leave as soon as she got the job and could afford to move.

Rain continued to fall but had slacked off to a dismal drizzle. The disturbance had moved out to sea, the thunder rolling like distant drums, becoming fainter and more muffled until it was only a sullen echo.

Ben drove around in the Village, unable to forget the short-skirted, booted, long-haired girl he had seen in MacDougal Alley. She piqued his professional curiosity and suspicions. Perhaps she could tell him something about Eddie Eden that he didn't know, throw some more light on his habits and character, for he was satisfied that they knew each other, probably intimately, since he could not imagine a guy like Eddie having any other kind of relationship with a doll like that. She might be his neighbor, although Ben had not seen her come out of any of the houses in his realm of vision. When he'd first noticed her, she was standing by a stoop, in the light of one of the perpetual gas lamps in MacDougal Alley, and it was unlikely she'd wait for anyone in a thunderstorm if she'd had a convenient shelter handy. More likely she had been hoping to see Eddie and had given up and settled for another acquaintance who had just happened along. She could be in a hundred different places now, and even if he accidentally located her, there was nothing he could do immediately. She was not alone, which eliminated the old ruse of striking up a conversation through mistaken identity. Certainly he could not approach her in a professional capacity, for if she knew Eddie she would surely mention the meeting to him, and if she didn't know him it would be wasted time and effort.

The storm had dispersed the protest rally scheduled to continue that evening in Washington Square, and it was deserted now except for the perennial stragglers and derelicts hoping to find a vacant and dry bench in the park. Ben knew that most of the night action was to be found in East Village, around which he had once cruised in a patrol car. She could be in any of the numerous bars, nightclubs, coffeehouses, movie houses, off-Broadway theaters. She could be in the boy's or someone else's apartment, at a private party, or even in night school.

He decided to park and walk awhile. He reached behind the seat for his hat and a tan raincoat, since it was still misting. The shop windows displayed more oddities than the Paris Flea Market. He wandered in and out of public establishments, remaining long enough only to reconnoiter the customers in search of a Titian head. He might glimpse her momentarily, or never again, but he wanted to be reasonably sure he would recognize her if he should. He rarely operated on hunches, there being more practical methods in the business, but occasionally he had an instinctive feeling about someone or something which he could not suppress or ignore. He had it about this girl now and, however nebulous or tenuous, had to pursue it.

The dampness intensified the myriad odors distinct and distinctive in the Village: musk and mildew and decay, old brick and stone, books and newspapers, oil paint, clay, fish, cheese, herbs and spices, poor plumbing, and cats. A potpourri of scents indigenous to the community, but which the natives didn't seem to mind and indeed rather proudly compared to the quaint bouquet of Montmartre and the Left Bank of Paris and breathed with the same nonchalance. This "exotic incense" was familiar to Ben and even nostalgic, recalling his own settlement there when he had first arrived from Vermont, naively hoping to be inspired by the memory of the literary greats who had lived and worked in Greenwich Village, before he had realized that inspiration sprang from within the private well, not the public fount, and talent, not environment, was the source. And nothing was eternal, not even love, especially not love; and this town within a town was a stinking milieu, a unique cesspool to trap unsuspecting victims in its slimy laterals.

He strolled past taverns and pool halls and pet shops, book stores and art galleries and studios of allied crafts, restaurants and delicatessens and bakeries, and houses and apartments sandwiched between the commercial and cultural establishments, remembering the marvelous plots he'd devised and the great expectations he'd entertained while papering the walls of his garret with rejection slips.

After three hours of searching Ben gave up and started for home. And then, as sometimes happened in such cases, he saw her quite unexpectedly, going into a house on Washington Square South. She was alone, and he wondered what had happened to the black-jacketed companion. He mentally marked the address and drove past without slowing his speed.

chapter
19

BEN READ THE NAMEPLATES on the mailboxes in the foyer of the red brick house on Washington Square South, which he had seen the girl enter last night. Millicent Rogers. No, she didn't fit that obvious nom de plume, nor the elegant alias of Daphne Duvay; and surely not Georgie Vanderbilt, or Davvie Copperfield. Christ, the imagination of some tyros, who apparently thought fame and success were all in the magic of a name!

A kid came out of an upstairs apartment eating a jelly doughnut and sliding his sticky fingers along the banister on his way down. Ben asked him if he knew a girl with long reddish hair, who wore short skirts and high boots. He was about to answer when the door above opened and a flour-faced woman, puffed as a Danish pastry, poked her head out and yelled, "Louie, how many times I told you not to talk to strangers!"

"He ain't no queer, Mom. He's lookin' for Tawny Mane."

Tawny Mane, Ben thought. That would be her, all right. Name and haircolor compliments of Clairol.

"That tramp," the woman above muttered.

"She turns Pop on," the boy taunted.

"Shut up and eat your doughnut," his mother said.

Louie winked at Ben. He was mature for his age; he thought he knew exactly what the stranger wanted and didn't blame him. If he was a little older himself . . .

"Lives in the rear, Mister," he said. "Number 11. A mole-hole in the basement. You can get to it through here, though. There's a back door."

"Thanks," Ben said, and nodded to the glowering gorgon hanging overhead. "And thank *you*, ma'am."

The courtyard was damp and steamy from last night's rain. Children played in the residual puddles. Sprigs of green, mostly grass and weeds, sprouted in the cracks, and the indomitable ailanthus stretched toward the sun. Pots and boxes of flowers marked some entrances, where the residents made an effort at beauty and homeliness. Number Eleven was bare, down a flight of moldly concrete stairs, with a rusty fire escape zigzagged on the wall above. Sometimes the children used the well as a toilet, neglecting to remove the evidence, and Ben had to watch his step. There was a box for mail, with her name over it, but no bell. Ben knocked several times and was about to leave and return later when the door opened a crack, held by a security chain.

Although it was eleven o'clock in the morning, Ben had obviously awakened her. She was in pink babydoll pajamas, her long rust-colored hair uncombed. She had a pert nose, a petulant mouth, and the attitude of an impudent child. Smudges of mascara and lipstick made her face look dirty, yet there was something wistful and appealing and even innocent about the wide dark eyes staring at him.

"What you want, mister?"

"Tawny Mane?"

She was cagey, in case he was a bill collector or summons server. "Who wants to know?"

"Didn't Eldie tell you?"

Her expression told Ben the name was familiar to her, yet she questioned it. "Eddie?"

"Eddie Eden, the Cajun Cat."

"Oh, that cat. No, he didn't tell me. But suppose you do, mister—?"

"Danti," Ben said. "May I please come in?"

She hesitated, shrugged, released the chain. "I got to put something on," she said, allowing him a long look before reaching for a leopard-spotted jersey thing that clung to her like a wet skin. No doubt the D-cup bra in Eddie's pad belonged to these breasts, although the hips would have much ado to squeeze into the black lace bikini panties. "Sit down, Mr. Danti," she invited. "Is that like the inferno?"

"No, I spell mine with an 'i'," Ben said.

"What's your first name?"

"Dino."

"Dino Danti? You don't look Italian."

"That's what my father said to my mother the day I was born," Ben said. "The bambino he no looka like me."

Tawny laughed. She liked his sense of humor, and she could do with some amusement this morning. She saw that he was glancing about the place, which was dank and damp and gloomy as a dungeon, and not exactly neat. Newspapers lay on the floor, clothes draped the furniture. Soiled dishes stood about on the tables and shelves as if they were ornaments.

"I sleep late mornings," she explained.

"What's your profession?"

"Well, not what you might think, mister."

"How do you know what I think?"

"I got ESP."

"Rhymes with POT and LSD."

"Whatta you, the fuzz? Some kind of social worker? If Eddie told you about me, how come you don't know what I do?"

Ben smiled smoothly. "Come on, Tawny. Quit stalling. You know why I'm here. You know the proposition."

"I told you, I ain't no prostitute."

200

"There're other kinds of propositions, honey."

"Maybe, but that's the only kind I seem to get." She scrounged for a cigarette, located a crushed pack in her purse, took one out and lit it. "If that's what you came for, you're gonna be disappointed. I ain't no call girl, and even if I was, I wouldn't do business before noon. Us chicks have gotta sleep sometime. I'm a dancer, an exotic dancer. I do a thing with seven veils, real artistic. Got the idea from Salome. In the Bible, you know."

"Very original," Ben said. "Wasn't she the bloodthirsty wench who danced for Herod and was rewarded with the head of John the Baptist on a tray?"

"I don't know about that, I just dance with veils. They're all sheer and white, but colored lights make them look different colors. You didn't catch my act at the Amber Alley? I was there before Eddie Eden. I hope to make a big club some day, and a musical on Broadway. And a popular TV commercial, so I can collect lots of residuals."

You and a million others, Ben thought.

"Good luck," he said.

"Thanks. I need it. Right now I'm between engagements, and my rent's due. Strapped for cash, but that don't mean I'm ready to solicit yet, and I'm gonna put a sign to that effect on my door: "NO SOLICITORS." She paused, waiting for his reaction to her pun, continuing when he smiled appreciatively. "Hey, you been here ten minutes already and ain't told me nothing but your name. You a friend of Eddie's, huh?"

"We have a business relationship at present," Ben said.

"You an agent?"

"Sort of," Ben said.

"Sounds like my agent," she said grimly. "He's a sort of agent, too. Not worth a damn."

"You know that hobby of Eddie's?"

"Photography?"

Ben nodded. "That's our connection."

"I get it," she said. "You want me to pose for you? You're an artist or something?"

"Something," Ben said. "You have a beautiful figure, Tawny. I bet Eddie's done some terrific nudes of you?"

She couldn't resist the flattery; she opened up like a flower to the sun. "He calls it art. He's got a briefcase of the stuff here. I never look at any except mine, though. Naked girls don't do nothing for me."

"I'm glad to hear that," Ben said. "They do plenty for most guys, though. Could I see some of Eddie's art?"

She hesitated, frowning. "I don't know, Mr. Danti. It's his private collection. He might not like sharing it."

"I'm a talent scout for a calendar company," Ben said. "Some girls have gotten famous that way, you know."

"Yeah, one in a million," she said realistically. "Most of 'em just get frigged. That'd be my luck."

"You've got to be more optimistic, Tawny."

"That's what my agent says, but after two years even he's getting discouraged. Last week he started giving me another pitch, about how much money I could make other ways. Said he could send me some clients, the pimp—at first I figured you for such a prospect. But I'm not that pessimistic yet. I still got hopes, though they're getting dimmer and dimmer."

Ben lit a cigarette, blew the smoke into the stale air. Why did New York tenements always smell of coffee, boiling cabbage, cats, and urine? And why didn't she invest in a bayberry candle, or one of those miniature incense burners that abounded in the Oriental gift shops? But maybe the stench was attar of roses to the poor kid, the essence of which dreams of success were made. . . .

"Where're you from, Tawny?"

"Terre Haute, Indiana," she replied. "Do I look and act like a corn-fed hoosier?"

"You know what pornography is?"

"You kidding? Sure. Dirty pictures."

"There's a big market for that kind of realistic art," Ben said. "Does Eddie have any in his collection?"

She gazed at him, smoking nervously. "I thought you were a talent scout for a girlie calandar company?"

"There're many kinds of calandars," Ben said. "Are you putting me on, Tawny? Eddie told me he was going to discuss this with you last night, brief you?"

"That explains it," she said, relieved. "I was gone last night. Matter of fact, I went over and hung around his pad awhile, in the storm. I hadn't seen him in a couple of weeks and thought he was trying to sack me. Sure enough, he had a broad up there. I could see her in the window, petting a mangy cat. I was furious at him, and went off with a guy I knew just happened along. We went to a movie and to his cave afterwards, but nothing happened because he's a homo, as fruity as a compote—just wanted me to sit and listen to his nutty poetry. God, was I ever bored and longing for Eddie. When you knocked, I thought it was him, although he has a key. But I figured he'd forgot it or lost it or something. He's kind of careless sometimes, never seems to know what he does with things. Absent-minded, if you know what I mean. I think the stuff he uses affects his mind. If it wasn't for that, and his other faults, I could go for him in a big way. He's some looker, but kind of weird. Know what I mean?"

"Yeah," Ben said. "How long have you known him?"

"Three months. Like I told you, I preceded him on the bill at the Amber Alley. Must have jinxed us both though, cause neither of us has worked since." She crushed out her cigarette in a filled tray. "Look, Mr. Danti. I need bread, and I'd pose for a *Playboy* layout or a legit calendar anytime, cause some lucky babes really have gotten famous that way. But I'm no cheap tits-and-ass tramp to hang naked in some kook's private parlor, just for his own crazy kicks. That's pornography, and I'll kill Eddie if he's been peddling my pics that way and not even paying me for posing!"

"You'd have to get in line for the killing," Ben said.

"But don't bother, Tawny. Eddie Eden's not worth it. Just get me the stuff and take yours out."

She was afronted. "You mean you don't even want to see mine?"

Ben smiled. "I didn't think you wanted me to, my dear."

"You ain't a bad sort, you know that? I like you, and I don't believe you'd be mixed up in anything wrong."

She knelt down and pulled a briefcase from under the couch, where it was concealed by a dusty dust-ruffle. She put it in Ben's lap. "I already took mine out. I did it last night after I got home, I was so mad at Eddie for not seeing me for so long and having that broad with him during the storm. I tore up the nude ones, kept those with veils to show when I go on auditions. I was gonna tear 'em all up, just for spite, but figured I'd better not. Eddie might beat me up, and dancers can't get bruised much." She waited as if for his agreement. "Say, I was just about to brew some java when you came. Would you like a cup o'mud?"

"Very much," Ben said.

"I'll fix it while you sample the merchandise."

There were a dozen or more different faces, figures, postures, apparently girls Eddie'd met on his tours, some lewd and obscene enough to pander to the most salacious appetite, others suitable for poster art and exhibition. Ben went through them quickly, disappointed not to find what he sought.

"Is this all?" he asked.

In the kitchen alcove Tawny was spooning coffee into a percolator. "Ain't it enough?"

"No."

"You can't use 'em?"

"Afraid not."

"Well, I don't blame you. Especially that skinny old one. Boy, she could haunt houses."

"There's no skinny old one here," Ben said.

"No deflated old bag of bones with white hair? Gee,

I must have left that envelope in the bedroom when I was culling 'em last night," Tawny said. "It was sealed and when I opened it, I knew why. You got to see it to believe it."

"Where is it?" Ben asked. "Do you know?"

"On the dressing table, I think. A brown manilla envelope, like they send bank statements in. Beats me why Eddie keeps that spook in his collection, unless he likes to scare himself once in awhile."

Ben went after it. Six pictures and negatives. But they weren't amateurish, and they weren't snapped with a Polaroid. He'd used a professional camera, flash bulbs, and he'd taken time to pose his subject in attitudes that could in no way be construed as cultural art. And Subject was going to be shocked, horrified, when she saw them. That delicate frame which made such an effective clothes hanger was pitifully thin minus the ornamentation, hip bones protruding sharply as plow-points, breasts immature as an adolescent child's. But the face looked far older than its thirty-five years: the kind of gaunt, tense, and intense face he'd seen in the city morgue when the victim had expired of malnutrition and in agony. It was not surprising that the girl from Terre Haute did not recognize the lady; not even the most candid news photos had been this cruel and harsh. If anything could frighten a woman into changing her way of life, pictures such as these should.

"Coffee's ready," Tawny called. "Find 'em?"

"Yeah."

Ben came out of the bedroom with the packet. He didn't want the coffee, but decided he'd better be polite and drink it after she'd gone to the trouble. He'd played his hunch, it'd proved correct, and now he was anxious to get out of there before some hitch fouled things up.

Tawny eyed the brown envelope with surprise. "You're taking that freak? Christ, you must have some ghoulish customers!"

"Takes all kind to make a world," Ben said.

"Sure. But you could do better than her in a mortuary, mister."

Ben burned his throat gulping the hot coffee. He stood, reached for his hat. "Thanks for the hospitality, miss. You've been a big help. But I've got to blow now. Business."

"You ever coming back?"

"You're Eddie's girl."

"Maybe, maybe not. Anyway, that don't mean you couldn't visit me if you want. But call me first, if you do. I'm in the book." She accompanied him to the door. "It was nice meeting you, Mr. Danti. Shall I tell Eddie you was here if I see him?"

"I don't think you'll have to," Ben said. "He'll figure it out himself eventually."

"I thought he sent you?"

"Yeah, but we like to play games with each other."

"Oh, I dig." She considered it a private joke, smiled. She had cute dimples. "You know I really do like you, Mr. Danti, so I'm gonna be honest with you. I'm not really from Terre Haute. That's a big town. I'm from a little jerkwater nobody's ever heard of, called Bee's Mill, and my name ain't really Tawny Mane. It's Agnes Mertz. I just made up the fancy handle to go with my hair."

"Really?" Ben smiled compassionately. In spite of the theatrical artificiality and the affected sophistication, she was naive and artless and she had no business in this town, trying to claw and scratch her way to a futile future. "You want some good advice, little girl? Go back to Bee's Mill. If you had a boy friend there and he's still available, marry him. Settle down and raise a bunch of hoosiers."

"I had a boy friend, all right. His folks are farmers. Corn and hogs. His ma'd flip her bonnet if she saw me now, though. I'd be the buzz of the county."

"I bet you were that, anyway," Ben said. "And since you've been so nice, I'll tell you a secret, too. My name's not really Dino Danti, and I'm not any kind of talent scout."

"What are you, then, and what is your name?"

"Ask Eddie," Ben said. "That's another little angle in this clever game we're playing. . . ."

chapter
20

"YOU GOT THEM! Oh, you're a marvel! I'm going to give you a bonus for efficiency."

Silver embraced Ben, planted an impetuously affectionate kiss on his cheek. Then she opened the envelope nervously, and stared incredulously at the contents. Her knees felt weak and watery, her face had drained white. She sat down for support. "You've seen them, of course?"

Ben nodded.

"Hideous," she murmured, aghast. "Simply hideous. Do I really look that bad—my face, I mean?"

Ben didn't know what to say. She seemed so stricken, so utterly appalled. "Those are terribly candid, Silver, as they were intended to be. You're thin, but you have an—an interesting face."

"Ghastly," she moaned, inconsolable. "Like a skeleton with parchment stretched over it. I look dead, Ben. Dead for some time . . . starved to death! If this is a true likeness, I should be buried without delay."

"It's the angle from which the pictures were shot," Ben rationalized. "And too much harsh light. Obviously Eddie wasn't trying for art and beauty—he just wanted to be sure he got the goods."

Silver reached for a cigarette from a teakwood casket,

decided against it, proceeded to the bar. She poured herself a potent potion of cognac. She looked at Ben somewhat wistfully. "You know the real irony of this, Ben? That he'd want to marry me after seeing these monstrosities. If I were a man, nothing could induce me to tie up with a spook like that. Not all the wealth on Wall Street . . . unless, of course, I were a ghoul of some kind, which I'm beginning to think Eddie is."

Ben joined her in the cognac, pouring his own. "Don't take it so hard, Silver, don't dwell on it. I've seen candid shots of some famous female stars that didn't look so hot. I remember one of Hedy Lamarr in *Life* Magazine, and another of Elizabeth Taylor. . . ."

"Thanks for the cheer, darling, but I'm not blind. They're weird. At thirty-five, I'm a grotesque old hag. That ought to be a lesson of some kind, a warning. . . ."

"I never figured you for the recanting type," Ben said.

"If there were a wailing wall handy, I'd hurl myself against it," Silver said soberly. "Not to mourn my past, but my future. Because I need the companionship of men, and the woman in those photos couldn't have much future in that respect. Do you suppose he has more of these horrors stashed somewhere to haunt me?"

"Not likely," Ben reasoned. "The negatives were with them, and he didn't have time to print more. We moved too swiftly for him. I believe we have everything, Silver."

She breathed a sigh of relief. "Where'd you find them?"

"He had them with a friend," Ben said. "I stumbled onto them by hunch and accident, mostly. Ten per cent sleuthing and ninety per cent lucky fluke. But don't ask me to divulge trade secrets." Recalling the voluptuous, fleshy young body of Tawny Mane, Ben knew he could never be cruel enough to tell her that part. He felt genuinely sorry for Silver Haddington; hers was a wasted life, and human waste was always sad and pitiable.

Disillusion etched a new dimension in her face, increasing the sharpness of her features, so they no longer appeared patrician or classic, but only gaunt and haggard. Her long thin fingers, exquisitely manicured as always, were like silver-tipped claws clutching the crystal snifter.

"No wonder you were immune to my passes," she mused. "I must have about as much sex appeal as a broomstick. How could any male but an insensitive gorilla be anything but repulsed?" She paused, sipped the brandy. "And yet Mother Nature, that perverse old bitch, equipped me with a desperate need for the opposite sex. How do you explain that, Mr. Hale? You're a bright boy. How do you figure *that*?"

Ben shrugged, embarrassed by her humility. He inhaled the fine bouquet of the excellent French brandy appreciatively, wet his tongue. "How do you figure nature, Silver? Takes a lot smarter guy than Ben Hale to crack those ancient mysteries. But fate gave you compensations."

"Like money, so I could buy the stuff that no sane man would want to give me? So I could compromise myself like a harlot in the market-place?"

"Come off the self-pity wheel, Silver. Just fatten up a bit, get off Metrecal and on calories. Put on some pounds. That's your only trouble—you're too goddamn thin. Skinny, to be brutally frank."

"An aging Twiggy?"

"Let the fashion fags call it slender and svelte and sylphlike, it's just hide and bones to the normal man. But like Twiggy, you have other fascinations."

"Money?"

"No, goddamn it! You have an obsession, a mental block about your wealth. Don't ignore your other assets, Silver. Contrary to what you might think in this self-belittling mood, you do have other attractions."

"An interesting face?"

"And more," Ben nodded. "You have a helluva fine brain too, though you don't use it. Why don't you try

210

using it for a change? Forget your goddamn body for awhile and give your mind a chance?"

"Go out for social work, civic stuff? I had the Junior League bit, Ben. A damnable drag."

"I don't mean that sort of thing, Silver. The superficial patroness of charity. You can't accomplish anything in that line with your person that you couldn't do better with your pocketbook. I mean use your head for something besides a chapeau prop."

"Oh, Christ! You're not going to give me a morals lecture, are you? The Find Yourself spiel? I'm not lost, Ben. I know who I am and what I am and where I am, and how I got there."

"Do you, Silver? Do you honestly?"

She mulled that over. Then she lifted her glass to the pastel portrait over the white marble mantel. "Look at the imperious bitch," she said. "That haughty disdain, that Mona Lisa smile, that smug satisfaction. As if she knew it all and was keeping it a big secret, especially from herself. I know I'm giddy and gauche to say this, but you just might be right, Ben. Maybe it could be a whole new adventure—the discovery of Silver Haddington."

Where did one start in such a quest? The usual dreary course was to make a pilgrimage to one's source, a sort of sentimental journey. But that would be treading familiar ground. She had forgotten nothing of her life, not one single episode or escapade, from the time she was old enough to record memory. Some people excused their ultimate destination by pretending they'd taken a wrong turn somewhere along the way, an unfortunate detour, and gotten lost. She had no such excuses for herself. She'd traveled her winding path intentionally and deliberately, intrigued and fascinated by the diversions it offered, the side excursions, and because it seemed right and logical and practical for her, in keeping with her emotional character; to alter it now would require alteration in her moral and mortal construction, and that was hardly possible, was it?

She could go home, to an elderly mother who was still one of Boston's great ladies, and an elderly father who was still one of America's financial giants and wizards, and what would that prove or accomplish? She did that, anyway, periodicly, and they welcomed her happily and generously, not as a prodigal daughter, but a beloved child with quixotic tendencies. For a few days she was a loved one home on holiday, and the ponderous old mansion hummed with activity. There were parties and plans and long intimate chats—and then the princess departed the ancestral castle and returned to her private tower in Manhattan, or some retreat in another country, on the periphery of society and sanity. Useless, inconsequential existence? Perhaps. But she liked and enjoyed it, had made it her special thing, her bag, and couldn't visualize herself making any grand gestures toward discarding it. That would not only be specious but self-defeating, surrendering to despair and futility, something the Haddingtons did not do publicly or privately, and hopeless unless she were somehow able to change her molecular and glandular structure. Even now, despising Eddie Eden, she longed for him. How did one reconcile and resolve that kind of insanity?

She was lying on the chaise longue in her bedroom when the bane of her existence came in, using his key. She had placed herself in this position after Ben Hale had left and had not moved since, not even to accommodate nature. She felt limp and languid, weighed down, as if an incubus rested on her breast. She had drawn the shades and the room was semi-dark, though the afternoon sun still brightened the outside, casting shadows across Central Park.

"Silver?" Eddie called softly. "You home, darling? Sil? Where are you, love?"

She did not answer.

212

Eventually he found her, switched on the lights. "Didn't you hear me call?"

"I heard you," she murmured.

"Why didn't you answer?"

Her look obviated a reply. She extended her hand. "Give me the key, Eddie."

"Why?"

"Your open sesame is over here." She waited. "Will you give me the key, or must I have the lock changed?"

"What's chewing you?" Eddie demanded. "I thought we ironed out the wrinkles in our relationship last night, and the bed was all roses again? What's with the thorns now? What're you lying here in the gloom for, looking and acting like a zombie?"

"I just had a vision of myself," Silver said.

Eddie perked up visibly. "No kidding? You mean you finally took a trip? Baby, that's great! Tell me about it. Where'd you go?"

"To hell," Silver said.

"That's tough," Eddie sympathized. "But sometimes the acid backfires. Only I wish it hadn't on your first journey. Now maybe you won't want to go again." He sat down on the chaise, took her hands in his. "Was it really that bad, Sil? Fire and brimstone? Did you meet the devil?"

"In person," Silver replied in a dull monotone.

"Old Diabolo, eh? Cloven hoofs, tail, horns, scales, and all? You really met the Master, Mr. Lucifer, Big Beelzebub?"

"He's sitting beside me now."

Eddie laughed, pleased with the compliment. "Well, he's an interesting fellow, *n'est-ce pas?* And you didn't expect St. Pete, did you? He'd have been an awful square, a holy bore. Insufferable."

Silver smiled gingerly. "You don't know what I'm talking about, do you?"

"Sure, doll. Your maiden voyage on the good ship LSD."

"You abysmal bastard," Silver muttered. "I'm talking about you, and the pictures!"

Eddie reared back as if he'd been struck. "You're lying!" But he knew better. That expression, that depression could mean only one thing: she had seen the evidence, the pathetic tragic horrifying evidence a good camera could capture and reflect more accurately than a thousand mirrors, where the beholder invariably practices self-adulation and personal beguilement and deception.

"Ben Hale?" he asked.

"Yes."

His respect for the man as a detective increased, along with his hatred and contempt of the man himself. "You sicked that hound on me after our beautiful ball last night?"

"*Before* it," Silver was pleased to announce.

"I see," Eddie said grimly. "But how—how in hell did he find them?"

"He knows his business," Silver said. "What did you use those horrors for, Eddie? To spook the kooks on your freakouts? Did they get lots of kicks and jollies out of them? What kind of Weirdo Wally are you?"

"A clever one, Countess, as you should know by now. And I have more," he bluffed. "That little group was only a sample. I have more and worse, Silver. Tucked away where nobody, not even the genius Hale, could find them."

Her passive face remained impassive, the green eyes glacial. That threat would never work again.

"What now?" Eddie asked bitterly. "*Fini?*"

"How perceptive." Her voice was sly with sarcasm. "Get out, singer. Leave and don't ever dare return. I have a gun, and I'll kill you if you do."

Eddie jumped to his feet as if he'd been electrically activated. "Oh no, Countess! The sign-off is not that easy or cheap. You settled a bunch of oats on your other stable-mates, legal and otherwise, and Eddie Eden doesn't get kicked out with nothing but manure on his face, pastured like some stud with blown balls. You think I enjoyed banging you? That you excited, thrilled me? Hell, it was an effort and a chore all the fucking way! That frame of yours is about as appealing and stimulating as a clothes-rack. I had to prime my pump with booze and pot to even get up the urge. You marveled at my staying power. Well, I had to whip and spur myself to keep riding my bony mount. And maybe I'm not a prize-winner in your stable, Miss Haddington, but I think I deserve something for perseverance on the track. But I'm not greedy or mercenary. I'll settle for a mere hundred thou."

His tirade did not disturb Silver, since it only echoed her own thoughts, and perhaps he did deserve some payment. "The stud fees on the Haddington Horse Farm are determined by the blood of the stallions. Thoroughbreds and champions naturally come high. But you have no pedigree, Eddie, you don't qualify in that class. Five thousand, as a nuisance value, take it or leave it."

"You insult me, *chérie*. Surely I was worth more than that paltry sum? Raise the ante to fifty, and it's a deal."

"I don't have to bargain with you, Eddie, or bribe you. You have no club over me now."

Eddie grinned, never more arrogant than in the face of defeat. "Sure I do, Countess. Big as ever. The same cunt club that initiated me in the first place. You're a phallus-worshiper, Miss Haddington. One of those females who make a cult of the male penis. You got to be laid, baby, and regularly, or you'll wither and die. And in spite of everything, I'm still willing to oblige. For a price."

"Oh, I wouldn't want you to prostitute yourself, *chéri*. Not when I disgust and repulse you."

"I didn't mean that, Sil. I just wanted to hurt you."

"You did," she conceded. "Feel better?"

"Not especially," Eddie admitted. "Maybe I am *weird*, Silver, because you still can and do affect me, bones and all. I bet you have a beautiful skeleton. Very chic. Can't we just forget all this nastiness and start over?"

"Now you disgust and repulse me," Silver said. "I'm not that desperate for your company, Eddie, and I hope I'm not that much of a drooling fool. You are persona non grata here, singer. Forfeit your key, or I guarantee there'll be a new lock on the door tomorrow."

"*L'amour force toutes les surrures, chérie.*" He smiled. "I can see by your blank face that your finishing school French fails you, so I'll translate: Love laughs at locksmiths, darling."

"Nevertheless, if you try to force your way in here I'll have you arrested for breaking and entry," Silver threatened.

"Ah, you're relenting," Eddie said, encouraged. "A moment ago you were going to kill me."

"The key, Eddie."

He refused. "Call your locksmith, Countess, because I'm not surrendering this little treasure. I intend to put it on a chain and wear it around my neck, close to my heart." He bent to kiss her hand, as one of her noblemen might have done, except that his gesture was mockery. "*Au revoir, Comtesse.*"

chapter
21

MARCIE WAS GONE. Bag and baggage, cleared out. It was Splitsville for good. Eddie was furious. This was more of Ben Hale's doing. Well, he'd show them, all of them. Nobody could get the best of Eddie Eden. Nobody could make a fool of Eddie Eden and profit by it. Not his wife, nor that two-bit Mike Hammer, nor that scarecrow in her perfumed tower, nor that tawny-haired babe in her putrid dungeon.

He scrounged the telephone directory for a number, dialed it, asked for a certain columnist.

"Earl, this is Eddie Eden."

"Who?"

"Eddie Eden. I played the Amber Alley several months. I'm a singer." He crooned a few notes. "Actor and entertainer, too. I'm sure you caught my act?"

"I'm sure I didn't," the columnist replied in a tone suggesting that he was busy and didn't care to be bothered. "Lots of nightclub acts in this town. Can't catch 'em all, pal. Only the big ones."

"Well, you'll catch mine one of these days, man, and there'll be SR only."

"Sure, friend, sure. Dream on."

"Get a scoop for you, Earl. You know Silver Haddington? *The* Silver Haddington?"

"Who doesn't ?"

"Well, she's responsible for Splitsville between me and my mate," Eddie said. "You can quote me."

"I'd rather quote her," the newsman replied.

"She won't admit it," Eddie said. "Would you expect her to admit it?"

"What's your game, pal?"

"Just trying to hand you an exclusive, pal. Some secret stuff." It was hard to maintain patience with so much deliberate denseness. "You want it or not? There're dozens of others in this berg who'd leap at it, you know."

"And I bet you dialed 'em all," the voice drawled. "You know, I think I do recognize your name, after all. Didn't you buzz me a couple of months ago with another 'scoop' about anonymous telephone threats on your life?"

"Not me," Eddie denied.

"It was you." Positive. Bored. "Crying wolf again in a different howl, eh? Didn't your mother ever tell you that old story, pal?"

"Look, you stupid sonofabitch," Eddie growled. "You wouldn't know a story if it kicked you in your fat ass!"

He banged the receiver down, tried another number from the yellow pages, a tabloid which had previously obliged him with an anon item: "A certain singer claims to hear gremlin voices bugging his wire ... could be feedback from a disgruntled mike."

But at least this gossip-monger would listen to him. "You say Silver Haddington's got a thing for you, Mac? The hotsies, no less? Will she confirm that? We got a couple of libel suits pending against us now, so I can't print any false info. Can't risk my job, I got an unweaned gut. I'll check it out with her, but if she denies it, the most I can run is the standard cliché clip: 'What well-known Jetter is rumored to be flying around with Eddie Arden.'"

"Eden," Eddie corrected and laboriously spelled it out,

astonished and annoyed at the absolute ignorance of some of these pen-and-ink people. "E-d-e-n."

"Like in paradise?"

"That's right. Eddie Eden, a Little Bit of Paradise, the Teche Troubadour, the Cajun Cat, according to my press agent. Spell it right, will you, Mac?"

"You bet. Sue me if I don't."

"Write it down," Eddie urged.

"I got a terrif memory," the reporter bragged. "Aren't you the guy that had gremlins on his line awhile back?"

"They weren't gremlins," Eddie said.

"The wonderful world of pot, eh?"

"You want Miss Haddington's private number?"

"I'll get it, pal."

"How?"

"The fourth estate has sources and resources. We could get the number of the Hot Line to the White House if we tried."

"Will this be in tormorrow's edition?"

"Maybe. Keep reading the rag."

"Thanks. At least you know a scoop when you hear it. That's more'n I can say for some of your competition."

"Call others, did you, before me?"

"No, no." Eddie bit his tongue, swore silently at his stupidity, almost hanging himself. "This was something else, a few weeks back. They wouldn't believe me."

"About the gremlins, you mean?"

Eddie ignored that, wishing he could choke the throat that kept uttering it. "I'll be reading you," he said before the connection was abruptly broken on the other end.

Well, that was that. All he had to do now was wait. Something would pop. Something would break, and he'd be on his predestination, courting that gorgeous goddess, Fate, who'd been so goddamn fickle and elusive to him so far, and he'd bring Dame Destiny to heel, too. Silver'd be begging him to call off the battle, bribing him. . . .

He wondered vaguely where Marcie'd gone. Probably back to Hale's old lady. He ought to barge in there and rip up the homestead, blow up a gale none of 'em would ever forget. But what the hell, he had more important things on his mind, bigger prospects in the beautiful breeze. And the next business on the agenda was one Tawny Mane.

She was in the shower when he arrived. Eddie used his key. Sometimes he mixed up the two keys, hers and Silver's. He had idiotically expected the latter to be gold-plated. He'd read somewhere that this was a romantic gesture made by wealthy women to their favorite lovers, a tradition since royalty had originated it centuries ago, and the "love-key" became a jeweler's item and a gentleman's toy. Silver Haddington had disappointed him in this respect, but Eddie did not believe she would actually have her lock changed, as she'd threatened; she liked what he had to offer and would not be silly enough to spite herself by refusing him entry. That would be stupid, and whatever else she might be, Silver Haddington was not stupid. Not like this dumb broad splashing away like a pigeon in a birdbath . . .

Tawny emerged from the shower with a towel draped around her sarong-fashion. She tried not to show either surprise or joy at his presence. "You get lonesome, lover?"

"Did you?"

"Dreadfully."

"Don't shit me, Tawny. You had some company."

"You mean your friend, Mr. Danti?"

"Describe him," Eddie commanded.

She did.

"You mush-head," he raged. "You hoosier idiot. That was Benjamin Franklin Hale, a private eye! How could you be dumb enough to fall for such a pitch? I ought to bang your head into aspic."

Tawny began to tremble and wail. "He said he was your friend, that you sent him! How'd I know who he was? If you'd told me something in advance—"

"How could I tell you something I didn't know? I've combed my brain, but I'm damned if I can figure how he connected you and me. You got any idea?"

Blanks and negatives were all Tawny could offer, although she tried to reassure him that his prized collection was still largely intact. "He only took the photos of that gosh-awful corpse," she soothed. "Who'd want that spook around, anyway? You didn't lose nothing, Eddie."

"Didn't lose nothing," Eddie mimicked and smacked her hard in the face. "Oh, Jeez! I'd like to pulverize you!"

"You got a glow for *her*?" Tawny asked in amazement, rubbing her stinging cheek. "Is that where you been all the nights you wasn't with me, banging that white-haired old harridan? Was she the one you bedded with during the last storm? I wanted you so much that night, lover. You know how wind and rain affects me. I wanted you so much, I went to your pad and waited around and was about to go up when I saw you had skirt-company, petting a mangy cat in the window. She didn't look scrawny like the pictures though, and she had dark hair. Guess she musta dyed it, huh?"

Eddie gazed at her. "That explains it," he said.

"Huh?"

"That wasn't me up there, squash-brain. It was Ben Hale. And the girl was my wife."

"Your wife! I thought she was in Dixie?"

"She ain't," Eddie muttered. "And I'm not gonna bother trying to explain the rest of this story to you, Tawny. There ain't enough time for that. But you fouled me up good, you know that? I had a sweet thing going for me, I was in lullaby land, and you loused it up." He cracked his knuckles, pounded one balled fist into the palm of the other. "I got to work you over, baby—you know that, don't you? I got to teach you a lesson you won't forget. It's school time, dunce, and here's the first bell. . . ."

"No, please," Tawny begged, cowering, suddenly terrified. "Don't hit me, Eddie. Don't bruise me. I got an audition tomorrow, a chance to dance, but if I'm bruised—"

"You'll be bruised, baby. Black and blue. You can bet on it."

Tawny dropped the towel to the floor, flung her arms around his neck, kissing him wildly, undulating her body against his, but still the blows fell, on her head and shoulders, breasts and belly. She continued her desperate attempt to seduce him, divert his violence to desire, but while he responded in some respects, he grew more brutal in others, hammering away until she collapsed and crumpled at his feet and lay whimpering like a whipped puppy. Then he stripped himself and ravished her and experienced a whole new range of emotions and sensations, a rapture unsurpassed in previous sex. Somewhere in the strange muck of his mind, in the erotic delirium of his lust, he knew that he had been cheating himself before, that brutality was his true sexual bag, and banging a babe physically contributed to the pleasure. He only hoped he hadn't killed her, because this savagery would happen again, this different desire would claim him again, and he had to know he had an outlet for it.

Tawny was bleeding from the nose and mouth. Her breathing was faint, shallow. She had ceased struggling, whimpering, and lay motionless as a lamb after slaughter. Her long coppery hair was spread out on the stained carpet, some strands matted with blood and tears. Her fingernails and toenails were turning blue, but her body was still warm to the touch.

Eddie rose and stood over her, feeling some revulsion and remorse now that it was over. He was drenched with sweat, it was streaming off him. He dried himself on the towel Tawny had worn, smoothed his hair back. He dressed and sat down on the couch and smoked a cigarette. Maybe he ought to pour some water over her head, revive her, but he was too tired to move. Exhausted. Not relaxed but spent. It was queer, the way he felt. That was a terrific drain on a man's system, his energy. Not revitalizing as normal sex, but devastating, depleting. He felt like a wrung out sponge. He'd have to reserve these experiences for special occasions, ration himself. I guess I'm some kind of pervert, he thought without either wonder or surprise. Swamp beast. *L'animal*, Grand'mère Baudard would say. Grand'mère? Why should he think of her now, at a time like this, that frail saintly little creature floating in the mists of the bayou, lost in the tangles and shadows of the Teche. . . .

"Tawny." He nudged her with his shoe, gentle, amazed at his tenderness now. "Get up, honey. It's over. You're bruised, baby, but you'll heal. Tawny, come on now, stop playing possum. . . ."

He waited, pulling on his cigarette. Her eyes were open, fixed on the ceiling as if staring at the cracks in the plaster. The blood was congealing in her wounds. Eddie bent to touch her. She was cool now, with a kind of clamminess to her skin, as if it had oozed moisture that had not quite evaporated in the heat. Eddie knelt beside her, tried to find a pulse in her wrist, her throat. He put his ear to her bare bruised breast to listen for a heartbeat. Negative. She wasn't faking. She must be dead. My God, he'd killed her! He hadn't meant to, but he'd killed her! Beaten her to death.

For a while his mind couldn't function beyond that one realization, nor his emotions react to it. The knowledge was stupefying. He needed a stimulant but there was no booze in the cellar, not even beer. Tawny was broke, out of work for four months, and on the verge of soliciting for a living. Maybe she had *sold* the pictures to Ben Hale! Silver would have paid any ransom . . . and maybe the money was here in the pad, for Tawny was too stupid to bank it.

He abandoned the liquor search for that of the hoped for loot, ransacking drawers and cabinets, pulling off chair and couch cushions, lifting the mattress of the unmade bed. He yanked the attaché case out from under the couch and rummaged through it, thinking she might have felt the money belonged to him since he owned the goods, and stowed it there. No such luck. Surely she hadn't obliged Hale for free? He rustled the closet, sweeping her clothes off the rack onto the floor. Pawing through them, he became entangled in her costume veils, bales of veils it seemed, and he had to fight his way out of the gossamer stuff before it suffocated him. But the harder he struggled the more involved he got, until it was like some wild nightmare of filmy spiderwebs that were yet as strong as steel mesh, and he was caught like a shrimp in a net. It was weird, crazy, maddening. If he didn't know better, he'd have thought he was on a trip that boomeranged.

"Get up!" he shouted at the still figure on the floor. "Get up, goddamn you, and help me out of this mess!"

It was funny, it was really hilarious. He laughed at his predicament, laughed until he cried, wiping his eyes on the tangled veils. Finally, he freed himself, got up and looked at Tawny again, hopefully. Her eyes and mouth were open, and he saw a gold crown on one of her teeth glittering eerily. She was icy-cold and board-stiff. He had to get out of there, get his pics and anything else that belonged to him and get the hell out!

He dragged the body behind the divan, threw a sheet from the bed over it and emptied a whole bottle of cologne over the sheet in hope that it would act as embalming fluid in retarding odor. He was glad he'd torn up the joint; that would indicate a motive of robbery and rape. He didn't even have to break a window, as the one on the entrance well, the only one in the apartment, was already open. He smoothed his hair again, straightened his clothes, and made certain there was no one in the courtyard before emerging from the stairwell. He slipped between the buildings, out to the street, where he dropped the key in a drainage sewer before crossing the square, and proceeded without undue haste to his pad in the alley. It was dark, except for the street lamps.

A positive identification would be impossible, even if he were seen leaving the scene.

Once in the safety of his studio, he broke out in a sweat as cold and clammy as that of Tawny's death. The bottle he'd bought to celebrate Marcie's homecoming— oh, brother!—was still on the table. He opened it, corked it again. He had to think, and that juice would only fog his mind. There was a way out of this, he was confident, if only he could keep his cool. When the body was discovered, he'd naturally be Ben Hale's prime suspect; he'd crack the case for the fuzz immediately. But it wasn't premeditated murder, at least. Manslaughter, at the most. Crime of passion, the rags would call it. Sex crime. But that was the worst kind, as far as juries were concerned. They'd throw the book at him.

First, he needed an alibi. Marcie, of course. A wife couldn't testify against her husband. He had to find her, get her on his side. Where the devil was she? Ben Hale would know, but that would blow the whole deal! He had to think of something else, and fast.

chapter
22

BUT GOD, HE WAS TIRED, sore and aching in every bone and muscle! He couldn't do anything, least of all think, until he caught some winks. His weariness baffled him, unaware of the morbid mind's need to rest, to seek recuperation in oblivion. He flopped on the bed, fully clothed. He dozed off, slept fitfully, in snatches disturbed by weird dreams. He woke at midnight, saturated in sweat, jittery as a jumping bean. Maybe some pot would help to calm and relax him? He had stashed away just such an emergency supply in the baggy folds of the closet wallpaper, and this was an emergency. A crisis. And Christ, the cache was empty! He ripped the rotten paper and canvas off the wall, as if he expected it had slipped into a crack or the pores of the wood. Nothing! What had happened to it, where'd it gone, his precious stuff? He must have used it, but when? Jeez, he was flipping, going ape! Losing his memory, his mind. No, by God, Ben Hale was the culprit. No doubt he'd searched there first for the pics and found the horde and seized it, probably turned it over to the fuzz, unless Marcie had managed to dissuade him. That man was a menace, his nemesis, his mortal enemy, the world wasn't big enough for both of them, and one day soon it'd be him or Ben Bastard Hale. . . .

Eddie threw himself on the bed again and feared he might go into delirium, hysterics, convulsions, or all three. He pounded the pillows in impotent rage, rattled the brass poles of the bedstead as if they were a cage confining him; he felt blown, brain and all. But it was only midnight, and things were just beginning to swing in East Village, and there were people there who would understand his bind and sympathize with him. He should've thought of that earlier, though, in case he had to establish an alibi. Now it would be risky, dangerous. Maybe he ought to backtrack to Tawny's sump, maybe by some lucky chance, some miracle, she had survived and still lived. No, returning to the scene, as they said, would be a mistake, the error that might trap and doom him. She was dead, all right, stone-cold stiff in rigor mortis. How long would it take before she was discovered? Not long, in this heat. Nausea seeped into his throat at the thought of the discovery. Why did it have to be summer? In winter, that brick basement would have preserved her like a refrigerated vault. Boy, he had nothing but bad breaks! The grinches were really after him, ganging up on him, working overtime to get Eddie Eden. . . .

Suddenly he remembered the swamps, longed for them as never before in his life. There were places he knew in Teche Country from childhood, where he'd be safe, impenetrable jungles surrounded by quicksand where he couldn't be traced and found even with bloodhounds. He could live for years in a shantyboat in the interior, off fish and game. Oh, the beautiful swamps! But he had to get there first, had to scrounge up the green somewhere and somehow for a plane ticket, his freedom-fare to New Orleans.

Five thou Silver had offered him, said she had the cash on hand in the safe. Why hadn't he taken it? His greed would finish him. But hell, she had more'n that, he'd bet, ten grand at least, and he knew the combination, had watched her open it to dole out bread to bail him out when he got sunk too deep in a game, and he'd memorized it, and later written it down so he wouldn't forget, on the hunch that he might someday have need of the knowledge. And this was the day! She hadn't had time to change either the lock on the door or the combination on the safe, even if her threats in the first direction weren't idle. That was the answer, the only answer!

But what if she wasn't alone? If she had company, a bash, or some other stud was already in her hay? It was a chance he had to take. Lately, it seemed, he was living on chance. Or had it always been so, and his whole goddamn life was composed of chance instead of opportunity?

Eddie dressed in dark clothes which he hoped would be inconspicuous and went out to hail a cab. None was handy, which was good, because it wouldn't do to be picked up too near his pad. He strolled leisurely toward Washington Square. The creeps and spooks were out in packs, it was the witching hour of Saturday night, but he didn't see anybody he knew or who was in any shape to recognize him even if they'd haunted the Amber Alley when he was its main attraction. The Christ Man was not preaching or pushing tonight, too bad, or he'd traffic with him for some stuff to take to the thickets; but on weekends the evangelists of pot and speed and free love practiced what they preached.

"Paper, Mister?"

The ragged newsboy, selling papers today and probably dope tomorrow. The waifs and urchins who used to symbolize something and were now frequently symbols of something else. Where did they sleep and when?

"No, thanks."

"Can't you read, Mister?"

Eddie wanted to cuff him. "Don't worry about your future, kid. With that attitude, you'll never grow up."

"Screw you," the newsboy said.

"What're you, a fag squirt?"

"Why? You lookin' for one?"

"Maybe," Eddie said out of curiosity.

"Well, you found him, man. For a price."

The poor little newsboy, the legend and inspiration of another day, another age, now peddling himself along with his papers. If any square thought times hadn't changed . . .

Suddenly Eddie remembered the columnist in the tabloid. "Gimme a paper," he said, digging out some coins, and the vendor completed the business transaction with sly contempt.

Eddie rummaged through the sheets under a street lamp until he found the column. There it was, sandwiched between an item about Taylor and Burton and Sinatra and Farrow: "Eden Arden's got the hotsies for one of the more with-it Jetters."

That dirty Commie columnist! Did he misspell Liz and Dick? Did he print Fink Sinatra or Mia Sparrow? No, but Eden Arden, who was *that*? It wasn't an honest error, either, he did it deliberately, like he kept bugging him about the gremlins. The dirty perverted sonofabitch!

Eddie swore violently, crumpled the paper, tossed it into the nearest garbage-can. What the hell! Maybe it was a blessing in disguise. Maybe not having his handle linked with hers publicly was the best possible break he could have now, and the bastard inadvertently did him a favor. Grand'mère Baudard would say his guardian angel was on guard. Grand'mère believed in such corny myths. Grand'mère was a klutz.

The newsboy grinned maliciously. "Whattsa matter, mister? Your stock go down?"

"Get lost, grinch."

The kid made the sign of the finger and repeated his earlier sentiments. "Screw you."

"Flake off, boy fag," Eddied muttered. "Go peddle your puky papers."

A taxi rattled into sight. Eddie signaled it to the curb,

got in, gave an address near the Regal Towers. The newsboy, still lurking curiously and perhaps hopefully about, saluted him obscenely in passing. Eddie hoped a garbage-truck would hit him before morning. But at least the cabbie kept his stupid mouth shut, otherwise Eddie might have clobbered him. He hated the world and everybody in it, especially reporters and newsboys and private detectives.

The cab disgorged him before the decoy address Eddie had specified, and the morose driver did not respond to the generous tip the passenger presented in appreciation for his grim silence. As the hack rattled away, Eddie walked along Fifth Avenue a couple of blocks, then turned back in the direction of the high-rise apartment-hotel.

The doorman! Damn, he'd forgotten about that sentinel. Lampkin knew Eddie Eden on sight. Of course discretion was nine parts of his job, and management would cut his tongue out for violations even if the residents didn't, but Eddie couldn't risk that hitch. He'd just have to stall until Lampkin took a break. He was human, after all; he had to visit the latrine occasionally, especially with all the cokes and instant coffee he consumed to stay alert on the dog watch.

Eddie posted himself in the shadows of the Park directly across the Avenue from the monolithic building. It was 1:35 by his watch. If the brass-and-braid general had just relieved himself, he'd have an hour or longer to wait. Jeez, if only he had a joint to keep him company!

At last, when Eddie was beginning to think the old boy was a camel incarnate, his bulky silhouette disappeared from the glass doors, and Eddie knew he had a few minutes to cross the street and enter the lobby. He took long strides, hurrying without appearing to do so. Inside, he caught the automatic elevator to the summit, pausing on several floors as a diversionary tactic should someone below be watching the ascent. For extra precaution, he stopped three floors shy of the pinnacle and continued by stairway to the penthouse. Leaving would be a cinch, for he was acquainted with the back exits, as he imagined most of Miss Haddington's male guests were.

He paused at her door and listened. All was quiet inside. He used his key. All was dark inside. He vacillated a few moments while a remnant of conscience nagged him, then brushed it aside like a cobweb, and proceeded determinedly. She owed him something, even she had admitted that, and he was here to collect. There was little danger of her waking, he'd realized this the night of the nudes, when he was popping flashbulbs all over the boudoir, without so much as a flutter of her eyelashes. She took barbiturates and chased them with brandy, virtually embalming herself with the lethal combination, which was precisely the effect the camera had captured. She'd know what'd happened tomorrow, but she wouldn't dare report the incident, for how'd she explain the delicate details of their relationship to the indelicate bulls? Eddie smiled at his ingenuity; it was like having a license to steal. No need even to work in the dark; he could throw a little light on the vault behind the portrait.

Keep smiling, Countess, he said with a wry salute. You'll never miss it. You got millions.

Five right . . . eight left . . . seven right . . .

Lovely seven. Lucky seven.

The shots rang out, four in rapid succession, like automobile backfires. Three of the bullets connected with their target, one in the neck, one in each lung. Eddie sagged, slumped, pitched, sprawled to the floor, mortally wounded. So fast, so fatally, he was unable to utter a single word, not even a dying gasp; and the heavily padded carpet cushioned his fall, so that it was a muted thump, almost soundless.

Silver Haddington stood near the body, holding a smoking revolver in her hand. Insensible with drugs, all she could think at the moment was that he was bleeding on the white broadloom. Her first rational impulse was to call Ben Hale, but she reconsidered. The police might wonder about her present connection with him. She dialed the operator. The inside of her mouth was cotton-dry, and she had to wet her tongue before she could speak, asking for the police. She stated her name and address and the nature of her call. Then she hung up and slipped into a pale gray satin robe that flowed over her body like a coat of liquid platinum, and was about to sit down and light a cigarette when she remembered the key. Slowly, calmly, like a figure moving in a dream, she retrieved it from Eddie's pocket.

The blood was spreading faster than the carpet could absorb it. A sudden wave of revulsion swept her. She backed away, feeling sick. Coffee might have helped, but she didn't feel like making it.

She met the law at the door, ushered them to the gory scene. The officer in charge introduced himself as Detective-Lieutenant Dean Morse, of Homicide, and questioned her while his assistants took pictures and fingerprints and whatever else they had to do. He examined the gun, a .22 pistol, and asked her if it was hers.

"Yes," Silver said. "Registered in my name, Lieutenant."

"How many shots did you fire?"

"I don't know. Several, I think. I didn't count. It's an automatic, and my finger just seemed to pull the trigger automatically. Is he dead?"

He told her the coroner would have to decide that. "You say you knew him?"

"Yes. His name is ... was Eddie Eden. He is ... was a singer. He entertained at some of my parties. My friends can verify that."

"Did he ever visit you in any other capacity?"

"What do you mean?"

"As a friend, an acquaintance?"

Her composure did not waver. "Naturally he came here to complete the arrangements for his act and to rehearse it, and we visited together in the interest of entertainment," Silver replied, which ambiguity she did not consider untruthful, for wasn't that essentially the purpose of his visits, to entertain? "But I never thought—I never dreamed he'd try anything like this."

"How did he get in?"

"Obviously, I forgot to lock my door."

"Obviously?"

"Well, apparently. I had a migraine headache last night—I'm subject to them, my doctor will confirm that—and I guess I wasn't thinking too clearly. I was tired and took some pills, a prescription for pain, and went to bed. I woke about three and noticed a light in the living room, which I didn't think I'd left burning, but could have forgotten as I did the door. Nevertheless, I didn't want to go in unarmed, in case there was an intruder. You see, my servants don't sleep in any more, and I'm alone. I have a great many valuable paintings and other art treasures, as you may know. Also some jewels—I don't go in for paste replicas—which I keep here in my vault, along with petty cash."

"How petty?" asked the officer.

"Five or six thousand."

Compared with millions, that amount could be considered pin-money. "Could Eden have known that you kept cash here?"

"Why, yes. I paid him in cash when he entertained, and he knew I got it from the safe."

"Why did you pay him in cash?"

"That's the way he wanted it," Silver said. "Moonlighting a little on his agency, I suspect. Or perhaps IRS. I don't know his reason, Lieutenant. I didn't ask him."

"Continue, please."

"Well, that's about all," Silver said. "I took my gun from the nightstand and crept into the living room and saw this dark-clothed figure fooling with the safe. I suppose I might have recognized him had I been cognizant, in full possession of my faculties, but the drugs were still in effect. Besides, his back was to me. I was dazed and frightened, and about the only thing that registered on my mind at the time was that there was a thief in my house, and I reacted instinctively to protect myself and my property. He was a big man, as you can see, and I'm a frail woman, as you can see, and I wasn't about to challenge him and give him a chance to hurt me—attack me or even kill me if he had a gun."

"He didn't," Lieutenant Morse said.

"But I didn't know that, Lieutenant. Criminals don't usually go abroad in the night unarmed, do they?"

"Not usually," he agreed. "And he probably was trying to rob you. If so, his prints will appear on the safe. But I can't help wondering how he knew where it was?"

"That's no mystery, Lieutenant. Aren't most home wall safes behind pictures or sliding panels? Besides, as I've already stated, I paid for his entertainment services in cash, which I realize now was probably foolish. Anyway, he *knew* the location of the safe."

"Did he also know the combination?"

"Not to my knowledge. I mean, I certainly never gave it to him. But he was in the room when I opened it. He could have memorized it, I suppose—although I wasn't aware that he was paying that much attention, if he was. There were guests present, and he appeared to be talking to them."

The camera flashed again, from another angle. Silver winced. "How many pictures do they need?"

"Does it make you nervous? I should think you'd be used to cameras, Miss Haddington?"

Silver considered that a cryptic remark and replied indignantly, "Not under these circumstances, Lieutenant."

The impassive expression he'd worn since his arrival did not change even fleetingly. He knew who she was, but if the identity registered it did not impress, and Silver felt somewhat slighted. He was here on business, not social interest, and he was showing her courtesy but

234

no privileges. And if he appeared to be questioning a suspect, conducting an inquiry rather than taking a deposition, that was just his method of interrogation, and he neither apologized for it, nor spared her any embarrassment when he considered intimate details and probing in order.

"They'll be finished soon," he said, scribbling on his form sheet, "and they'll cover the corpse. The coroner will make an autopsy—it's routine. Do you know if he had any next-of-kin?"

"A wife, I think."

He gazed at her levelly. "Know how we could locate her?"

Silver returned the gaze unflinchingly. "Afraid not, Lieutenant. I don't even know her."

"Where's he from? I mean, what's his home town?"

"Some place in Louisiana, according to his publicity. Naturally he worked through an agency, most show people do, you know. I'm sure they could supply further details of his life and habits." Her temples began to throb again, it was not pretense; she pressed the palms of her hands flat against them. "My headache is returning. I'll have to take some more medication. May I call my physician?"

"Sure, if you feel you need him. You might want to call your attorney, too."

"Will I need him?"

"There'll be an inquest, ma'am. Routine procedure in violent deaths. It's the law."

"I don't suppose there's any way to keep it out of the papers?" Silver asked hopefully.

His look suggested that she was being naïve. "The crime reporters have better communication systems than the police, and they monitor them as vigilantly. They heard this dispatch as soon as our boys did. They're gathering before this building right now. Some of 'em even beat us here."

"I won't see them," Silver declared emphatically. "I shall lock myself in and refuse to see them."

The officer's shrug indicated that it was her decision, her choice.

"If I don't talk to them they'll speculate, of course," Silver relented. "But they do that, anyway."

"Well, you're accustomed to publicity, aren't you?"

Silver wondered what he was getting at with these sly digs, which were about as subtle as a spading fork; and again she reiterated, careful to neutralize the acid in her voice, "Not this kind, Lieutenant."

"Well, it's too late for the Sunday editions, anyway," he offered by way of consolation.

The medical examiner listed his information in a special report. A black grease pencil was used to outline the position of the body, since chalk would not have registered on the white carpet. Then a sheet was thrown over the corpse, but the gore had spread beyond its reaches. Ironically, Silver remembered Eddie Eden's angry prediction a few days ago, during his scuffle with Ben Hale, when he'd accused her of having a fetish about that white carpet: "One of these days, I'm going to dump ashes and blood and crap all over it." And her own grim prophesy: "You do, Buster, and it'll be your blood."

"My carpet is ruined," she said inanely. "The stains will never come out. It'll have to be replaced."

Lieutenant Morse thought that a strange worry in such a situation, but then he'd heard that Silver Haddington was eccentric, along with a lot of other things.

"That's the trouble with blood," he said. "It's hard to remove. Difficult to wash off anything, including the hands."

Another of his clever innuendos, his professional cryptograms? She would not like to tangle with this guy legally.

"My hands are clean, Lieutenant. I didn't commit a crime, did I, protecting myself?"

"That's not for me to decide, Miss Haddington."

236

Too sad. And then when I married a man with Acadian blood, it seemed sort of prophetic. That's silly, isn't it?"

"Romantic, perhaps. But Evangeline didn't marry her lover. Gabriel fell for someone else."

"I know. I was luckier than she."

"Were you, Marcie?"

She stared at him, brows curiously arched, eyes deep purple in the twilight. "What?"

Ben shrugged. "Nothing."

Fireflys appeared in the settling dusk. Mosquitoes began to swarm and drone. The redolence of honeysuckle was closing in on Ben. He was relieved when her aunt announced supper.

chapter
23

IT WAS EARLY SUNDAY MORNING, and church bells were ringing over the city. Marcie could hear them from the room in the women's hotel, where she had moved yesterday afternoon. The accommodation was compact and utilitarian, on the order of a nun's cell in a cloister convent. The narrow single bed would have ensured the occupant's chastity, even if the puritanical house rules had not. A dresser painted white, a small desk, an uncomfortable chair, all made Marcie feel as if she were doing some form of penance. The walls and ceiling of the ten-by-twelve cubicle looked as if they'd been whitewashed, a Venetian blind let in bars of sunlight through the solitary window, and a faded candle-wick spread and drab curtains completed the decor. Tomorrow she would apply for the job at Dibrell, Cantrell, and Larson, and go apartment-hunting. Today she had a sentimental desire to see some of the sights and attractions of this town for which she felt neither sentiment nor affinity, but only a sense of wonder, bewilderment and awe. Ben had insisted on accompanying her, and now she was dressed and waiting for him in the lobby, according to the covenant of the establishment.

She had eaten breakfast—eaten but hardly enjoyed the

stale sweet roll and tepid coffee in the hotel dining room, which was as austere and ascetic as the rest of the place, its customers mostly elderly residents, old ladies on pensions and annuities resigned to vapid vacuity; and bored and impecunious young ladies stuck there by circumstances or anxious relatives who considered it a proper address for a virtuous lady living alone in New York. It was an Amazon-like community staffed entirely by females, including the bellhops, one of whom Marcie suspected was a latent Lesbian. She wondered if there had ever been any genuine romantic excitement in this sterile atmosphere, or indeed any kind of excitement. Ben had been somewhat chagrined when she had selected the Abbey, considering it a personal affront.

The management provided Sunday papers for the guests, and Marcie thumbed through the *New York Times,* which was almost as thick as a Sears catalog. One could not hope to digest that amount of newsprint in a day and must be content to assimilate a part of it. She read the headlines and the front-page stories, noted interestedly the advertisements which promised bargains in clothing and shoes in some of the department stores, where most of her future shopping would probably be done. Soon she found herself glancing hopefully at the portals of the Abbey and eagerly rushing to meet Ben Hale the moment he entered; pleased that other heads, young and old, swiveled in his direction, some with obvious envy.

Ben had parked the car down the block, and on the way to it, remarked moodily, "God, what a grim place, Marcie! You might as well have entered a nunnery."

"It'll serve the purpose until I can afford something better. But I'm glad I don't have to spend the day there. One of the bell girls has been giving me the eye."

"A Lesbian's paradise," Ben said.

"Not with the Medusa that manages it," Marcie said. "I bet that misfit will be fired by nightfall. Where're we going first?"

"I've seen it all," Ben said. "But most visitors start with the Statue of Liberty. Anyway, it's as good a beginning as any, although there's going to be a crowd. August is tourist time in this town, and Sunday is the worst day of the week. We have to take a ferry from the Battery. I hope the wait isn't too long."

"So what? We've more time than money."

"That's no lie."

"I bought a guidebook in the lobby," Marcie said. "New York on five dollars a day. Who're they kidding? I paid seventy-five cents, plus tax, for a cold cross bun and a cup of anemic coffee."

"Well, I'll stake you for the rest of the day," Ben said. "You can put the savings in your piggybank."

"And rob it tomorrow," Marcie said. "Unless I get that job and an advance on my salary, I'll have to sell the car, Ben. Pronto."

"You know your radio is on the blink?"

"Oh, it just has a temperamental tube or something. A jolt or bump in the street can make it stop or start playing, depending on its mood. But I'm glad I brought it and it's paid for. It's some security, anyway."

"If Eddie doesn't try to claim it," Ben said.

Marcie sighed. "I dreamed about him last night, Ben, a wretched dream. Maybe I shouldn't have moved out that way, without even leaving a note."

During a stop for a red light, Ben turned to her. "Do you honestly think it would make any difference to him, Marcie, if you'd left a complete memoir?"

"I guess not," she agreed. "But it was an impulsive act, after I learned about the pictures. I didn't actually believe they existed, Ben. Why wouldn't you show them to me?"

They were moving again, down the island, toward the Battery. "Confidential material, Marcie, between client and agent."

"Was Client happy Agent found it?"

"Relieved," Ben said, ignoring the sarcasm.

240

"What made you suspect that girl, Ben?"

"A hunch, mostly. I had an idea she knew Eddie, after watching her watching his pad. That was another little hobby of his you weren't aware of, Marcie."

"His affairs?"

"His interest in pornography."

Marcie shivered in spite of the heat already steaming up from the asphalt, which was mushy in places, cracked and buckled in others like over-baked dough. The sun-glare and reflections off the concrete and pavement made her dig into her tote bag for her dark glasses.

"I wonder if Her Highness tossed him out of the tower?"

"Probably, although she's a little unpredictable herself."

"What'll he do now?"

"That's his problem, Marcie. Let him live by his wits. He'll manage, don't worry about that. My God, how can you still worry about him?"

"Habit," Marcie murmured.

"One he never formed about you, I'm sure."

"No, but he's incapable of feeling any deep emotion or concern for anyone or anything but himself, Ben. I think I've alyays known that but tried to ignore it. Eddie's utterly selfish and self-centered and weak—quite a miserable, desperate person, actually. And yet it's not entirely his fault, Ben. He's sick."

"I'll go along with that, Marcie. But can't we forget him for today? I've had my daily quota of Eddie Eden."

Luckily they didn't have to wait too long for space on the ferry to Liberty Island. Leaving the dock, Marcie watched the skyline of the city, made famous and familiar on millions of postcards, some of which had found their way to Rainbow. Just yesterday she had mailed one, with a brief message, to Aunt Beth. She thought of her aunt now, walking to church in her Sunday dress and little Milan straw hat with the faded silk violets. She thought of the dark-mirrored bayou and the quiet, shadowy swamp. It seemed years ago that she had left Louisiana, a lifetime in which she was a different person.

"You should be looking ahead," Ben told her. "Fore, not aft, Marcie. Face this way, toward the Statue."

She obeyed the urging of his hand on her elbow. He was right, of course. There was little to be gained looking back, except experience of a nature she hoped she'd never have practical need of.

The people were packed like cattle on the ferry, and they thundered down the gangplank when it landed. Then came the mad rush to line up for entry to the Statue, the hurrying through, the view from the upper reaches, the hurrying out again, and the stampede to the returning ferry. Maybe some were impressed, inspired, imbued with proper spirit, but most seemed to be more concerned with finding the restrooms, buying souvenirs and mailing cards and snapping pictures. Marcie observed their expressions and postures, slack with relief, as if to say, "Well, that's over. What's next?"

Marcie was one of the few who paused long enough to read the legend at the base of the Statue. She glanced up at the flag and the outstretched, torch-bearing arm and felt appropriate stirrings, almost embarrassed at her emotions, which were probably on the schnook-side these days.

"That poem ought to be compulsory in every public school," she said, "memorized along with the Pledge of Allegiance."

Ben smiled at her naiveté. "Some organization or other would protest to the Supreme Court until it was declared unconstitutional. The Lord's Prayer lost out to democracy, you know. How could a patriotic poem win?"

"I guess you're right," Marcie agreed. "Well, that's over. What's next?"

"The ferry."

In the car again, driving uptown, Ben said, "Grant's

Tomb is on most tourists' agendas, but some Southerners are not too keen about it."

Marcie knew he was teasing but scolded him, anyway. "Another crack like that, Ben Hale, and I'll get out and take a Greyline Tour."

"I can think of better things we could do today, dear."

"Shut up and drive."

"Yes, ma'am."

The long flights of steps to the Tomb tired Marcie, and it was really nothing but a gross monument, a granite sepulcher pretentious in its monolithic bulk and severity, and she was glad to proceed to the more interesting—architecturally, at least—Cloisters and the magnificent gardens of Fort Tryon Park. Ben took her to the observation terrace for a better view of the Hudson and the Palisades, and Marcie was thrilled.

"It's beautiful, Ben. I guess there's some beauty in this town, after all."

"If you know where to look," Ben said.

Marcie could have lingered there for hours and left reluctantly, marking it as a place to return. There was more than could be seen in a day, a month, a year. The United Nations must be reserved for another time. And Central Park. And Rockefeller Center, where she would probably work. And all the rest for other long lonely Sundays which would make up her personal calendar.

Now she was hot and weary, hungry and thirsty for a hamburger and a soda, and Ben suggested Coney Island, a mistake he knew the moment they arrived, people and umbrellas and towels and picnic baskets covering every square inch of space, every dry grain of sand, so that the only beach visible was that bordering the water. That's what the population explosion was all about, and it was not a new thing, it had been happening for years, as these hordes testified, and after fighting their way to a snackstand for some sustenance, Ben drove up Long Island for miles and miles, until he found a secluded stretch of duneland, where he dropped anchor.

"Nice," Marcie said. "Like the Gulf of Mexico."

"A sea is a sea is a sea," Ben said. "You know where I'd really like to take you?"

Marcie nodded. "Vermont. Mountains are mountains are mountains, Ben."

"And you were queered on them in the Smokies, is that it?" Marcie didn't answer, and he persisted, "I was born in Vermont, Marcie, and lived there for twenty years. I'm going to live there again someday, and I expect you to live with me."

"Why talk about it, Ben, when you know it can't happen?"

"It can, after the divorce."

"What divorce? It hasn't even been discussed yet, much less filed. And how can it be, if Eddie doesn't even know where I am to talk about it?"

"Let's walk awhile," Ben said abruptly.

"My feet hurt."

"Take your shoes off. Go barefoot, the way you were the first time I saw you."

"That was unfortunate," Marcie reflected.

"What was unfortunate, Marcie? Your being barefoot, or our meeting?"

Why did he always want explicit answers? Why couldn't he just accept the obvious? She shrugged, sighed, gazed out at the white-crested swells rushing toward shore. Ships moved on the horizon like pantomines on a watery stage, and airplanes soared overhead casting shadows like giant birds.

"It set off a series of events, Ben. A kind of chain reaction that's irrevocable and endless."

"All things end, Marcie. There is no perpetual motion."

"And how will this end, Ben?"

"How do you want it to end?"

"What difference does that make? You talk as if we were masters of our own fate."

"We can be," Ben told her somberly.

His voice had a sepulchral tone. Marcie glanced at him sharply. "How?"

"I want you to be free, Marcie. I want it so badly, I'd be willing to do almost anything to accomplish it." He hesitated slightly. "Even kill."

"Oh, for heaven's sake, Ben! That's idiotic, and you know you don't mean it."

"But I've thought of it, Marcie. Not in cold blood, not premeditated murder. But I'd like to find him in a situation or force him into one where it would be justifiable."

Marcie turned to the sea again, which was crashing ashore now, foaming and frothing at the edge. "I can't believe you're saying this, Ben, or that I'm sitting here listening to you. We must be mad, utterly mad, the two of us."

His eyes lingered on her, slate-gray and brooding, and then he laughed shortly. "Yeah, nuts. But circumstances like these are enough to drive people loco, Marcie. I want you so wildly, and you won't even let me touch you any more."

"Good grief! If that's the reason for your insanity—"

"It's not the only reason," Ben interrupted and opened the door swiftly. "Get out, Marcie. Let's walk."

"Yes, I think we'd better. Maybe we should go swiming? Cool off a bit."

"Did you bring a suit?"

"No."

"Would you go nude? In the broad daylight?"

"Would that be a crime?"

"It's against the law on a public beach."

Marcie gave him an oblique smile. "I'm glad you said that, glad you wouldn't want to break the law."

He looked sheepish. "So I was raving. Desperate with desire, as the effete novelists say. Forget it."

They walked for an hour, Marcie splashing barefoot in the surf, short skirt lifted shorter, delighting in the feel of the sand and water between her toes, the sea-spray on her thighs. She felt fresh and alive and hopeful and inexplicably free, unencumbered. She supposed the euphoria was generated by the vacant beach, the boundless water, the restless breeze in her hair, the gulls free-winging in the cloudless blue sky. Why weren't things as they appeared on the surface? Why did this have to be only a respite, an interlude, a brief escape from reality, like her former retreats in the Teche?

She posed the questions to Ben, but he had no satisfactory responses. He was still morose and pensive, seemingly sunk in despair over their dilemma, and his mood distressed and frustrated Marcie. "If I could squeeze that sour expression into a glass and add sugar, we'd have lemonade," she chided. "Is it a concentrate of unrequited love?"

"Just concentration," Ben said. "I'm meditating."

"On murder?"

"I told you to forget that."

"Why? It's obvious you haven't."

"All right, I'll admit I've considered it, and I think I'm capable of it, but that doesn't mean I'll do it, Marcie." He paused for emphasis. "Every human being is capable of murder, you know. That's a psychological fact I learned in criminology. Even you, my dear, have the potential. Didn't you consider killing me in the Smokies?"

"Why did you have to bring that up, Ben?"

"To make my point," he said.

"But I didn't kill you, Ben. I couldn't do it."

"Even if I had attacked you? I think you could have, Marcie, if you thought your life was in danger, that it was you or me. That wasn't the case, but it doesn't prove or disprove anything. Survival is the first instinct, and self-preservation the first law, and both as primitive and natural and normal as life itself."

"Perhaps," Marcie conceded. "But Eddie isn't threatening our lives, Ben, only our love."

"That's a pretty vital instinct too, Marcie."

"I don't want to talk about it any more," Marcie broke off abruptly. "Take off your shoes and roll up your pants, Ben. Walk in the water with me. It's great fun. Cooling, refreshing, cleansing. Makes you feel like a kid again. Come play with me."

"If you'll play with me later."

"All right, but where? We can't go to your place, and men aren't allowed in the rooms at mine. They don't call it the Abbey for nothing."

"Why did you choose it?"

"Because it's economical, and I thought it would be a deterrent to sin. I guess I should have known better."

"There's a blanket in the car," Ben suggested.

"For unexpected blizzards?"

"For anticipated heat waves."

The sun had moved westward, slanting over Connecticut and New Jersey. But darkness was still hours away, and the lovers were impetuous and went into the dunes.

"This is the second time on the ground," Marcie said.

"We didn't have a blanket the other time."

"It's rough as cockleburs. Scratches."

"Wool. GI issue. Courtesy of Uncle Sam."

"Stolen love on stolen property."

"I think I earned it," Ben said. "The blanket, not the love."

"But isn't it illegal on a public beach? Indecent exposure or something?"

"Something," Ben said. "Illegal entry, maybe. It'll be rape if you keep stalling."

"You told me in Alabama that you weren't a rapist. You said you'd never raped a woman."

"I said a lot of things."

"You mean you have?"

"Not technically, no. But there's a first time for everything."

"I know," she said. "It happened to me."

"Eddie?"

"Yes. Our wedding night. I was eighteen and still a

247

virgin, naive and reluctant. He got tired and frustrated and impatient."

"I know the feeling."

"I hated him that night but I loved him, too. You can hate and love at the same time."

"Yes," Ben said. He had felt that way more than once with Dale. Like all emotions, love and hate had many nuances and crescendos, sometimes so closely related in cause and effect, so intermingled in essence as to be indistinguishable. "Maybe that's what makes it so interesting."

Marcie slipped off her panties, a wisp of white nylon, and then was embarrassed because she didn't know what to do with them. It seemed immoral to leave them in sight. She tucked them into her tote bag. "Maybe we should get in the car?" she suggested.

"No, too hot and crowded. And teenage stuff."

"Drive-in movies," Marcie nodded. "I knew some girls in high school who never saw the pictures they went to see. Some of the more enterprising kids sold résumés for a quarter. I used to wonder what I was missing."

"Now you know."

"It's better in bed."

"Relax, baby. Release yourself."

"I can't. All those planes overhead."

"Air traffic is heavy today. Tourists."

"Do you think they can see us down here?"

"Does it matter?"

"Not really."

"Marcie, you're not going to talk me out of this."

"I'm not trying to, Ben."

"Well, let go, then. You're tense and tight. We'll be here for hours."

"You think so?" She opened her mouth to his, tasted his tongue. "Salty," she murmured.

"Your's too. But sweet, like salt-water taffy."

"I love you," she whispered, as if she feared someone might hear as well as see them.

"Why are you whispering?"

"It just seems to go with the occasion." Her fingers traced his lips, the contour of his jaw. "I guess this is what love is all about, really. Worry and wonder and whispering. Wanting and needing. Pain and grief and hunger."

"Pain?"

"Yes. It hurts, Ben. Not physically, but it hurts."

"I know, darling. Oh God, how I know!"

"Love me, Ben, and don't play Yoga this time. Finish with me, together."

"Tell me when."

But the act was not without its tragedy, its pathos and poignancy. Some disenchantment invariably followed the enchantment. Marcie did not know why this should be, why something so seemingly perfect must have imperfections, she only knew it was so for her, and she could not face him immediately afterwards and kept her eyes averted.

"Turn your back," she said.

"Why?"

"I have to put on my pants, and you have to zip yours."

"You're embarrassed," Ben said. "Why are you always embarrassed afterwards?"

"I'm not, always. Just in the woods and on beaches."

"You're inhibited."

"Only with lovers."

"You want me to apologize?"

"Of course not."

"We've got to get married," Ben said. "You couldn't take a long affair."

"Let's not go into that again."

"Into what?"

"Removing the obstacle."

"Marcie, don't spoil this," Ben pleaded. "It was wonderful—don't ruin it now, please."

"Oh, Ben!" She caught him to her breast. "Forgive

me, forgive me. It was beautiful, darling. Lovely, lovely. But it's over, and I have to go back to that awful hotel, and I'm afraid it'll always be that way, it'll never be any different."

"Hush," Ben said roughly. "Hush, Marcie, or I'll change things tonight."

"No, that's not what I meant!" she cried and held him tighter. "Promise me?"

"All right, darling, all right. But you've got to get an apartment."

"The rent will have to be reasonable."

"I'll pay it," Ben offered and knew it was a mistake even before she looked at him. "Okay, I won't pay it. You're difficult to do business with, you know that?"

"Really? I thought I was pretty easy. Besides, why buy the cow when you can get the milk free?"

"Goddamn it, Marcie!"

She laughed and kissed him. "Turn your back, lover."

chapter
24

THEY WERE CROSSING the Queensborough bridge when a sudden application of the brakes jolted the inert radio into action in the middle of a newscast. There was a communiqué from Vietnam, a comment from the President at the White House, and then the announcer's voice assumed a bored air of repetition, as if he'd been reading the next bulletin periodically for hours and was weary of it.

"Silver Haddington, well-known member of the International Jet Set and heiress to the Haddington Enterprises, multimillion dollar corporation, shot and killed an intruder in her Manhattan penthouse early this morning.

"The victim was Eddie Eden, singer and nightclub entertainer. According to Miss Haddington's statement to police, she had a casual acquaintance with Eden, whom she had engaged to entertain at some of her parties, but apparently Mr. Eden decided to try a Raffles act and victimize his wealthy patroness, who awakened at about three o'clock this morning to find him attempting to burglarize her private safe.

"Miss Haddington, the former Countess de Martinique, who just last year figured in a sensational divorce trial from the European nobleman, told police that she had taken some pain pills for a migraine headache earlier and, dazed with drugs and sleep, did not recognize the handsome young singer before firing the fatal shots. Miss Haddington's physician was later called to the scene to administer a sedative, and she is in seclusion in her tower now. Police are conducting an investigation. Further details as we have them. Now here's a word about an effective remedy for headaches and other minor discomforts. . . ."

Ben silenced the commercial. Marcie was stunned, speechless and immobile, shocked into a kind of catatonic mood. Traffic from Long Island into Manhattan was extremely heavy at that hour of the evening, and it was awhile before Ben could exit from the main artery and park on a side street, and by then Marcie had recovered somewhat.

"He's been dead all day," she said incredulously, "and I didn't know it. I didn't even know it!"

This in itself was strange and bewildering, as if they'd been castaways on a remote and inaccessible island somewhere, and were just now returning to civilization. How could such a thing happen in this day and age of rapid, almost instant communication? How was it possible that they had not so much as heard a transistor radio while on the sightseeing tour or the beach at Coney, or paid any attention if they had? How was it possible to be surrounded by millions of people and yet be alone? She had heard that this was a phenomenal fact in New York, but until now she had not believed it.

Trying to comfort her, Ben said an uncomforting thing. "It was inevitable, Marcie. With a man like Eddie, it was inevitable. He was destined to die violently."

Marcie couldn't weep for her husband just then; she knew she would later, but now stronger emotions claimed her. "Do you believe her story, Ben? You know Silver Haddington—do you think she's telling the truth, that it really happened as she says?"

"Yes, I do, Marcie. She had no reason to kill Eddie

once she had those pictures. His hold over her was gone, but he still did not have what he wanted most from her. She refused to cooperate with him in any of his desires or demands, and he was desperate enough to try to take what she wouldn't give. There'll be an investigation, of course. But she won't be indicted, and even if she were, no jury in the land would convict her."

"I'm not sure I agree with you, Ben. She's rich and probably very clever, but I don't believe she's completely innocent in this. I think Eddie was victimized as much as she, and I think she knew what she was doing when she shot him."

"You thought she knew about the photos in advance too, remember? But I assure you she didn't, Marcie. She was asleep, either drunk or drugged, but definitely oblivious. If you'd seen them you'd know."

Marcie felt chilled, as if a cold wind had swept up from the East River. She shivered and bit her quivering lips to steady them. "Do you think she still has them?"

"I don't know, but I imagine she destroyed them," Ben said. "She'd be a fool not to, and she's not a fool."

"You seem to admire her?"

"I respect her intelligence," Ben said, "although she doesn't always use it. I hope she will in this instance. At any rate, she has a battery of attorneys at her service should she need legal or moral advice and assistance. A crime has to be either admitted or established before a person can be accused and formally arraigned, Marcie. And the only witness she needs in her behalf, the only evidence necessary to support her testimony, are Eddie's fingerprints on her safe. I'd be willing to bet they were there."

"You're defending her!" Marcie accused. "You're on her side!"

"The law is on her side, Marcie. I'm just trying to show you that."

"And where would the law have the victim now?" she asked angrily.

"The city morgue," Ben replied.

"And he's been there all day, lying in an icebox while we were diddling on the dunes?" The memory repelled her now, was suddenly repugnant and even sordid, as such spontaneous sexual indulgence frequently was in retrospect, and her face burned with shame. "Oh, God."

"There has to be an autopsy," Ben explained calmly, "or already has been. His next-of-kin will have to identify and claim the body before it can be released for burial."

Marcie swallowed a convulsive sob. "That's me."

"Yes." Ben pressed her hand, and like an impulse lever his touch triggered her tears. He held her gently until she quieted. "I'll go with you."

"No! They'd wonder about our connection. That'd be incriminating."

"We're not guilty of anything, Marcie."

"Aren't we, Ben?"

"Love is not a crime."

"But it has led to crime, hasn't it, directly and indirectly? We'd have to do some confessing of our own, wouldn't we? Tell the whole story?"

"No," Ben said, "only the part that concerns Eddie and us. His connection with the Dobbs Agency will naturally come out in the investigation, but it won't do any damage unless the grand jury doesn't accept Miss Haddington's account as conclusive."

"And what if she's lying to protect herself, Ben, or telling only half truths? What if Eddie's fingerprints are *not* on the safe?"

"They are," Ben said confidently, as positive as if he had found them there himself. "All of her story may not be true, but you can count on that part."

"Why?" demanded Marcie. "If he really intended to rob her, wouldn't he have worn gloves?"

"Did he wear gloves in summer?"

"No, but he didn't go around robbing safes, either!"

"There're lots of angles to this, Marcie. He probably didn't consider it robbery in the strict sense and didn't

254

expect it to come to light, since Miss Haddington would have found it tedious to report, to say the least. Furthermore, she takes drugs to sleep, and he knew he'd have time to wipe off his prints if he thought it necessary. But I don't doubt that he knew the combination of that safe, Marcie. He'd gotten money from it before, but Silver gave it to him. Payment for entertaining her, in more ways than one."

"Did you have to say that?"

"You knew it, Marcie. I told you before."

"Well, I won't lie about us, Ben. If I'm questioned, I'll tell the truth."

"Certainly. But don't go to pieces and volunteer information that has no bearing on the case, Marcie. Don't cast doubt and suspicion where none exists. We're not directly involved in whatever happened in Silver Haddington's penthouse this morning, and there's no legal reason to involve us."

"What about moral reasons, Ben? We're morally involved in this mess whether you think so or not, and whether we like it or not. How will I explain my presence in New York? How will I explain not living in my husband's apartment in the Village, why I moved only yesterday to the Abbey? How will I explain my whereabouts and actions today?"

"Good Lord! You're not accused of anything, Marcie! You don't have to explain any of that unless you want to. You can drag us into this, sure, but it won't change what's happened, and it damned sure won't make it any easier for anyone, least of all you. You have no experience in this game, Marcie. The reporters will make mincemeat of you."

She began to cry again. "Oh, Ben, help me!"

"You're just having an attack of conscience, darling," Ben said, embracing her again. "You need a sedative. Have you any tranquilizers with you or in your room?"

"No, I don't use them."

"Well, maybe some aspirin would help."

She had aspirin, carried it in her handbag, and gagged trying to swallow a couple of tablets without water.

The city had entered its hectic evening pace. Glaring lights and blaring sounds. Flashing neon tubes, spasmodic bulbs. Traffic noises, hurrying humanity, a ceaseless cacophony alien to Marcie's ear. Wild music, wilder laughter, the intense frenzy, the infectious hysteria of nightfall, the special madness of Manhattan. It was like being caught in the midway of some gigantic carnival, Marcie thought; trapped in a broken Ferris wheel that threatened to spin endlessly in eternity.

"Feel any better?" Ben asked solicitously.

"Not much," she answered. "Sort of dizzy."

"It's ironic," Ben mused. "Eddie wanted publicity, preferably notoriety. He wanted his named linked sensationally in the news with Silver Haddington's. In a way, he got his wish. He'll make the headlines, all right."

"Take me to the police station, Ben."

"Not yet, Marcie. Wait a little longer. You have to get better control of yourself."

"Ben, this is just procrastination. You know I have to go there sooner or later."

"Yes." He started the motor. "And you'll have to make a statement for the record, Marcie. So will I. Routine procedure. I used to be on the Police Force, you know. I still work on cases with the Department. Answer all questions truthfully, but don't deviate and don't volunteer irrelevant material. Above all, don't mention the pictures unless you want Eddie to appear to be a pornographer and a pervert, in addition to a thief, and turn this whole affair into the damnedest scandal this scandalous town has ever seen."

Marcie sighed forlornly. "I couldn't do that to Eddie's family. I couldn't add that horror to their grief. This is going to be difficult enough for them to bear. They're such religious people."

"Too bad their son wasn't," Ben said.

Lieutenant Dean Morse, who had gone off duty at seven o'clock that morning, was back on again, and very glad to see Mrs. Edward Eden, whom the police had been trying to locate all day. Her appearance in the company of Ben Hale added an interesting aspect to this bizarre case, which he suspected had more facets than those reflected in the Haddington penthouse, further intriguing him, but he was well aware of his limitations in a situation of this sort.

Extending his sympathy to the young widow, he thought she looked stricken but not especially surprised, almost as if she had expected her husband to meet such an end. In twelve years of relaying such tidings to the next of kin, Lieutenant Morse had become adept in detecting every nuance of reaction, from genuine shock and bereavement to relief and even gladness. What he recognized in Marcie Eden was acceptance, resignation. He said they'd tried finding someone from Mr. Eden's agency who could assist them in their search for her, but Sunday was a bad day for getting information, most business establishments being closed and people away on pleasure. Which was the perfect lead for Marcie to explain her whereabouts and Ben Hale as her escort. Fortunately, Ben knew Dean Morse well and took over when Marcie faltered.

"The hell of it, Dean, is that we only learned of this half-an-hour ago. Didn't tune in the car radio all day, because it was acting up—a loose connection or filament somewhere that comes and goes. I was trying to show Mrs. Eden something of the town and its environs, and we were driving back from Long Island when the news program came on. Naturally I brought her here immediately."

"How do you happen to know each other?" Morse asked.

"It's a long story," Ben said.

"I got time, and I'm paid to listen."

Ben smiled at his old friend, with whom he'd worked on many cases during his tenure on the Force and since. "Would you like a formal report, Dean? From the time Eddie Eden hired me to escort his wife from Louisiana to New York?"

This interested the officer. "Escort?"

"Yeah, check with Harvey Dobbs."

"Why, if you say so, why should I check? You're saying that Mr. Eden hired protection for Mrs. Eden?"

"That was his contract," Ben said.

"Why?"

"The reason he gave Dobbs and me was that he didn't want her traveling alone by car."

"There are other ways of traveling," Morse said.

"She happened to be coming by car," Ben said. "Eden hired Dobbs' escort service. I got the duty."

"When did you and Mrs. Eden arrive?"

"Last Wednesday, about midnight."

The lieutenant addressed Marcie. "You staying in your husband's apartment in Greenwich Village, Mrs. Eden?"

It was obvious that they had tried finding her there, and Marcie answered without evasion. "Not since yesterday."

"May I ask why not?"

Marcie gazed down at the small white hands lying limply in her lap. "We quarreled. I moved to the Abbey."

"Why did you quarrel?"

"I found some things that made me suspect that my husband was seeing another woman or women," she replied.

"What things?"

Without mentioning his name, Marcie ennumerated some of the items Ben had discovered in his search of the studio.

"Do you have any idea who this party or parties might be?" Morse inquired.

Marcie shook her head negatively.

"Answer verbally, please. It's hard to record a motion."

"No, I don't know the party or parties. But it wouldn't have been an unusual situation for my husband, Lieutenant. He frequently had girl friends on his tours."

Ben tried to catch her eye subtly. She was forgetting his admonition, volunteering unrequested information.

Morse proceeded, "If that's the case, why was he solicitous of your well-being on the trip up here, Mrs. Eden? That seems a little incongruous to me."

Marcie considered her words before replying. "I'm not sure solicitous is the right word, Lieutenant. He really didn't want me to come at all. But I had a vacation, and I was determined. We'd been apart for three months, and frankly our marriage was in trouble. It had never been too solid, and it was shakier than ever. But I couldn't possibly mend or stabilize it from that geographic distance, and I thought the trip was my last hope. Evidently, I was wrong. Mistaken. It only split us farther apart."

Without glancing at Ben, Morse continued, "And so you turned to Mr. Hale for comfort?"

"If you want to put it that way, Lieutenant. I didn't know anyone else in New York, and this can be a terribly big and lonely place if you're alone."

Ben was proud of the way Marcie was handling herself now; he tried not to betray his pride through his own conduct.

Morse persisted, as if there was something he couldn't quite put his finger on, a missing key or link somewhere which puzzled and intrigued him. "That still doesn't explain why your husband hired Ben Hale in the first place."

"Doesn't it, Lieutenant? It was so apparent to me, I imagined it would be to anyone. As I said before, my husband didn't relish the idea of my coming to New

York. even on vacation, but he also knew that he couldn't keep me away, once I'd made up my mind. I can be stubborn about things I believe in, and I believed our marriage was doomed unless we could get back together and try to salvage it. My husband knew Mr. Hale slightly and told me on the telephone that he was sending a friend to escort me to New York, since I insisted on bringing the car, and he didn't want me alone on the road, this being summertime and there being riots and all that sort of commotion in this country now. I'm sure my husband knew that if he'd told me Mr. Hale was a private detective it wouldn't have stopped my plans, I'd just have taken a plane and arrived even sooner, which he definitely didn't want. In addition, I think he hoped that Mr. Hale and I would become friends during the journey, thereby lessening his responsibilities and obligations to me when I arrived in New York. And for this he was willing to pay a fee."

"And did you and Mr. Hale become friends?"

"Fortunately, yes," Marcie answered clearly and firmly. "I'd have been lost here otherwise, because my husband simply did not want to be bothered with me."

"I see," the Officer said and Marcie expected him to pursue the issue further, but he tried another tack. "Did you know that your husband knew Silver Haddington?"

"I knew that he had entertained at some of her social affairs," Marcie replied evenly. "He was proud and pleased at the opportunity."

"Did you suspect that there might be more than a business relationship between them?"

Marcie's hesitation suggested a wife's natural reluctance to face such a possibility. "I suspect that my husband might have preferred more than a business relationship with a woman of Miss Haddington's prestige and prominence."

Bravo! Ben thought. He hadn't needed to worry about her control in the clinches, after all. She never lost her cool for a moment, gaining in poise and imperturbability as the relentless law pressed and progressed, and again Ben had to dim his personal beam of pride in her. Let Dean Morse, the old pro, the old vet, make what he could of that, which was nothing.

His next inquiry was directed at Ben. "Eden wasn't working steady, Ben. You got any idea where he got the money to hire a private eye, whatever his personal reasons? I know the services of Dobbs' boys come high."

Ben shrugged. "Dobbs' boys don't have access to client's bank accounts, if any, and Eden's financial condition is a mystery to me. But I do know that he liked to gamble. Maybe he hit a lucky streak. Actually, he never paid Dobbs the full fee, only a small part of it for traveling expenses."

Dean Morse put the tips of his long bony fingers together, his hands forming a tepee structure which he appeared to contemplate. Ben was familiar with this habit of his, a trick he employed when he had run out of pertinent questions and was hoping for volunteer information. But inadvertently—or perhaps not so inadvertently—Ben Hale had given him a possible motive for Eddie Eden's attempted burglary: he could have been under pressure to pay a gambling debt and driven by desperation to his own funeral.

"That everything?" he asked finally, shifting his eyes from one to the other of them. "Want to add anything?"

Ben said he couldn't think of anything more he wanted to include, and Marcie said she couldn't, either. The statements would be typed up for their signatures.

"Well," Morse said, "I guess that about wraps it up, except for one thing."

Marcie started visibly and turned pale in the face, the normal reaction to the ghastly prospect, and Lieutenant Morse wished he could spare her.

"Sorry, Mrs. Eden, but we need your identification," he explained. "It's the law."

Marcie nodded. "I understand, Lieutenant."

"Help her, Ben," Morse said, and Ben, who'd been exerting effort to remain physically detached, now took Marcie's arm and urged her to her feet for the grim journey to the morgue.

chapter
25

EXCEPT FOR THE BROAD GENERALITIES of war and catastrophe, it is people, not events, that make news, and Silver Haddington was a newsmaker supreme. Her birth had hit the front pages, and every event of interest or consequence in her life since had been printed, along with many of no significance. She was the kind of character out of which contemporary writers made fortunes in poorly camouflaged "biographical novels." She had enjoyed little privacy even in her cradle, her first steps and words zealously if not always accurately recorded in the women's sections of the leading papers and magazines, her wardrobes from her layette on described in the fashion-books. Kidnaping attempts had shadowed her childhood, and she had been surrounded by bodyguards and watchdogs. Protection accompanied her to and from school, on the playground, in the swimming pool, on the bridal path. Her debut was the social affair of the season, her first serious romance avidly awaited, her first marriage an international event, her first divorce an international scandal. She had no private life and no one, least of all the reporters, seemed to think she was entitled to privacy even when she went to bed or bathed or made love. People wanted to know if she slept nude, what kind of soap she used, and who was her latest lover.

Ordinarily the inquest would have been a routine formality required by law in the death of persons from other than natural causes, and largely ignored by the press. Because of Silver Haddington's involvment, no such anonymity was possible in the case of Eddie Eden, and by association a largely unknown person was suddenly thrust into prominence. Intrigue and conspiracy were hinted at, old myths and legends revived, and assumptions twisted into as much sensationalism as could be invented and printed within legal propriety. There was little doubt among the members of the media that Silver Haddington was capable of murder, premeditated or otherwise, and Melissa Stone, for one, would have happily tried, convicted, and executed the lady in her *Sun-Globe* column if that were only possible and permissible. The enmity between the two women was a long-standing feud, an active vendetta, dating back to their Radcliffe days, where some of their friends thought that Melissa Stone was pursuing a career in journalism primarily as a means of plaguing Silver Haddington.

And in this one instance, at least, she had Marcie Eden's support, even though Miss Stone did not show Mrs. Eden much sympathy or compassion, either. She referred to Marcie as "the hapless widow in this bizzarre happening" and to Ben Hale as "that handsome bloodhound whose keen nostrils sniffed out the unsavory evidence that allowed the former Countess de Martinique to slough the nobleman with the customary recompense and slay his character if not the man."

Silver Haddington, flanked by an attorney and a physician, had long since developed, if not an actual immunity to this form of pen poison, an effective antidote to it. She knew she was suspect in the eyes of the more jaundiced journalists, and felt that she might as well be accused of murder and forced to stand trial, and that even acquittal would not acquit her. Nevertheless, she endured the ordeal with practiced grace and acquired equanimity (hysteria and its attendant emotions having been bred out of the distaff side of the Haddingtons generations ago), and it was precisely this nonchalance, bordering on insouciance, which Marcie resented the most. How calm and cool she appeared, even frigid in her glacial white linen, which Melissa Stone, who knew about such things, described as an original by Jackie Onassis' favorite designer, Givenchy. Reigning royalty could not have affected more imperious imperviousness. She could blast that serenity, Marcie thought vindictively, crack that composure if she chose. And once she had to suppress a vicious impulse to mention the photographs, not out of a sense of justice but a feminine, wifely desire for revenge. This serene slut, this tranquil trollop, who looked like a marble statue brushed with silverdust, had stolen her husband, seduced and shot him, and whatever the circumstances, Marcie Eden, like Melissa Stone, did not believe that Silver Haddington was entirely guiltless and thought she deserved some kind of punishment.

"This inquest is a travesty of justice," she complained to Ben during a recess.

"No, just a satire of it."

"A mockery," Marcie insisted. "And she's enjoying it, Ben. She's the star in a new drama. She'll probably take curtain calls when it's over."

"Is that what you think? You're wrong, Marcie. She hates publicity. But she's learned that old adage about accepting what you cannot change."

"You're defending her again," Marcie accused angrily. "Miss Silver Pure in her immaculate white."

"I'm just accepting what *I* can't change, Marcie. Why don't you? It's sound advice."

"Words, Ben. *Bon mots* and bagatelles. They sound good in a writer's vocabulary, but they don't have much meaning outside of fiction."

"You're being stubborn," Ben said.

"That's just a word, too," Marcie told him. "I can't

help what I feel, Ben, and I feel that she is guilty as sin. I think she killed Eddie in cold blood."

"It doesn't matter what you think or feel, Marcie. Intuition doesn't count for much in a situation like this. Facts determine the outcome. It's a case of law."

"And the law is never wrong?"

"I didn't say that."

"Then you admit she could be shading the facts, if not actually twisting them? Lying?"

"That's not for me to decide."

"Oh, don't quote the law to me again, Ben! There are loopholes in that statute of self-defense big enough for an elephant to jump through, and you know it!"

Ben pushed his cigarette into a jar of sand. "The hearing is about to resume. Come on, Marcie. Let's go back inside."

Marcie went reluctantly. She resented Ben's obstinate defense of Silver Haddington, as if he were under a strong compulsion to believe her innocent. But perhaps he was just grateful to her, she rationalized, as the principals filed back into the chamber. And why not? She had removed an enemy he himself had contemplated eliminating. He had murdered Eddie in his heart and mind, which should make him morally guilty of his death. And what about her own mental murder of Ben Hale in the Smoky Mountains? They were all culpable, all guilty. They should all be punished.

But the coroner's jury weighed only the facts in hand, and found no evidence that a crime had been committed. The victim's fingerprints on the Haddington safe were irrefutable proof that he had attempted to burglarize it, and Marcie still wondered why he hadn't bothered to wear gloves if that was his intent and purpose. The doctor's testimony on the medication his patient was under at the time and its effects on the faculties, corroborated Silver's account of her irrationality. The attorney's inventory of some of the valuable possessions in the penthouse substantiated her need for a weapon of protection. How the culprit had entered the premises, how he had known the location of the vault, how well the owner had or had not known him, seemed inconsequential to the law. A potential thief had been caught in the act, and Silver Haddington had acted in defense of her person and property. And the law was specific in this respect, clearly defined, pragmatic. The case was adjudged justifiable homicide, and closed.

But it did not end there.

Ironically, Eddie Eden had created a sensation in death that he couldn't in life and attained a following in memory that evaded him in reality. Almost immediately a cult formed to venerate a man whom most had not known, seen, or even heard of before his notoriety. His pictures, along with Silver Haddington's, appeared in papers across the country and abroad. *Life, Look, Time* devoted space to the curious incident, and even the *Wall Street Journal* speculated on its market effect on the Haddington Enterprises stock. Feature writers besieged Eddie Eden's agency for information, any bits and pieces of personality, any swatches of character fabric to fashion into "human interest stories." A publisher approached the widow with a contract to write The Happening, lending her name, that is, to a ghost-written tale. A couple of flop records on an insignificant label were resurrected, hundreds of thousands more pressed out and peddled, and the "in" disc jockeys spun them as frequently and fervently as ever they had the hits of Elvis Presley, the Beatles, Fabian, and others. The nightclub which had canceled Eddie's act weeks before, now capitalized on his former appearance at the Amber Alley as "the scene where Eddie Eden sang his swan song." He was a posthumous success, a *cause célèbre*, a NAME, a VIP, because one had killed him. And when finally his coffin was loaded aboard a baggage car on a southbound train, a *Variety* reporter commented sentimentally, "Eddie Eden takes his last trip." A fitting tribute, Ben Hale thought grimly, for a devotee of LSD. Nevertheless, the

Cajun Cat had finally achieved a measure of fame and immortality. The Teche Troubadour glowed temporarily with a fallout of luminous stardust.

Silver Haddington had done that much for him and through Ben Hale had offered to do more, in financing his funeral expenses, including a bronze casket and shipping costs, but Marcie had scorned this generosity, shocked and indignant.

"Blood money," she said bitterly. "I won't let her ease her conscience that way, Ben. I've sold the car, and his agency assures me there'll be royalties from his records. I might even accept that publisher's advance for his life story. I just might get mercenary and greedy, after all."

"Don't talk that way, Marcie, even if you don't mean it," Ben said at the railroad station. "And I know you don't mean it." He touched her hand. "Let me go with you, Marcie. Let me see you through the rest of this."

Marcie shook her head. "No, this is something I have to do alone, Ben. There are some things all of us have to bear alone, and this is my thing and my time." She held out her hand. "Goodbye, Ben."

"This is not goodbye, Marcie. If you don't come back to me, I'll come after you. That's a promise."

She smiled wistfully. It sounded like a scene from a novel he had written, or might someday write. The whole affair seemed unreal to her, like something out of a book or a play or a dream.

"Life is full of promises, Ben."

"I usually keep mine, Marcie."

The conductor was giving his last call to board the train. Marcie glanced around her, in the hope of seeing some sunlight. But the depot was underground, and there was only shadow.

"We'll see," she said. "We'll see."

Although her exit from earth was more gruesome and in a sense more spectacular than Eddie Eden's, Tawny Mane, neé Agnes Mertz, didn't fare as well in her publicity. She received only scant notice on the back pages of the dailies. Her landlady had discovered the body, already partially decomposed, when she had come in the hope of collecting some overdue rent. Receiving no answer to her knock, and detecting an odor which she thought might be a dead cat, Mrs. Hibble had used her passkey to enter the basement flat, and immediately summoned the police.

Lieutenant Dean Morse, assigned also to this case, conducted the customary investigation. Did Miss Mane have any enemies? None that Mrs. Hibble knew of. Any boy-friends? Several, one fairly regular one lately. Did Mrs. Hibble know his name? Well, she wasn't sure, but tenant rumors said he was a singer from the club where they'd both worked.

The law proceeded diligently to the Amber Alley to question the proprietor. Yeah, he knew Tawny Mane, sure he knew her, the kid had danced there awhile, did a thing with veils, not very good but she was well-stacked, played the bill before Eddie Eden. Yeah, them two knew each other, sure they did, and even seemed to be making out, if the Lieutenant knew what he meant.

The Lieutenant knew even without the myopic wink.

"But say, do me a big favor, will you, and don't mention this to the papers? I mean, about her playing here. I wouldn't want it to get around. One violent death—that's good for publicity. But two—you know how superstitious show biz folks are, they wouldn't believe it was just coincidence. Hell, I couldn't get none of them kooks to play here until the hex was removed, and I might go broke meantime. You know what I mean? You understand?"

Lieutenant Morse knew and understood, but it went into his report anyway, and that was as much as was ever done about the Tawny Mane case, which, with its only clues pointing to a dead man, would remain unsolved in the files of Homicide. In a city which averaged over six hundred murders per year, one more wasn't noticed much when the victim was a nonentity. The press wasn't interested, and the public just then was still too busy reading about Silver Haddington and Eddie Eden to pay attention to the few lines devoted to the ill-timed murder of an ill-fated dancer with the improbable name of Tawny Mane, and her body traveled westward to Bee's Mill, Indiana, soon after Eddie Eden's went south to Rainbow, Louisiana.

chapter
26

SILVER HADDINGTON WAS HOLDING a press conference. The news coterie had begun to gather in the Regal Towers at eight that morning, presenting their press cards like calling cards to the uniformed maid at the door. The subject was not scheduled to appear until ten, and even then she was late, letting them squirm and speculate, aware that they were more eager for the meeting than she.

When finally she appeared, she was impeccably groomed as always, but more severely attired than any of them had ever before seen her, in a high-necked, long-sleeved black silk dress and black accessories, without so much as a single ornament to detract from its severity. Her couturier considered this an appropriate costume for one about to embark on a distant journey to a demure destination, a land of remote monasteries and sacred shrines, which was the advance information provided the press.

"Shades of Shangri-la!" Melissa Stone had exclaimed upon first receiving the news at her office in the *Sun-Globe*. "I bet the Dalai Lama is a muscular beast."

Her secretary said, "This is the Tashi Lama, and the info says he's an old man. An ancient."

"Don't contradict me," her boss snapped. "Anyway, why couldn't she go to that yogi's ashram on the Ganges, like everyone else? Why does she always have to be different and hibernate in some goddamn stone-pile in the Himalayas? I didn't even know they accepted students or disciples or converts or whatever the hell you call 'em! She must own the mortgage on the monastery."

Miss Stone was miffed because Miss Haddington's proclivity for initiating fads rather than emulating them would result in extra work for her. She had done research on the Maharishi Mahesh Yogi, the Guru from Rishikesh, for articles on Mia Farrow and the Beatles and other famous personalities, and could have whipped out a feature on Silver Haddington in no time with a few pertinent changes. Now she'd have to bone up on the history and philosophy of Lamaism, about which she was comparatively if not totally ignorant, and the prospect annoyed her.

"She's not going to the monastery proper," the secretary dared to differ again. "It's a colony supervised by the lamas of this particular sect, a retreat for laymen. Something new, I understand. A sort of experiment."

"Competition for the yogis, that's all," Melissa Stone declared authoritatively. "Everybody's getting into the act, out to lure the celebrities and all the publicity they can for their crazy cults and creeds. But if moral impetus is a requisite for success, they're going to experience a miserable failure with this prospect."

Now, loaded with ammunition, Miss Stone awaited her turn on the firing line with her comrades-in-arms, unimpressed by the surroundings, since she lived in comparable elegance herself. Her dress was a Dior original, her hat by Dache, and her alligator shoes cost eighty-five dollars. She sat with pencil poised over pad, thinking that the pen was not really mightier than the sword, after all, for despite her many hopefully fatal throat slashings of Silver Haddington, she still lived, perched on her pinnacle from which not even "justifiable homicide" had removed her, symbolizing the perpetual power and indestructibility of wealth. A less affluent figure would have long since toppled and crumbled under the repeated attacks. She did her heritage proud in this respect, if no other, in that she was apparently as invincible as her Revolutionary War ancestors, formidable as the Plymouth Rock of her foundation.

A description of the target's ensemble busied Miss Stone's shorthand. In all honesty, she could describe it as no less than elegant in design, dramatic in simplicity. Contrived and affected, obviously, but *effective*. If she were going to an abbey to meditate on her past, to repent of her sins, she was certainly not going in sackcloth and ashes—nor did she imagine that forsaking her jewelry was the supreme sacrifice and penance. She was sedate, subdued, but hardly demure, and definitely not prostrate.

Ben Hale, the only person present whom Silver Haddington had personally invited to her farewell party, stood at the back of the gathering, leaning against a brocaded wall, observing the bizzarre proceedings with interest and curiosity, wondering what the finale would be, what Silver Haddington could possibly do for an encore.

"Miss Haddington," said Miss Stone, who had consistently refused to address her any other way even when Silver was a baroness and a countess. "Could you tell us exactly what prompted this decision? I mean, it's not in keeping with your religion or philosophy, is it?"

"It's in keeping with my desire for a period of rest and seclusion," Silver replied to her arch enemy. "A time in which to meditate and re-evalute my life."

"Sort of a spiritual retreat from reality?" asked another columnist, a bored man who had not bothered to bare his head in obeisance to nobility, and was plainly disappointed, actually disgruntled, because he had expected to be treated to champagne and caviar on this bon voyage wing-ding.

"You might call it that," Silver answered. "Some religious orders do this periodicly, you know."

Cynicism pervaded Melissa Stone's smile. If she were referring to convent orders and trying to affect a habit in her severe garb, nuns everywhere would be shocked and insulted. But she had to give the creature credit for courage and originality. No ingenue, this one, but an accomplished actress portraying "Another Silver" and inviting the press to witness the debut of her new personality.

"Do you plan to fast and abstain?" she asked. It was a loaded question.

"I shall follow the prescribed diet and routine," came the amiable answer, "whatever it entails."

"How long do you expect to remain in seclusion?" a male voice in the group inquired in a tone suggesting that he hoped forever, since this sort of insignificant stuff disgusted him.

"As long as it takes to find what I seek, Mr. Davidson. Peace of mind, heart, and soul."

"That's a large order," a cynic observed.

"I shall be happy and content and grateful to fill only a small part of it," Miss Haddington qualified.

"Would you call this a pilgrimage, essentially?"

"Essentially," Silver nodded.

"I understand one of the beliefs of Lamaism is reincarnation. Do you share that belief, Miss Haddington?"

"I haven't thought much about it." Silver said.

"Do you plan to embrace mysticism?"

"Why not?" Melissa Stone murmured in sotto voce. "She's embraced everything else."

A titter ran through the group which escaped Silver Haddington's hearing in the fore, but not Ben Hale's at the rear. He couldn't help admiring the accuracy of the dart, if not the viciousness of the thrower.

Melissa Stone signaled for attention, raising her hand as if requesting permission to speak at a forum. "Miss Haddington, did the recent unpleasantness have any bearing on your decision to go into temporary seclusion?"

Until then, no one had mentioned "the recent unpleasantness," perhaps because all knew that Miss Stone would eventually and inevitably do so. She was not about to pass up the opportunity out of kindness or any other motive that might possibly be construed as compassion or generosity. Melissa Stone was first and foremost a journalist, and privately her colleagues thought that printer's ink flowed in her veins, inherited from her father, who had also been in the business.

"Yes, of course. A great deal. It was a tragic, devastating experience. Traumatic."

"Did you say dramatic?"

"Traumatic, Miss Stone."

"But why should it be so demoralizing? You were acting within your legal and moral rights, weren't you, in self-defense, or so it was ruled at the inquest."

"Legality has nothing to do with the sensibilities, Miss Stone. I should be less than human to be unaffected by that unfortunate occurrence. And contrary to some printed images of me, I am neither a cynic nor a stoic."

Miss Stone scribbled rapidly. Tomorrow these phrases would not be quoted verbatim, but twisted neatly and cleverly, given her own personal touch of acid-etching and unique green patina: "In discussing the recent death of Singer Eddie Eden by her own hand, Silver Haddington admitted that the tragedy had affected her emotionally, deeply, traumatizing her, in fact. And as she spoke, one had the feeling that she felt, in addition to sorrow and humility and remorse, somehow responsible for the incident; as if she had killed, not an intruder in her home, not a potential thief of her riches, but an intrepid trespasser on her most sensitive soul and human heart, her sensibilities." What could the lady's attorneys do with that ambiguity?

"Are you taking any recommended literature with you, any preparatory material?"

"I've read some books on the subject," Silver admitted. "And I understand there's an ample library in the colony, and mentors to aid in the selection of proper reading."

Silver allowed them one hour to torment her, during which she endured the ordeal like a veteran of many wars, and then clammed up and ushered them out. Only Ben Hale was permitted, indeed requested, to remain.

"Well," she said, beckoning him to the bar, "how did I do, Mr. Hale?"

Ben, who had seen her in action before, during and after the fierce legal battles with the Count de Martinique, grinned his approval. "Heroically," he said. "The Haddington mint should strike another gold medal for exceptional valor in the face of the enemy."

"Your tongue is a double-edged sword," Silver observed. "You know it was a confrontation rather than a conference. A conviction, and they'll crucify and hang me upside down in their columns. Especially Melissa Stone. I won't recognize what I've said after that bitch gets through twisting it."

"Sue her for libel."

"It won't be libel. She's too smart for that, or her editor is. And she's a wizard with words. I'd hate to play Scrabble with her." She sighed. "I feel as if I'd fought The Hundred Years War in sixty minutes. I just hope it's as peaceful as they say in that hermitage in the Himalayas. Not that I expect to find Utopia or Nirvana, or even a halycon interlude. I'll be satisfied with just solitude." She paused. "Would you like to come along, Ben?"

"On what basis?"

"Bodyguard. Traveling companion. Sounding-board. What basis do you want?"

"I thought you were going to meditate, Silver?"

"I am, dear boy. I just thought you might like to meditate with me?"

"I've got work to do," Ben said.

"Are you going to be a detective all your life?"

"I hope not."

Silver sipped her favorite sherry. "How would you like to write my life story? The only authorized biography of Silver Haddington. It could launch your writing career, if you're still literary-minded, in style."

Ben acknowledged his appreciation. "It's a tempting offer, but I don't think I could do it justice, Silver."

"How do you know, unless you try?"

Ben pondered his bourbon. "If I agreed, I'd insist on complete and absolute honesty from my subject," he said tentatively. "Could I depend on that, Silver?"

She looked at him, almond-shaped eyes slanting under oblique brows. "What do you mean?"

"You know what I mean, Miss Haddington. What really happened with Eddie Eden? I know what you told the police and the coroner's jury, but was it the truth, the whole truth, and nothing but the truth?"

Her gaze was adamant. "You doubt it?"

"Answer my question."

"What do you think happened?" she parried.

"I think he was trying to rob your safe, all right," Ben conceded. "But I find it difficult to believe that you didn't recognize him before you fired those shots."

"Really?" she asked archly.

"Don't be coy with me, Silver, and don't fence and feign. Save that for the press. I'm serious. The cleaners managed to get the blood off your carpet, but if there's any on your conscience—"

"Don't you think Eddie deserved to die, Ben? He tried to blackmail me and then to steal from me."

"I know all that, Silver. After all, I recovered the evidence for you. But you still haven't answered my question, and I'm going to keep posing it like a D.A. until you do. Did you kill Eddie Eden deliberately?"

The pearlized tip of one finger traced a dark vein in the white marble bar-counter. "I loved him, Ben. In spite of what he was, in spite of what he tried to do to me, in spite of everything, I loved Eddie Eden."

"That's an old scene from an old movie, Silver. I saw it just the other night on the late, late show. Bette Davis, in *The Letter*. 'With all my heart, I still love the man I killed.' Dramatic. Poignant. Brilliant acting. But that's all it was, acting. And she did deliberately kill her lover."

"What hurts most is that you doubt me," Silver said sadly. "I have many acquaintances, Ben, but few friends. Few people I really trust and admire and respect, whose friendship I value and would like to keep. You're one of them."

"Thanks," Ben said. "But you're dissembling, Silver, and I want the truth. I've got to know if I did the right thing in concealing the knowledge of those pictures from the law."

"You did, Ben. Of course you did. But why are you doubtful and concerned now? You had your moment at the inquest, the same as I."

Ben told her about Tawny Mane, the insignificant item of her death which he'd just stumbled across in the paper. There was no way on earth to prove it now, but Ben suspected that Eddie Eden was guilty of that crime.

"Oh, God," Silver murmured, visibly shaken. "You mean you think someone else might have died because of me?"

"She was raped and murdered," Ben said. "Brutally beaten. The police have no positive clues, but they know she knew Eddie Eden, that they'd met at the Amber Alley, where she was billed before him."

Silver's mouth was a wry twist. "And the Cajun Cat was stalking us both at the same time?"

"Apparently."

"Why should you have qualms about that?"

"Because that tawny-haired little pussycat had your pictures," Ben explained to her instant horror and dismay. "Eddie had a collection of such art, Silver. You weren't his only hobby. I entered her apartment under false pretenses and persuaded her to let me take yours."

"She must have thought you had strange taste in females, to say the least."

"She was surprised, I'll admit. But if it's any comfort to you, she didn't recognize you."

Silver reached for the wine decanter. Her hands trembled as she replenished her glass. "You think Eddie killed her for giving you the pictures?"

"He had a violent temper, Silver, and he was capable of cruelty and murder. Some other sadist may have beaten and raped her, of course, but I think it was Eddie, and I feel responsible for what happened to her."

"That's ridiculous, Ben! You were hired to get them, it was your job."

Ben's saturnine mood deepened. His hands clinched his glass, pressing hard enough to splinter the crystal. "That doesn't help much, Silver. That poor ignorant girl is dead, because I tracked her like a hound a rabbit to its burrow and tricked and conned her into giving me the goods."

"That's rationalization, Ben. You're belaboring yourself for doing your duty."

"Maybe."

"Forget it, Ben. It's unfortunate and tragic, but she's dead, and Eddie's dead, and how and why it happened won't change anything, won't bring them back to life. But it might help you to go away and meditate and come to new terms with yourself."

Ben sat quietly on the bar stool, seeming to contemplate her suggestion, then hit her with another shocker. "Suppose I told you there were more photos than the six I delivered to you, Silver? Suppose I told you there were twelve, and I still have the remainder?"

She stared at him, blinking her eyes as if there were a strong light in them. "I'd think you were an odd duck."

"And suppose I told you," Ben continued in the same even tone, as if there'd been no interruption, "that I've put a price tag of one hundred thousand on each, a grand total of six hundred thou for the bundle?"

279

"I'd say you're teasing, and I don't appreciate your sense of humor at the moment," Silver said.

"Did you kill Eddie Eden?"

"No, no, no!" Silver screamed her denial, and then dropped her head onto her arms on the bar. Her thin shoulders quivered under the black silk gown, and she wept. "Why won't you believe me?"

"I believe you," Ben said softly. "I just had to be sure, that's all, Silver. I'm sorry for the third degree."

"A rubber hose and Klieg light couldn't have been more effective," she sobbed. "You're not very subtle, Ben."

"Please understand, Silver. I *had* to know. I have to live with myself. I have to shave every morning and look in the mirror. It hasn't been easy lately. I've cut myself a few times, bad enough to bleed. Silver?"

When she lifted her face, it was wet with tears, the flawless makeup streaked, mascara smudged. "Surprised? You didn't think I could cry?"

"What did you tell Melissa Stone, about being less than human if you were unaffected by what happened? Up until now, I didn't think you were affected, Silver. But you are, and you'd be less than a woman if you couldn't cry about it. I had to see those tears, Silver. They're the only real thing in this performance you've been giving, and I believe them."

"Thanks," she murmured. "My plane leaves in three hours, Ben. The champagne flight. Please come with me. I need you. I need someone. I feel so desperately alone and forsaken."

"You just need a new perspective, Silver. I hope you find it in Tibet." He paused thoughtfully. "I'm taking a sabbatical myself, retreating to a little domestic Shangri-La of my own. A farmhouse in a valley in the Green Mountains."

"What about Marcie Eden?"

"Nothing's changed in that respect," Ben said. "I'm in love with her. But there has to be what's commonly called a decent interval—her sentiments, not mine. I suppose she'll meditate in her own special temple on the Teche." He waited. "What would you consider a decent interval?"

"About a week, give or take a few days."

"It'll be longer than that for Marcie," Ben said. "She's a Southern lady, you know."

"A lady," Silver said. "Worth waiting for, Ben."

"I think so," he said.

"Will you drive me to the airport, Ben? My luggage is already there, though I probably won't need most of it. Maybe they clothe themselves mostly in humility."

"I'll drive you," Ben said.

"Pardon me while I repair the ravages of my unbridled emotion," Silver said. "Some of those hawk-eyed reporters are bound to ambush me at Kennedy, and I can't appear less than poised and perfect."

"Poor little rich girl," Ben teased.

"Shit," Silver muttered.

chapter
27

BEN LAUGHED AND WENT OUT ON THE TERRACE
while Silver repaired to the boudoir. Was this what
Eddie Eden had coveted so desperately, he wondered,
this view of heaven and earth and the unattainable
world between? Was this what the poor devil had died
for, essentially? He could almost pity him.

Presently Silver rejoined him. "Inspiring, isn't it?"

"I'll admit it provokes thought."

"Does it tempt you?"

"To jump?"

"Silly. I'm offering you the use of my pad during my
absence, Mr. Hale. Isn't that what every writer dreams
of, his own private tower?"

Ben smiled. She would probably find it difficult to
believe that he had no aspirations in that direction, did
not entertain idle dreams of an ivory tower. His concep-
tion of an ideal studio was a log cabin in the Green
Mountains, or possibly a remodeled grist-mill on a clear
stream, or even one of Vermont's unique old red barns
built of native woods and painted with a mixture of
oxide of iron and skim milk that had endured for centuries. But he would have felt ridiculous explaining to
this sophisticated woman, this cosmopolitan, that he was

bucolic at heart, provincial in mind, and rustic in spirit. He said simply, "I couldn't produce anything worthwhile in this atmosphere, Silver. Too much luxury can have a sterile effect on a man."

"Oh, you could adjust to the higher altitudes of ambition if you made an effort, Ben. Few men are that inflexible. And it isn't as if I'm making you an indecent proposal, trying to compromise your manhood, or hobble your free spirit. It would be a gift, in appreciation. I owe you a great deal."

"Nothing you haven't already paid for, Silver."

"You're a rare gem," Silver observed. "A whole treasure chest, in fact. I just hope Marcie Eden recognizes your intrinsic value. She couldn't assay her husband's true worth, you know. Eddie was brass and zircon and quartz. Pyrites, fool's gold. But I'm serious about the loan of this place, Ben. I'll give you a key, gold-plated if the gesture appeals to you, and no strings attached unless you want to attach some. The lease is paid up for another nine months, and I'll even keep a servant or two on for your convenience. A woman can produce a child in that length of time, a man should be able to produce a book. I promise not to disturb you. I don't know where I'll go after the Himalayan experiment—buy myself an island somewhere, perhaps, and build a castle with the whole sea for a moat. I only know I'm not coming back here to live, ever. So you're welcome to this eyrie, even if you choose to be a lone eagle."

"Why aren't you coming back, Silver? Afraid of ghosts?"

She nodded: "My own, not Eddie's. I'm the one haunted, Ben. Since his death, I reside in a chamber of horrors."

"Then you really did love him?"

"I've already told you that, Ben. And you want to hear something even more spooky? I'd have married him eventually—that's the real and terrible irony of this. He could have had this pad and anything else he wanted, if he'd just been patient. It was his pushing I resented, his trying to force and coerce me into marriage with every foul trick and trap in the lovers' book. Oh, why was he so impatient! This outfit is actually a mourning costume. If I were truly honest with myself, I'd be wearing a long black veil. I feel like a widow, and I'm not dramatizing, Ben. But I seem to have the Circe touch to men. Somehow I manage to turn them into despicable creatures. Swine or beasts of some sort."

"Not Eden," Ben said grimly. "He was those things before you met him, Silver."

"But I was fatal to him, Ben. I did destroy him."

"He'd have destroyed himself eventually," Ben said. "His contract with life contained a suicidal option, and he'd have exercised it sooner or later, one way or another."

Silver stood with both hands on the concrete parapet of the terrace. Up in the clouds, she sometimes felt elevated and isolated from the earthlings, like a goddess on Olympia, or so Eddie had accused her. To him, this tower represented Mecca and El Dorado; it epitomized all his hopes and dreams and ambitions. And it had killed him as surely as if he had fallen off it to the pavement forty stories below.

"Even so, I precipitated his decision and his destruction," she brooded. "Like that spider that eats her mates— is it the black widow? Lures them into her web, uses them ... and then zap." She snapped her fingers, a hollow sound at that height. "Once we were standing here like this, Eddie and I, and he remarked that it was a long way down. I called him Humpty-Dumpty and said it was also a hard fall. Oh, I was so damned witty and prophetic! I feel now as if I'd pushed him, Ben. Do you think he suffered any pain?"

"No," Ben conforted her. "The medical report said death was instantaneous."

Silver shuddered, still horrified by the memory. "I

ought to swear off pills. I was in such a daze, such a stupor, like a somnambulist. You do believe me, Ben?"

"Yes," he reassured her.

"Adjusting to it is going to be a long slow process," Silver anticipated. "That's why I have to go away, Ben. For more than just a new perspective. I hope they have solitary cells in that colony for voluntary confinement, and intricate labyrinths in the gardens where I can lose myself, and all the guests are hermits and recluses. I have much to ponder and sort out in my mind." She paused to retrieve her thoughts which were constantly straying. "Do I sound as if I'm reciting my *mea culpa?* Well, I had another birthday last week. Maybe I'm mellowing with age. Horrible thought, isn't it?"

"Mellowing?"

"Aging."

"Not necessarily. Women, like wine, are supposed to improve with age."

"Do you think so?"

"One of the most beautiful women I ever knew was eighty years old." Ben said. "My grandmother."

"What a wonderful tribute! I envy her, because I'll never have a grandchild to pay me such a marvelous compliment. See how rich she was, and how poor I am by comparison?"

"Now you're moralizing," Ben said.

"The parson's son, born to poverty and piety, and suspicious of anything outside of it? Are you afraid of the Circe curse, Ben? Afraid I'll corrupt and castrate you in some way? Sterilize your mind and emotions? Is that why you won't accompany me to Tibet, or accept my generous offer here?"

Ben was surveying the eight-hundred acres of parkland below them. Grass, trees, flowers. Meadows, ponds, outcroppings of rock. Incongruous in this commercial complex, these concrete canyons. "Maybe I just want to own myself, Silver, and that's not possible with you. When you take a man, you take every part of him, including his soul if he has one. I couldn't stand that kind of possession."

"Oh, come now! Is Circe also some kind of she-dragon that devours her lovers?"

"No, she just absorbs them by some peculiar osmosis, dissolves them until they're not men any more. They become blots, blobs, blurs. Shadows.

"That champion boxer, for example. Know what he is now, after blowing his million buck settlement? A punch-bag for other champions at a training camp in the Catskills. And that football hero—that magnificent male specimen who was the idol of the college-girl crowd? He's a bouncer in a Thrid Avenue bar. The actor is doing character bits on TV, along with an occasional toothpaste commercial, though I hear he doesn't even own his teeth or his hair any more. Christ, Silver! He was Number One Star in box office heaven before you shot him out of the sky. I don't give a damn about the noblemen, because neither of them had anything to offer or share except a title. But you sure played hell with the others."

"They were well paid," Silver reflected grimly. "They could have lived like kings and potentates for the rest of their miserable lives, all of them, if they'd known how to manage. If they hadn't been dopes and duds and was-trels to begin with. But I seem to have a penchant for picking the wrong mates."

"At any rate, I don't envy or covet their fate."

"Possess me not, eh?"

"Something like that," Ben agreed.

"Strangely enough, I don't like to be possessed, either, Ben, even by myself. That's why I fly around so much, trying to escape Me as much as anyone or anything else. Sometimes I succeed, more often not. I have no illusions about my life, Ben. I know it's been as useless and wasted and futile as Eddie Eden's. Never a big important thing but an infinity of little things—petty, pica-yunish for the most part, blown up out of all sense of proportion and reality by an imaginative and frequently myopic press, until sometimes I feel like one of those crazy balloons in the Macy's Thanksgiving Day parade.

"When the effigies and caricatures become too grotesque, I take to my magic carpet and zoom off to some envisioned Utopia that never quite materializes out of the hopeful mists. If I were a drinking woman, I'd probably hibernate with a jug and sink in my cups until overcome by the raptures of the deep. This trip may be just another dry run, another flight to Mirageland, but I have to take it, Ben. I don't delude myself that I can change my image. I'm afraid the mold is too long set to be melted and remolded, except in the crucible of fire, and I'll leave that for the Big Blacksmithy in the hereafter. I'm just escaping again, only this time I know I can't leave myself behind. I have to take Me along, no matter where I go. How's that for a capsule analysis of self?"

Ben could have put it in one word: resignation.

"You are mellowing," he said.

Silver laughed ruefully. "God forbid. You know what happens to fruit after it mellows? It decays. Rots."

"You're full of wisdom today."

"And you're full of philosophy."

"Maybe were both just full of prunes," Ben grinned. "But I hope your pilgrimage proves rewarding, Silver—that you find whatever you're seeking."

"I'd have to know what it is first," she said realistically. "So far its as mythical and elusive as the Holy Grail. And are you sure you know what you're hunting, Sir Lancelot, since it's obviously not Guinevere?"

"Nobody's ever sure about anything," Ben said. "That's what's meant by the uncertainty of life."

"I guess," Silver conceded.

Ben consulted his watch. "We'd better leave, Silver, or you'll miss your magic carpet."

Silver sighed wistfully. She was weary and discouraged already, and she wasn't even airborne yet. "I'm so tired of flying, Ben. I wonder what mode of transportation they use in the Himalayas."

"Yaks, I think."

"Just so it's not jets," Silver said.